St. Anthony's Piglet

By

Rex Merchant

Copyright © Rex Merchant 2006
ISBN 978 1 902474 175

Published by Rex Merchant
Norman Cottage
Oakham
Rutland LE15 6LT. UK.

rexmerchant@btinternet.com
www.rexmerchant.co.uk

British Library Cataloguing - In – Publication Data.
A catalogue record of this book is available from the British
Library.

Typeset, printed and bound by Rex Merchant at Norman
Cottage.
Cover designed and printed by Rex Merchant at Norman
Cottage.

St. Anthony's Piglet

A Medieval Mystery.

By
Rex Merchant

Published by
Rex Merchant at Norman Cottage.

Author's Notes.

This story is set in the Lincolnshire fenland town of Spalding in the year 1290AD. At that time Edward the First was battling with the Scots and the Welsh and taxing his subjects heavily to finance these wars. The Lincolnshire farmers were suffering under the heavy burden of taxation.

In those days Spalding was a busy port on the River Welland with a fleet of fishing boats that fished the Wash and the North Sea for herring. The town was also a very important crossing point with a stone bridge over the Welland.

The Prior of Spalding was Lord of the Manor and head of a very rich church foundation. The priory was one of the richest in the land and often played host to important men, such as the King himself.

At this period the fens were often overrun by the sea when high tides breached the sea banks, causing death and destruction.

Prologue

When Ivo Longspee, a Norman Landowner and kinsman to the Earl of Lincoln, dies of poisoning on his Lincolnshire holding, Giles Fisher, a young Spalding fisherman is suspected of the crime.

Gilles is imprisoned in the gaol at Spalding Priory, awaiting trial at Lincoln castle.

Hugh Pinchbeck, a veteran bowman of the crusades and a healer, has one niece of whom he is very fond. The niece, Elizabeth, is in love with Giles Fisher. Hugh is convinced of the young fisherman's innocence and sets out to prove it.

The story unfolds against the background of King Edward's wars with the Welsh and the Scots, and the heavy burden of taxation falling on the general population to finance these wars.

Chapter One

The east wind freshened off the North Sea, reaching into the sheltered waters of the Wash, whipping the salt water into frothy white peaks and deep grey troughs. Strong gusts whistled through the rigging, swelling the square linen sail, driving the squat wooden cargo boat towards the Lincolnshire coast of England.

"Look out for pirates." Erik van Driell shouted to make his voice heard above the noise of the sea. The small Flemish krugge ran before the wind towards the South Channel and the mouth of the Welland estuary. "Take the helm, Hugh. I will keep a lookout." Erik handed over the tiller to the grey-haired Englishman at his side.

Hugh Pinchbeck grasped the tiller and set himself to take the strain, stumbling momentarily on his damaged leg as he took the weight.

Anxiously the five members of the crew scanned the horizon and the coastline. They were well aware that their cargo of wine and woollen cloth, bound for the priory at Spalding, was valuable and well worth stealing. They also knew that piracy was common in the area and they could pay with their lives.

"Over there! A sail! Could be pirates!" Erik shouted and pointed towards the distant mud flats of the Lincolnshire coastline. A narrow fishing boat put to sea from one of the numerous salt-water creeks and sped towards them. Erik glanced up at the sail above him, which was billowing in the fresh wind. He listened to the cracks from the timbers as they shifted and struggled to cope with the strain. He knew he was already asking too much of the old cargo boat. "They're too fast for us. These krugges are fine beasts of burden but they're not built for racing!"

"It's full of men, master. Ten of them at least. Shall we arm ourselves?"

"Aye. Break out your weapons. Look sharp about it. I'm sure they're looking for trouble." Erik licked the salt from his parched lips and wiped his mouth with the back of his hand "Not a very good homecoming for you, Hugh. The first trouble we meet since leaving Amsterdam has to be in your home waters and from your own countrymen."

Hugh shook his head in dismay. His heart sank. He had been delayed in Amsterdam by bad weather and needed to get back to Spalding quickly. It was

4

important he arrived home with his goods intact, he had spent most of his savings on this buying trip in a desperate attempt to make some profit and stay out of debt. He knew only too well that the waters off the Lincolnshire coastline had a terrible reputation. Piracy was rife there because there was no organised resistance to it. King Edward was too busy with his wars in Scotland. The Prior, Lord of the manor of Spalding, enforced the peace on land, but he was powerless to intervene at sea. There was a busy trade between England and the Low Countries. Wool, cloth, wine and grain were shipped regularly between the ports, so there were rich pickings to be had, and each cargo boat had to look to its own defence. Living in Spalding near the waterfront, he heard all the gossip and news from the seafarers; he knew merchant ships were frequently raided and many seafarers lost their lives. Shielding his eyes from the sea spray he searched the coastline to get his bearings. His own holding was somewhere to the south of them but it was difficult for him to recognise landmarks at that distance and from the unfamiliar viewpoint of the open sea.

"Must I man the tiller, Erik? You know I brought my bow and a sheaf of arrows with me, just in case."

Erik grinned. Hugh had been an archer in Prince Edward's army in his younger days. He'd fought the infidels in the crusades, at the battle of Acre and at Nazareth. Even though he was now older, he had a cool head. He was a useful man to have by your side in a tight situation.

"You'd better take the platform at the prow. Your skill will be more use there." The tall Fleming took the tiller from Hugh and swung it across the deck to turn the krugge away from the coast and its pursuers. The wide, flat-bottomed, craft did not respond; it was sluggish and too heavily laden with cargo to be easily manoeuverable.

Hugh took his bow and iron tipped arrows from their waxed linen bag and limped to the prow. He walked unevenly on his stiff left leg, the result of an infidel lance in his knee when he'd fought in the crusade alongside Edward Longshanks at Acre. The rolling of the cargo boat as it bucked in the strong wind, made it difficult for him to keep his balance. He mounted the low platform at the bow of the boat and pressed his back hard against the ropes, which supported the mast, then braced his legs against the near vertical sides of the boat to firm his stance. From the raised platform he had a clear view of the sea all around him. The fast boat pursuing the krugge, was getting nearer by the minute.

Erik's voice rose above the sound of the wind. "Two men to each side. Wait 'til we see exactly what they intend to do."

Hugh strapped a leather brace onto his left wrist then strung his longbow, lodging the tip under the instep of his stiff leg, easily bending the bow as he slid the string along it. As a young man he'd spent all his spare time at the archery butts. He'd concentrated on upper body strength to develop the muscles in his arms and shoulders. With his bow at full draw he pulled well over a hundred pounds. Such power made his arrows fly straight and fast, their iron tips capable of piercing even stout metal armour. Constant practice had honed his accuracy. Even in his later years he kept his eye in by setting up a straw target in the yard at his home and loosing a few dozen arrows into it whenever the fancy took him. He counted his arrows as he slotted then through his belt.

Only twelve! What had seemed an ample number when he set out from home, was now far too few. Each shaft would have to play its part and find its mark if he was to come through this encounter safely.

"Pirates! Scum!" Hugh spat the words into the wind. "I haven't worked and scrimped for thieves to take my goods."

As the intruders drew nearer, the krugge's crew caught glimpses of the glint of steel blades and helmets above the wooden sides of the boat.

"They look as if they mean to board us. We can't outrun them but we have an advantage; the sides of our boat are much higher. They will have to fight uphill and we will give them a battle to remember." Erik sounded almost cheerful at the prospect of trouble. In his native Amsterdam the young man was well known for enjoying a brawl in the local taverns.

Hugh turned back to the sea and concentrated his attention on their pursuers. Looking across the narrowing gap between the two vessels, he estimated the distance between them. When the fishing boat travelled another hundred yards towards them, it would be within range of his arrows, a little nearer and he could hope to be more accurate and hit one of the crew. His thoughts went back to the many battles he had fought. Automatically he held up a hand to check the strength and direction of the wind and estimate its effect on the flight of his arrows, but he immediately dropped it to his side, realising such extreme conditions were beyond calculating. All he could do was breath slowly to calm his racing heart, dry his hands on his sheepskin jerkin and rely on his instincts. As the strip of water between them narrowed, Hugh could make out individual crewmen on the pirate boat. He could see that most of them wore steel helmets and a few had body armour. They would be difficult to wound. He knew he must hold back his arrows until they were much closer.

By this time, the leader of the pirates had taken the helm. Even though he was beyond earshot, Hugh could see the man gesticulating as he bellowed orders to his crew. He was a thickset individual, wearing a chain mail tunic and steel headgear. He looked much bigger than most of his companions. His muscular shoulders were even broader than Erik's although he appeared to be shorter in height. The man's burnished steel helmet glinted in the grey light.

Hugh slipped his draw fingers through a protective leather tab, nocked an arrow on his bowstring and drew the shaft to his ear. As his thumb nestled against the angle of his jaw, he felt the familiar touch of the grey goose fletchings brushing against his cheek. He held his stance at full draw and sighted along the slim shaft, watching the tip of the steel arrowhead rise and fall as the krugge rode the swell of the sea. Hugh instinctively calculated the flight his arrow would travel before it reached its target. In his imagination, he loosed several shots as he worked out the best trajectory to use.

"Near enough yet?" Erik shouted from just behind him. The Master had roped the tiller fast and armed himself with a long spear.

Hugh, concentrating hard on his first shot, didn't answer. As the two boats rose and fell in unison, he loosed his first arrow, which sped towards the pirate boat and thudded harmlessly through its side, penetrating the hardwood plank but missing its human target.

"Good! You've got their range." Erik raised a fist to encourage him.

Hugh nocked another arrow, pulled the fletching back to his cheek and aimed again. The krugge rose and fell to the rhythm of the waves. The pursuing craft drew nearer by the second. He took aim at the helmsman, knowing he would do most damage if he disabled the leader of the pirates. The arrow arced away towards the faster boat and found its target. There was a metallic clang as it glanced off the steel helmet, pushing the big man off balance. The helmet clattered to the deck. They were now close enough for the sound to carry clearly.

The helmsman staggered and let go of the helm, his shaven head clearly visible for a few seconds before he replaced his protective headgear. With no one at the tiller, the pirate boat momentarily bucked and hesitated in the rough sea as its prow swung away from the krugge and into the swell. The pursuing crew seemed taken aback by such accurate shooting, but the helmsman only shook his fist at the Flemish boat and shouted more orders to his men.

Hugh could not make out individual words because of the sound of the wind but he was near enough to hear the anger in those bellows.

Hugh followed that first hit with two arrows fired in quick succession; his second arrow leaving the bow before the first one found its mark. This ruse worked well and confused the enemy. With satisfaction, he saw one of the crew throw up his arms, heard him scream with pain and saw the man drop his sword over the side, as the second arrow thudded deep into his shoulder.

"Good shot! Keep trying." Erik shouted encouragement.

Hugh lowered his bow. "I'll save the rest of my arrows until I can make each one tell."

The pirate boat raced towards them in a broad arc, aiming to come alongside them. The helmsman dared not ram them for the krugge was built of heavy oak planks and would have splintered the lighter boat. As the pirates came up level with them, trying to manoeuvre alongside, Hugh loosed another two arrows and wounded one more of their pursuers. The helmsman shook his fist at the lone bowman and ordered his men to crouch below the wooden sides of their boat as they veered away.

"Next time they'll try to board us." Erik yelled to his crew. "We must keep them off. There are too many for us to take on in a close hand to hand fight."

To emphasise his words and set an example, he gripped his spear and thrust it over the side of the krugge, preparing to keep off any attempt at boarding.

The pirate boat turned in a broad arc, gaining rapidly on the sluggish krugge. Hugh whispered a prayer to St. Sebastian, the patron saint of archers, and wiped his fingers again on the salt-encrusted fleece of his sheepskin tunic. All five members of the Flemish crew manned the south side of their boat, where they anticipated the marauders would come alongside. Hugh took one of his remaining arrows and nocked it onto his bowstring, where it hung limply awaiting the draw and loose. He would use his last few shafts at close range, to ensure every single one scored a hit.

The pursuing vessel drew alongside them again. With the gap narrowed, Hugh could see the grappling irons and ropes in the crew's hands. A score more yards and they would be fighting hand to hand. Nervously, he fingered the pommel of his sword, lifting it half out of its scabbard and letting it slip back again. Behind him, Erik shrieked a challenge, a Flemish war cry, mounted the narrow platform that ran around the outside of the deck and brandished his spear at the enemy. Hugh smiled to himself, in spite of their imminent danger. With his long hair and brown muscular arms, Erik looked exactly as one of his Viking ancestors must have looked, challenging the enemy from a longboat. Those pirates must be wondering just what kind of a cargo boat they had chosen to attack.

The Flemish crew braced themselves for the final onslaught. The pirate boat drew still nearer, its crew crouching out of sight of Hugh's deadly arrows. He pulled his shaft to full draw, prepared to loose at the first human target that presented itself. For several minutes he took the strain of the bow across his shoulders, oblivious to the aching in his knotted muscles as he concentrated on the approaching danger.

The pirate vessel was sailing parallel and close to them. It seemed to hover about ten paces distance waiting like a falcon, judging where to plunge its talons into its prey. Suddenly it pulled away. The pirate boat was so close that Hugh heard the burly helmsman speak and point out to sea behind them. This disengagement was totally unexpected. Surprised at this sudden retreat, the archer lowered his bow and allowed his eyes to stray from his target. He shot a quick glance in the direction the helmsman's finger had pointed and saw what no one else on the Flemish boat had noticed. There was another sail fast closing on them! He shouted to the rest of the crew.

"Another boat coming up behind us."

The pirate boat dropped away. This newcomer was obviously not with them. All eyes on the Flemish boat now focused on the new arrival, trying to gauge its intentions, for it was gaining on them rapidly from the open sea and would be alongside within minutes. As the second boat sailed towards them, they were able to make out the details of the craft and could see there was some kind of a white painted emblem on the prow, just above the water line.

"It's a Spalding fishing boat." Hugh yelled joyfully as he recognised the image of open fish jaws, on the front of the boat. I'd know that boat anywhere. It's one of the Fisher's fishing boats. It's a common enough sight in Spalding docks."

Erik lowered his spear and grinned in relief. "Praise be to St Brendan for their arrival." He had been ready to fight, but he knew his crew was outnumbered by more than two to one, and their adversaries were heavily armed and well protected. He untied the helm and steered the krugge towards the mouth of the Welland estuary and the shelter of the land.

Hugh unstrung his bow and rolled it with his remaining arrows in their linen pouch. He watched as the fishing boat passed them on the seaward side and made for the mouth of the river Welland. One of the Flemish crew handed him a jug of wine, which they were passing amongst themselves. He drank deeply to wet his dry mouth and throat. Brushing the wine from his lips with his hand, he exclaimed "What a homecoming!" A rough sea crossing from Amsterdam and a brush with pirates. It was too much excitement for one day. His thoughts turned to his home at Eau Side and his people there, hopefully they were having a less stressful time.

Erik took the jug, drank the last dregs then broke into Hugh's thoughts. "We are at the junction of the Boston Deep and the South Channel into the Welland. We'll soon be at the Lord Prior's wharf at Wykeham. I know you're anxious to be home. You can leave the boat as soon as we dock and go on to Spalding on foot, if you like."

Hugh smiled; it was a good feeling to be within easy distance of home.

The rest of the journey was uneventful. As they travelled up the river, the wind dropped. They made good progress on the incoming tide until they were within sight of their first landing place.

"Another delay, Hugh! It seems you are not destined to get home today." Erik shook his head in disbelief and put a consoling arm around his friend's shoulder.

Hugh stared ahead at the Wykeham wharf, at the fully laden boat already moored there. There was only room for one boat to unload at the prior's wharf and they would be unable to dock until it left. To make matters worse, nothing was happening at the wharf. There was no sign of work taking place. The crew of the first boat was sitting idly on their cargo. By the time Erik delivered his consignment, it would be dark and the tide turning. They would have to spend the night moored at Wykeham.

"Now I'm within a few miles of home, I can't wait. Tomorrow my rent is due at the priory. I must be home tonight." Hugh thumped his fist on the boat side. "Can't you get me closer to the bank so that I can get ashore?"

Erik considered the request. "Maybe we could let her drift a little nearer to yon craft. Could you swing onto the other boat if we narrowed the gap?"

Hugh nodded. He was willing to try anything to get on the road home.

Erik cupped his hands and shouted to the first boat. "Hello there! One of my crew needs to get ashore urgently. Can he use you as a bridge?"

The master of the other vessel agreed to the request and threw a rope over to the krugge.

Hugh gave the waxed linen bag containing his bow and arrows, to Erik for safe keeping, fastened his short sword to his belt and tied a small leather bag of cloves, the most valuable of his small shipment of spices, around his neck. He would have no problem swinging over to the other craft but he feared his damaged leg might make landing difficult when he reached the other side. He swung across the gap over the river and thumped heavily against the hull of the waiting boat. There was a moment when he feared he might finish in the river but eager hands grabbed him and hauled him onto the deck.

"God speed, Hugh. I hope you find everything well. We will see you in Spalding today if we can, but if it gets too dark before we unload, we'll travel down on the morning tide." Erik shouted his farewell through cupped hands.

Hugh scrambled down a mooring rope onto the wooden planks of the Wykeham wharf. He dusted himself down and waved goodbye to his friends.

The prior's wharf was built alongside the old Roman bank of the river Welland. It was a relatively new structure, built by Spalding priory to serve the rural retreat that Prior William of Littleport had built a few years before. Hugh walked up the riverbank and stood on the top of the incline, looking out over the fields of his native fens A mile inland he could see the grand house, with its formal gardens, wide moat and gatehouse. There was a newly constructed dirt road leading to it. Looking the other way, towards the town, he could see a wide avenue with newly planted trees lining its sides. The Lord Prior had excelled himself with this country retreat, where he could escape the pressures of the town. Suddenly,

Hugh heard the sound of horses and wagons on the road immediately below him. He glanced down and realised a party of men had come from the house to meet the cargo boats. He started to descend the oak plank steps, set into the steep bank, treading carefully, one step at a time, to avoid slipping on his crippled leg.

"Stop! Where are you going?" A fresh-faced young cleric, dressed in the black, Benedictine habit, barked out this command and barred his way.

"Into town." Instinctively Hugh stepped back and fingered the pommel of his sword.

A man at arms drew his sword and stepped up to support the monk, who stood his ground and held out his hand, palm uppermost. "Any stranger travelling through Spalding must pay the prior's through tax."

Hugh glanced down at the outstretched hand and grinned disarmingly. "I'm not a stranger. I live here."

The cleric eyed him suspiciously. "I am new at the priory. Who are you? What is your business here?"

Hugh looked at the young man more closely. He knew most of the Priory monks but this one was new to him. "My name is Hugh Pinchbeck. I live in town by the river. I have just returned from business in Amsterdam. I'm well known at the priory. You've only to ask Brother Mark, the healer, he's a very good friend to me."

The monk frowned at the mention of Brother Mark. He hesitated, stared into Hugh's eyes then looked away. Raising a finger, the man seemed about to say something, but appeared to think better of it. With a gesture of dismissal he pointed towards Spalding. "Go to your home, Master Pinchbeck. We will not delay you. We have much business to do here."

Hugh walked slowly along the new roadway, pleased to be on dry land with the prospect of an easy route to town, for the prior had constructed a good road. He was pleased to be on his way home but felt disturbed by the attitude of the young monk who had demanded the through tax. Hugh turned and looked back at the Wykeham quay and was surprised to see the monk was still staring after him. The young man was taking an unexpected interest in him. He shrugged his shoulders and strode out for home, hardly limping now he was on the even ground. As a young man he had sailed the Middle Sea as far as the Holy Land and had never given home a second thought. Now that he was older his views had changed. It was good to go to Amsterdam, where Erik's father had made him very welcome and had procured for him all the herbs and spices he could afford, at prices well below those in London, but it was much better to be home again.

Chapter Two

The crowd of people shuffled forward a few steps at a time. Progress towards the gates of Spalding priory was painfully slow, for at that early time of the morning lay workers were going into the priory grounds to start their day's work. On that particular day, the Michaelmas quarter day, the crowd was swollen by many of the priory's tenants, needing to settle their autumn rents. Among these was Hugh Pinchbeck.

"Uncle Hugh." A young woman ran up to him, stood on tiptoe and threw her arms around his neck. He bent forward and kissed his niece on her cheek. Wisps of her long dark hair brushed against his neck. She giggled and broke away from the embrace, rubbing her face where his stubbly chin had scratched her skin.

"How's my favourite niece today?"

"I'm your only niece!" She scolded, putting on a make believe frown.

"Stop it, Elizabeth! You look just like your mother when you do that. If the wind blows you will stay like it."

She looked up at the old man and smiled. "I'm well, but I shall tell mother you said that!"

Hugh smiled fondly at the girl. She did indeed look as pretty as his sister had looked at that same age. If he had been blessed with a daughter, he would want her to look just like Elizabeth.

The crowd shuffled forward again, but only a few paces. He glanced over the heads of the patiently waiting people and realised the guards at the gates were stopping every visitor that morning and checking them thoroughly before allowing them to enter the priory grounds. It looked as if the prior or his steward had been reminding the men at arms of their duty to keep the area safe.

"I want you to meet Giles. We are betrothed. We are going to be married one day, when he gets a fishing boat of his own." Elizabeth beckoned a young man forward.

"Giles?" Hugh eyed the tall, skinny youth.

"Giles Fisher, sir. You must know my father and mother, they have the fish stall on the market stead."

"Ah yes! I knew your grandfather better. He fished the Welland and the estuary washes when I was a young man."

The morning crowd edged nearer the priory gates. The young couple chatted to the old man. Elizabeth, full of her good news, hovered close to Hugh, sometimes standing beside him and holding his hand, sometimes dancing backwards, in her excitement. Giles said little, but grinned happily, letting Elizabeth do all the talking. They had almost reached the entrance to the priory when the happy mood abruptly changed.

Elizabeth did not see the horseman approaching. The rider spurred his mount towards the gate, recklessly ignoring the people waiting patiently there. He was almost on top of the girl when she noticed him and screamed. The rider pulled hard on the bit. The frightened horse reared up, then plunged towards the girl. Hugh leapt forward, throwing himself between his niece and the danger. He grabbed the animal's rein and jerked the head down, almost throwing the rider to the ground. Giles stood open mouthed, rooted to the spot. Hugh had moved so quickly and decisively to bring the courser under control, everyone was taken by surprise, especially the rider.

"Unhand my horse!" The man shouted furiously, as he tried to regain control of his mount.

Hugh made no move. He tightened his grip on the bridle and stroked the frightened animal's head, speaking to it soothingly in a voice that was low and honeyed, but his eyes were ablaze with anger as he stared up at the arrogant horseman.

"I think you had better dismount before someone gets hurt."

The horseman glared back angrily. Hugh stood his ground. The rider gripped the pommel of his sword and started to draw it, but the priory guards surrounded them both, their swords already drawn. The crowd melted back and watched in sullen silence.

"You cannot bring weapons into the priory grounds." The head guard held out his hand for the man's sword. "The Lord Prior forbids it."

Hugh let go of the horse's rein and stepped back into the crowd happy to let the proper authorities deal with the newcomer.

"Do you know who I am? My kinsman, Henri de Lacy, will hear of this." The man screamed at the men at arms.

"Lord Prior's orders. No one is exempt." The bailiff had come running from the gatehouse as soon as he became aware of the fracas

The horseman dismounted, but continued to argue with the bailiff as he walked through the priory gateway. Someone in the crowd murmured how unfair it was to let some people go straight into the priory while others had to wait their turn, even if the intruder was related to the Earl of Lincoln.

Giles moved forward and enveloped Elizabeth in his arms. She was still tearful from the shock of the incident. He held her until her crying subsided, then dried her eyes. Hugh stood beside them, concerned for his niece.

"That's Ivo Longspee." Giles hissed in his ear. "He's a right Norman bastard! Thinks he's so important, just because he's distantly related to the Earl's wife."

Hugh stared at the man with renewed interest. He had heard of Ivo Longspee. The Norman farmed the holding next to his own in the fen, but Hugh had never met the man. As he lived and practised as a healer in Spalding town, Hugh was happy to leave his reeve to oversee the day to day running of the farm, nevertheless he had heard of the man's bad reputation. Joseph, Hugh's reeve, had hinted that their neighbours were not above sheep stealing or even piracy. Rumours were rife among the local seamen, of a boat full of armed men, putting out to sea at all hours of the day and night. That behaviour hardly seemed like legitimate fishing expeditions. The wide, sea-water, creek, which separated Hugh's holding from Ivo Longspee's land, had already been given the name of Thieves Creek by the local fishermen.

"He operates out of Thieves Creek." Giles whispered. "I've seen him there when we're putting to sea to catch herrings."

His interest aroused, Hugh took careful note of the man's appearance. Ivo was a thickset individual, with a bull neck and muscular shoulders, reminding Hugh of the wrestlers he had seen performing in the Eastern street fairs, when he had accompanied Prince Edward on the crusade. This impression of power was strengthened by the hardness of the Norman's face, with a cruel, hooked nose, high cheek bones and deep set, dark eyes. The strong face was crowned with a bare head, completely shaven of hair. Hugh frowned and stroked his chin. This was the first time he had met the man but there was already something vaguely familiar about him. Suddenly an intriguing possibility dawned on him. This could be the helmsman on the boat that had attacked them at sea! Ivo Longspee, kinsman of the great Earl of Lincoln, could be the leader of a pirate band!

My neighbour at Wykeham is not a pleasant individual, Hugh thought grimly. He's a bully and he will surely regret it if he crosses me again. Dismissing Ivo from his mind he turned to his niece and hugged her reassuringly. Thank God she was unharmed. Standing to one side, he let the people pass him by as he talked to the young couple.

"You must be used to handling horses, sir, the way you stopped that one." Giles put a protective arm around Elizabeth's shoulder, as he spoke.

"Uncle Hugh fought in the crusade with the King. He was wounded in battle and trained to be a surgeon. He's done most things."

Hugh smiled indulgently at his niece. No doubt her mother had told her about his past and had exaggerated the stories in the telling. "I was wounded in that battle and was no good for fighting, so I helped the surgeons to save the men and I helped the farriers to heal the wounded horses."

"He helped operate on the king when he was stabbed with a poisoned knife by an infidel assassin. He actually cut a piece of bad flesh out of the king's arm!"

"Enough!" Hugh held up a hand for silence. "I must see the prior's steward today and pay my dues. If you had your way, Elizabeth, I'd be prattling here 'til nightfall and evicted from my holding for non-payment of my taxes."

Elizabeth returned his grin, but she said no more because she knew from his tone of voice, that he meant what he had said. As they were speaking, another horseman approached the gates. They turned apprehensively, at the sound of the animal's hooves just behind them, but this rider was approaching more slowly, leading a packhorse on a rein.

"That's Ivo Longspee's groom." Giles whispered.

Hearing that name yet again, Hugh took more interest in the man, who was sitting slouched forward in his saddle. Hugh thought he looked a cowered individual, not the sort to have a mind of his own or to cause trouble. The packhorse was more interesting. It was heavily laden, with two huge earthenware jars slung across its back; one hung in a net at each flank. Hugh's eyes narrowed as he recognised the spherical jars. They were spice containers used in the Spanish trade. He had seen them frequently on the merchant ships in the Middle Sea. They looked strangely out of place on a packhorse at the gates of the Lincolnshire priory. The groom shifted listlessly in his saddle and looked down, avoided the hostile stares of the people around him as he waited for his master to complete his business at the priory.

"I will call at the market tavern for my mid-day meal today. Tell your mother to expect me." Hugh called to his niece as he finally parted from her and entered the priory gates.

The steward's office was a single story, stone structure with a thatched roof. It was situated well away from the main part of the priory. Hugh walked between the tall buildings, picking his way around the stone masons and the piles of Barnack Rag sandstone being dressed for yet more new building. The locals had nicknamed Clement of Hatfield, the present head of the religious house, the Building Prior, because of his ambitious rebuilding program. Hugh had mixed feelings about the expansion. It enhanced the priory and gave work to the local stone masons, but it meant the steward was keen on getting in the increased rents and tithes. All this building work must be emptying the priory coffers. The Lord Prior was Lord of the Manor of Spalding and the principle landlord in the area, so he levied the rents and collected the taxes. The pressure on small Lincolnshire farmers was forcing more and more of them to borrow heavily from the Lombard bankers. Many were losing their lands because they could not meet the repayments. To add to their problems, there were new taxes being levied because King Edward always needed more money for his wars. Although Wales was now subdued, the Scots were proving more difficult for the king to conquer.

Between the greed of the church and the ambitions of the crown, we will all be driven to starvation, Hugh thought. Thank goodness I have escaped the Lombards' embrace so far, but that's only because I have simple tastes as a single man, and I can eke out a living by selling my healing skills as a surgeon as well as farming the holding.

When he eventually entered the outer room at the steward's office, Hugh was surprised to see Ivo Longspee was still sitting there, waiting to see the prior's chief officer. The old soldier explained his business to the clerk, chose a seat on the opposite side of the anteroom from the Norman, and sat down to wait. In a few minutes the door to the inner room opened and a tenant came out. The clerk took the opportunity to go in and speak to his master. Hugh watched Ivo out of the corner of his eye. He could see the man was becoming more and more agitated, sighing and grunting to himself and tapping his fingers restlessly against his outstretched leg. He gave the impression he was not used to being kept waiting. As soon as the clerk returned, Ivo jumped up and strode towards the inner office door.

"Hugh Pinchbeck. The steward will see you now." The clerk ignored Ivo and smiled at Hugh.

"I have been waiting here far too long!" Ivo protested.

Hugh frowned. Ivo Longspee's voice certainly had a familiar ring about it. That sound confirmed beyond reasonable doubt that this was indeed the leader of the pirate boat. He shrugged his shoulders, dismissing the thought for the moment, but promised himself he would take the first opportunity that presented itself to get even with the man.

From the inner office an educated voice rang out. "You will wait a little longer, Longspee. I decide who I will see, and in what order." Then the steward himself came to the door and beckoned Hugh. "Come in, Hugh. I suppose you've come to pay your dues on time. I wish some others would do the same." The door closed behind them as that barbed comment echoed around the anteroom. The Norman valued himself well above his real worth, but his highborn connections obviously did him no good at the priory

Thomas Bohun, the priory steward, sat down heavily behind his ample table. The man dominated the small room. His large frame filled the oak carver chair. His podgy hands flicked through the parchments strewn on the desktop, searching for the roll of the Wykeham holdings. His plump fingers counted the coins Hugh had placed before him on the desk.

"Ah! Up to date, as I expected. You're a model tenant. We could do with more like you." Thomas sat back in his chair, winced as if a sudden pain had struck him, them gingerly eased his large frame forward.

Hugh noticed the signs of discomfort but chose not to mention them. "It's not easy these days to find the rents, but I pride myself on paying my way. The King was good enough to procure me the rights to that holding when we returned from the crusade. The least I can do is keep my side of the bargain." Hugh was tempted to add that his grant of land had been against the wishes of the prior, who would have jumped at the chance to reclaim it for non-payment of dues, but he thought better of it and held his tongue.

"Yes. That was before my time as steward..." Thomas hesitated then continued in a lower voice. "Your name was mentioned at Chapter this morning. The prior remembers you and wants you to call on the new hospitaler when you can make time."

"New hospitaler? What's happened to Brother Mark?" Hugh was shocked that his friend Mark had been replaced and rather surprised that his own name had been mentioned at the prior's meeting.

"Brother Mark is dead. He passed away suddenly, a week ago. We have an untried lad replacing him from our mother house in Anjou."

Hugh took this sad news in silence. Brother Mark would be missed. He ministered to all the sick brothers and was an experienced herbalist. Hugh had often exchanged medicaments with him from their physic gardens, when one of them was short of a particular remedy. This was bad news for the people of Spalding as well as the priory, for Mark had worked unstintingly at the leper hospital of Saint Nicholas in the town. His replacement might not be as willing or as able. Hugh considered the implications for himself. If the Lord Prior had mentioned him at Chapter they must be thinking of asking him to temporarily fill the gap. He was not sure he was young enough or fit enough to take on all of Mark's work, but he was wary of antagonising the Lord Prior. He voiced some of his fears aloud.

"I suppose the new recruit will want some help? I'm not sure I'm up to taking on much extra work."

"He's a nice enough lad but he'd only just started helping Brother Mark when he died. I for one, would prefer someone with a bit more practical experience to care for me." Thomas said pointedly. "Which reminds me, when you have time, I will consult you on a small health matter."

Hugh was not entirely surprised at this request. Thomas Bohun had been unusually friendly during their meeting that morning. The steward did not normally praise tenants for paying their dues, neither did he show favours, calling one man into his room, before another who had been waiting longer. This turn of events needed careful thought. He would have to visit his old friend, Brother James, the priory librarian, and find out exactly what had been said at Chapter and what might be expected of him.

When dealing with a powerful man like the Lord Prior it paid to be well informed.

The priory had a new library. A move had been forced on them because the old building had been much nearer the river Welland and was prone to flooding, which was a constant danger to the priceless books. Brother James was overjoyed at the move, for he regarded the books as his children and lavished as much care and attention on his charges as any doting parent would on his family. When Hugh walked into the library, the old monk was treating the leather binding of one ancient volume with a beeswax dressing. Hugh stopped just inside the doorway and took in a deep breath of the aromatic air. The pleasant smell of beeswax pervaded the library like the odour of polish in a joiner's workshop.

"That's an evocative smell, Brother James."

The monk looked up from his labour of love to see who had entered the room "Hugh! Good to see you. I was only speaking of you this morning."

"So I hear."

Brother James put down his polishing cloth and nodded knowingly. "Been to see Thomas Bohun, have you? He said you would be in to pay your dues promptly." He moved to the far corner of the library and opened a small, oak cupboard with one of the iron keys hung at his waist. "You will join me in a cup of wine? It's the cellarer's best red from Anjou."

Hugh smiled his thanks. He and James had enjoyed many a good wine in the library, for the priory kept an excellent cellar and the cellarer was a particular friend to the librarian. He watched as Brother James said a brief prayer of thanks then handed the drink to him.

Hugh brought the conversation back to himself. "I understand I was the subject of some speculation at Chapter."

"Brother Mark has passed on unexpectedly, bless his soul. Brother Godfrey, his trainee, is very new. The Lord Prior asked after you. I think he had already broached the subject with our new healer." He held his drink up to Hugh as if he was offering a toast. "You have a reputation among the town folk for common sense healing, and Brother Mark, God rest his soul, always spoke highly of you."

Hugh raised his cup and silently toasted his old friend, Mark. The last time he had met the hospitaler had been in that very room, when they had come together to consult one of the herbals on a medical matter. They had stood side by side at the oak table, pouring over the hand-written texts and discussing how to interpret some of the more obscure observations. Hugh smiled to himself at the recollection. Brother Mark was such a knowledgeable and helpful man. He would be sorely missed.

"I told the prior you could be relied upon to give sensible, down to earth, medical advice." James said.

"I'm not a trained doctor of medicine, if that's what you mean. I can't cast your horoscopes before I treat you, neither do I argue about the state of your humours. Just a bit of minor surgery, blood letting, or a herbal remedy, if my experience suggests it might help. The body can heal itself well enough, given the chance, and God willing."

"Will you help?" James had detected the reluctance in his visitor's voice.

"I'm not a young man, as you are aware. Neither of us will see fifty again. I can offer advice, especially if you will let me continue to consult your herbals in the library, but young Brother Godfrey will have to do the bulk of his own work."

"That's more or less what I suggested to the Lord Prior. By the way, he wasn't aware that you already consult our books from time to time, but I'm sure he will not object now you'll be helping the priory."

Hugh lifted the wine to his lips and drained it in one gulp. "Refill my cup and I'll drink to that."

Chapter Three

By mid morning, Hugh had returned from his visit to the priory to his home on Eau Side. He had called at Brother Mark's old dispensary to meet the new healer, but had not found him there. He waited among the drying herbs and spices but there was no sign of Brother Godfrey. Finally, one of the lay workers, who was autumn digging the herb beds, explained that Godfrey was out of town treating a patient at the prior's Wykeham retreat. Hugh decided to leave his business until another day and made for home.

He strolled home via the docks, hoping to find the Flemish krugge moored at the priory wharf and Erik's men unloading his cask of wine, his olive oil and his dried herbs, but the dock was full of barges from inland, from the Stamford stone quarries. The unloading of the massive stone blocks of Barnack Rag was proceeding very slowly. The whole river was choked with boats waiting to moor and discharge their cargoes. He stood on the bridge and looked down river for signs of the Flemish boat but there was no sight of it, just a tangle of masts and boats as far as his eyes could see. Disgruntled at this delay, he walked home along the towpath, entered the back of his house from the yard and went to warm his aching leg in front of the fire.

"John, put a fresh turf on the fire and bring a dry log as well. I'm feeling my age today." Hugh shouted down the yard for the boy to make up the fire in the main hall. John came running from the stable as soon as he heard his master's summons. Hugh stood with his back to the smouldering turf and warmed himself.

"Tell your mother I will not be in for dinner today. I am going to my sister."

John ran out of the hall and into the kitchen where Margaret, his mother, was busy salting fish for the winter.

"All the more for you and me." The housekeeper whispered to her son.

Hugh stood in the hall, deep in thought. The log so recently placed on the fire, burst into life, lighting the gloomy room with a flickering yellow glow. The long oak table and the single carver chair reflected the flames in their dark polished surfaces. Even the dusty threadbare tapestry, covering the bare wall above the table, took on some of its former glory as the faded colours came to life in the dancing light of the fire. But he ignored the room and dwelt on the sad news he had heard earlier that morning. Brother Mark had not been an old man, probably no more than forty summers, but he had worn himself out tending the sick. It was a sad loss to the community and a personal loss Hugh felt strongly. They had worked together for several years and were comfortable in each other's company. This new, young healer would probably bring new ideas from Anjou. Hugh felt especially sad that he had been away in Amsterdam when Mark had died. He had missed the funeral and an opportunity to say farewell to such a good friend.

Suddenly, John burst into the room, disturbing his master's thoughts. "Sir! There's a horseman at the bottom of the yard. He wants to speak with you."

Hugh snapped out of his contemplative mood and followed the boy down the yard towards the river where two men on horseback stood waiting for him. He hesitated half way down the cobbled yard as he recognised Ivo Longspee and his groom. He'd already seen evidence of the Norman's character and was wary of him. What could the man want? Hugh didn't like the situation at all. He stopped several paces away from the visitors and asked. "Yes? You want me?"

Ivo got down from his horse, smiled disarmingly and offered his hand in greeting. "I understand you use herbs and spices in your medical work. I have some Spanish spices to sell."

Hugh eyed the packhorse suspiciously. He saw the two earthenware jars were still suspended in their nets at the horse's flanks. The groom sat very upright in his saddle, watching the ships sail up the Welland to the docks, as if he had no interest in the conversation, but Hugh could tell from his tense manner that he was listening intently to every word.

"I rescued them from a sinking Spanish merchant ship in the Wash. We were too late to save the crew but we salvaged these jars and a few other items."

"What's in the jars? Did they get contaminated with sea water?"

"I believe they are full of cloves. We can break the seals and look if you are interested in buying them."

Hugh was even more wary. Clove was a very expensive spice, used by the richest houses to flavour their food. He used them when he could afford them and prescribed them sparingly as a treatment for toothache and stomach ache, but the high cost ruled them out for most of his patients. He inspected the jars thoroughly, noting that the wax seals with their deeply impressed coats of arms, were still intact. He could see the jars were of unglazed pot. If they had indeed been rescued from the sea, the salt water would have quickly seeped through the porous earthenware body and spoiled the contents. He also knew that there must have been at least one other similar jar, which has been opened, because Ivo Longspee knew what the consignment contained. Search as he might, he could see no signs of a watermark on the pots. They had certainly not been in the water for very long, if at all. It all sounded very suspicious to him.

"You say you came by them legally? I hope so, because I am not interested in stolen goods. I may be interested in buying, but only if you can convince me they are indeed yours to sell."

Ivo hesitated at this veiled accusation. An angry frown passed over his face then he switched on an oily smile and went into an explanation that sounded a little too well rehearsed for Hugh's liking.

"My men were fishing off the Lincolnshire coast when we saw this merchant ship in distress. There had been a bad storm the night before. By the time we reached them it was too late. We would have rescued the poor souls who sailed the ship, if they had been alive when we chanced on them. The ship sank with all hands. No one survived. God preserve their souls." He crossed himself religiously and turned his face upwards to the heavens. "There were these two containers and some sacks of grain floating on the wreckage. We hauled them aboard."

Hugh remained silent. He was not convinced by this story, especially as he had personal experience of the man's piracy. But he realised the circumstances described would give the man a legal title to the goods as they had not been washed ashore, where they would have become the Lord Prior's property by shipwreck rights. It all sounded far too convenient. There were disturbing questions still not answered. Why were there no signs of the jars being in the water? Hugh turned the evidence over in his mind and decided to give the man the benefit of the doubt, for how else did a landowner, who could not even pay his rent, come by such a rich haul of cloves?

"Do you want to buy the cloves, or not?" Ivo had misconstrued Hugh's hesitation as reluctance to purchase. He shifted his weight from one foot to the other and looked very ill at ease.

"Let me see them first. I will fetch a blanket and you can tip some out of the container onto the yard." Hugh sent John to the house to collect a clean woollen blanket, which they spread on the cobblestones

Ivo smiled with relief. He cut the nets and took the jars down, one at a time, encircling them with his muscular arms and lifting them easily, in spite of their obvious weight. He cut into the soft wax seal of one of them with his dagger and tipped the cloves out in a steady stream.

Hugh picked up a handful of the spice and held it to his nose to check the freshness. The cloves ran easily from their container. They had a healthy bloom and a deep purple sheen on their dark skins. There was no sign of damp and the jar emptied completely and easily. Hugh realised the cloves were of the very best quality and probably destined for some important household, before they came into Ivo Longspee's hands. He was tempted to buy, but only at the right price. He reminded himself of a saying the Middle Sea merchants were fond of quoting. 'An item is only worth what someone is willing to pay for it.' He asked. "How much did you expect to get for them?"

"Make me an offer."

Hugh considered the situation. So many cloves could not be sold in Spalding. That huge quantity would keep the few rich customers in the area supplied for several years. Even the priory, the most likely buyer, would buy only a fraction of this amount. He took his time considering his reply.

"Well? Do you want them or not?" Longspee asked aggressively, his short temper beginning to fray as he found Hugh's silence very disconcerting.

"There are too many for me to use. There are too many for me to resell in Spalding. If I buy them, I will have to export them to London or the continent and that costs money..." The Norman, hearing the doubts in Hugh's voice, folded his arms over his chest, his face black as thunder.

Hugh continued unabashed "...And there may be many awkward questions asked."

Ivo's expression changed abruptly. "Awkward questions? I've explained how we came by them." He looked towards his groom for support, but the man turned a deaf ear to the conversation and studiously ignored his master, gazing up river as if his life depended on seeing a particular ship come into view.

"The wax seals will identify the source and the actual shippers. Someone will be very interested in what happened to that merchant ship." Hugh explained.

Ivo fell silent. His face flushed.

Hugh decided to make him feel even more uncomfortable. He asked innocently. "Have you told the priory of this windfall? They are the biggest users of spices in the whole area. They cook for many hungry mouths." Hugh knew he had hit his target when he saw how startled Ivo looked, at this suggestion. He guessed the man was still in debt to the priory and the steward would confiscate the goods in lieu of payment, if he learned of their existence. He waited patiently for his advantage to sink in.

Ivo was in an obvious dilemma. Indecision showed on his face. He realised that Hugh was his only hope of a cash sale in Spalding. Dragging the jars back to his holding would be useless. In no time at all they would be damp and unusable. As he wrestled with the problem Hugh named his price.

"I'll pay you two shillings."

"What! Is that all?" Ivo choked on the small offer. He stamped his foot and clenched his huge fists "So little; it's not even the price of a quarter of wheat...it's...it's... robbery! So little money for a jar of excellent spices!"

"Correction, my friend. The offer was for both jars of cloves. You must decide to take it or leave it. I have pressing business elsewhere." Hugh turned on his heels and started to walk slowly back up the yard, towards the hall. He was not bluffing when he had offered only two shillings, for after settling his dues at the priory, that was all the money he had left. He had taken only four steps when Ivo Longspee shouted after him.

"I'll take it! But I want coins of the kingdom in my hand before I part with the jars. I'll take none of the Lombards' promissory notes!"

Hugh smiled with satisfaction, but made sure he removed all traces of triumph from his face before he turned back to face the man.

"I will fetch your payment." He said, soberly.

The Norman took the coins without a word of thanks and mounted his horse. Satisfied he had been given the right amount of money, he pointed towards the market place and rode off, followed by his groom. No further words were exchanged. There was not one backward glance from either of them.

Hugh watched the two men until they were out of his view. The sight of the Norman's shaven head and the gesture he made as he pointed towards the town, reminded him again of that same gesture used by the pirate helmsman when the krugge was under attack at sea. Hugh shook his head in disbelief. How could a man of noble birth stoop to such crime?

When the sound of their horses had died away, Hugh shouted for his boy to help him replace most of the spices into the jars. He kept a small amount back for his own use. The task took some time for the cloves were much easier to pour out of the narrow necks than they were to get back in again. When the jar was almost full, Hugh pressed the wax seal back in place, smoothing over the cut with a warm knife blade. With John's help, he carried them up to the house, where he stored them under lock and key, in the dry storage room below the hall. With the spices safely locked away, Hugh made his way to the kitchen to find a jug of beer to celebrate his windfall. He was feeling very pleased with himself.

"Beer for the master, Margaret. I'm in a celebratory mood." He slapped her playfully across her bottom, a thing he would never normally have done.

Margaret giggled and filled a jug from the stock barrel. She was flattered by his attention and felt emboldened to ask a favour of him.

"Can I beg a favour, sir? As you are in such a good mood."

Hugh threw up his hands as if nothing would be too much trouble, and took the jug from her.

"It's about my son, John, sir."

Hugh, who had already raised the jug to his mouth and was taking his first sip, removed his lips from the spout and wiped his hand across them. "Good lad. He's a good lad. A credit to you."

"I'm pleased you find him helpful. He was wanting to learn to use a bow and had begged me to ask you to teach him properly."

Hugh smiled broadly. Archery had been his passion in his younger days. The bow had been his weapon on the crusades. If the boy wanted teaching, he had asked the right man.

"Of course. I'll set a butt up down the yard and teach him all I can."

With his housekeeper's thanks ringing in his ears, Hugh went to the solar and poured himself another mug of beer. He was very satisfied with his morning's work. The cloves were worth ten times what he had paid for them. Much more to his satisfaction, he had managed to trick Ivo Longspee, taking some small revenge on the man for the incident at the priory gates that morning and their meeting at sea. The Norman may be physically strong, and he may have good family connections, but he was no match for a wily old soldier with a good head for tactics. Hugh raised his mug to the rafters and silently congratulated himself on his windfall.

Chapter Four

Hugh sat sprawled on his chair beside the fire, enjoying a second mug of beer and talking to his friend, Will the fletcher, about old times. The two old soldiers were good friends; indeed, Will's son, Joseph, had become the reeve on Hugh's Wykeham holding.

"Do you remember that house at Acre, where those Greek girls entertained us?"

Hugh grinned. "Trust you to remember them. You spent all your wages there."

Will slapped his thigh and laughed aloud. "Those were the days. I wish I was twenty again and making war arrows for the King's bowmen." He drained the beer from his mug and threw the dregs onto the turf fire where it spat and bubbled. "I wish I was still earning a soldier's wages as well." He shrugged his shoulders at the thought.

"Another?" Hugh enquired. Without waiting for a reply, he shouted for his housekeeper. "Margaret. Bring us another jug of beer." Then he continued. "You've just reminded me. I used several of your arrows on my Amsterdam trip. I could do with another dozen when you have time."

"Oh! Did you get to use your bow in anger again?" Will sat upright on his stool, his interest aroused, but before Hugh could answer him, Margaret appeared from the kitchen bearing a large earthenware jug, which she placed by the fireside.

"Anything else, sir?"

"No." Hugh shook his head.

Will forgot his questions about the lost arrows and eyed the housekeeper as she walked out of the room.

"What did she say? 'Anything else, sir?' I'd soon find her something else to do, if I were in your shoes. She's a handsome girl is Margaret."

Hugh smiled but said nothing. He was well aware of Margaret but it didn't do to get romantically entangled with your own staff, besides which, he regarded himself as past all that at his age. Even so, he had to admit, Margaret, who was a good twenty-five years younger than him, was a well-made lass.

"Lovely shaped backside and a well-turned leg. Just made for bedding; she being a widow and all," Will added.

Hugh was not amused. Holding a finger up to his lips, he said. "Hush, Will. Keep your comments to yourself. You'll give her the wrong ideas." But secretly he was feeling quite protective of his housekeeper and perhaps a little jealous.

Will, sensing his old friend was not to be drawn on Margaret's charms, changed the subject abruptly. "Tell me, how did you get on in Amsterdam?"

"Fine."

"Did you do the business? How is it that you used those arrows? I know you put much store by the venture. Was it profitable?"

Hugh nodded noncommittally at this barrage of questions. His continental trip had replenished his stock of herbs and he had bought a small amount of spices that he could sell in Spalding. His windfall from Ivo Longspee was worth far more, but he had no intention of drawing anyone's attention to that. He decided he would not mention his brush with pirates in the Wash for he and Will had been in far worse situations on the crusade.

"I got what I went for."

"Good. Joseph will be pleased about that."

Hugh nodded again. His reeve had obviously mentioned that the Amsterdam trip was necessary to bring in some much-needed money.

The two old soldiers slipped into a comfortable silence. Will recalling his long past youth and daydreaming about a Greek girl he had known, who was very like Margaret. Hugh was wondering how he could best dispose of the cloves. He came to the conclusion it would be best to sell a small amount of the Spanish spice locally, to get some much-needed ready money, and to ship the bulk of it to the continent where no awkward questions would be asked. He was already planning to ask Erik to sell the cloves for him in Amsterdam.

"You were very fortunate getting a holding from the king when you returned from the east. I came back to nothing. I have often thought it was lucky you got that lance in your knee." Will's reminiscences about the old days were rudely cut short by the sound of persistent hammering coming from the front of the house.

Hugh put his drink down by the fire, held up a silencing finger to his friend and listened intently. From the frantic knocking, interspersed with the sound of a high-pitched voice, raised loud enough to penetrate the thick oak door, he guessed it must be an emergency. Grumbling under his breath he struggled up from his chair and ambled towards the noise. As he walked into the hallway and neared the front door, he could make out the actual words being shouted and he recognised the female voice shouting them.

"Uncle Hugh! Uncle Hugh! It's Giles! Help!"

Recognising his niece's cries, he rushed the last few steps, drew back the bolt and flung the door open. Elizabeth stumbled over the threshold and collapsed into his arms, almost catching him off balance. He stared at her in astonishment. She was distraught and panting, her face tear stained and her cheeks blood red. He held her close and gently patted her back to reassure her.

Finally, Elizabeth recovered a little, regained her breath enough to speak, and tried to explain. "Uncle Hugh..." She gulped and swallowed a sob. "...It's Giles...I think he's been murdered!" That final effort seemed to drain all her energy. She crumpled against him and started sobbing again. In spite of the pain in his leg, Hugh lifted her in his arms, took her into the hall and placed her in the oak chair, where she sat hunched up like a small child.

Will, realising this was a private, family crisis, was already on his feet. "I'll go Hugh. I'll see you later at the tavern, if you can make it... I'll let myself out."

Hugh turned his attention to his niece. "Steady now my girl. Get your breath back then tell me all about it." He offered her a mug of beer but she brushed it aside. He waited patiently while Elizabeth gulped in several deep breaths and gradually calmed down. Finally, his patience was rewarded and he had an explanation.

"You must come to the market tavern. Giles has been struck down. He's not moving! I'm sure he's dead!"

Hugh thought quickly what he should do. He rushed upstairs, the pain in his leg temporarily forgotten. He threw a few of his herbal remedies into a bag, then hurried back to his niece. By this time, Margaret and her son had heard the noise, even though she was busy in the kitchen and he was cleaning out the stable down the yard. They both ran into the house just as Hugh reached the bottom step of the stairs. He shouted to them. "Here John. Bring this to the market tavern. Follow us." Turning to Margaret he added. "I'm going with Elizabeth...some kind of emergency." Hugh threw the bag of remedies into the boy's hands and grabbed his niece. Grasping her hand firmly in his, he hurried to the market stead.

Elizabeth led them down the side passageway and into the back room of the tavern, where they found Giles still lying motionless on the earthen floor, looking as pale as death. Shocked that he was still not recovered, she burst into tears again and hid her face against her mother's shoulder.

Hugh knelt down beside the still body and placed his hand inside the young fisherman's tunic, desperately searching for a heartbeat. He found what he was seeking and let out a deep sigh of relief. Giles was not dead but he was still unconscious, so there must be some hope for his recovery. Hugh continued his examination, leaning closer to the young man's mouth to check his breathing. It was only when he moved Giles head, he noticed the long red weal down the side of the youth's deathly pale face. Obviously, the boy had been struck on the face a very hard blow or he had fallen heavily on that side. Satisfied the patient was still alive, Hugh turned Giles onto his side and considered his options.

"Get me a goose quill and a light."

Elizabeth hurried to obey, pleased to be doing something to help. She watched apprehensively as Hugh lit the goose feather and let the smouldering quill smoke under the unconscious man's nose. The acrid fumes worked their magic in minutes. Giles coughed violently and began to regain his senses. He opened his eyes and blinked at the light and the figures bending over him, then struggled to move, his face still blank and uncomprehending. Hugh gently restrained him.

Elizabeth and her mother bent over the patient as soon as he showed signs of recovering. Giles recognised them and tried to speak, then he tried to sit up, but as he regained consciousness, the pain flooded over him and he collapsed.

"Sit still, man. You'll do better if you'll only give yourself time," Hugh assured him. "Elizabeth, help me sit him upright in case he vomits. Sometimes a blow to the head can cause that."

Between them they pulled Giles up to a sitting position and propped him against the wall. The angry red bruise on the side of his face was growing darker by the minute. Hugh checked the wound and was pleased to find there was no bleeding from the damaged area, or from elsewhere. He knew from his experience on the battlefields, that bleeding from the ear could mean a broken head and herald more serious problems.

Giles was by then fully conscious and suffering intense pain. He moaned as he gingerly explored the damaged side of his head with the tips of his fingers. Even his own gentle touch made him draw in his breath with the pain.

"Can you open your mouth for me?" Hugh was relieved as the patient performed that simple task. Even though the boy winced at the attempt, he managed to do it successfully.

"Good. Nothing appears to be broken. You have been very lucky, judging by the size of that bruise. Now you must rest. Rest is always the best healer."

Elizabeth, who had been watching and listening intently, turned to speak to her mother. "Giles can sleep in my bed tonight...I'll sleep down here." She kept her gaze on the floor as she spoke but she shot a furtive glance at her mother as she added. "If you and father agree, of course."

"Of course. The lad can hardly walk home in that state."

They carried him upstairs and put him onto the bed, where he lay on his side, very still because any movement made his head throb unbearably. Hugh followed his sister and niece downstairs and shouted for John and his bag of nostrums.

"Will he live, master?" John had stood in the doorway, watching all the while his master had been examining Giles. He was too frightened to enter the room.

"I think he'll recover. Now let's see what we can give him to help him with the pain." Hugh searched in his bag and took out two small containers. He removed the closures and checked the contents by sniffing at each one before he handed it to his sister.

"Here, Maud. These are the best I can do for him." He held up a small, glass bottle of a thick, clear liquid. "This is poppy syrup. It will make him sleep soundly and take away his pain. It's very strong. Give him a quarter of the bottle as a single dose if he can't sleep tonight." He held up a warning finger. "Don't give him any more than that dose, and only use it if he can't sleep without it."

Elizabeth took the syrup from her mother and curiously held it up to the window.

Hugh held up the other small container, which contained a dark brown unguent. "This is a salve to apply to his face. It will soothe away the pain and help the bruising. Don't get it near his mouth or use it on broken skin. It's very poisonous if taken internally."

Maud raised her eyebrows in question.

"It's monkshood salve. You'd know it as wolfsbane. Rub a little of it on the bruising twice a day, when he can bear to be touched. Apply it on a piece of clean linen cloth. It's best applied at night and in the morning. Make sure you clean your hands thoroughly if you get it on your fingers." Elizabeth took the second pot from him and quickly passed it to her mother.

"Don't worry yourself, daughter. I've used it before. It's safe as long as you don't get it in your mouth. It's good for bruises and blains."

Hugh repeated his instructions. "Don't forget. Rub in the salve twice a day. In a day or two Giles will be able to do it himself." Then, overcome with curiosity, he asked. "How did Giles come to have such a serious wound. Surely he didn't just slip and hit his head?"

"No, he did not!" Elizabeth exclaimed. "He was struck down deliberately!"

Hugh frowned in disbelief. The customers at the market tavern were usually sober and quiet, especially at mid-day.

"It was that mongrel, Ivo Longspee!" She spat out the Norman's name.

Whenever that man's name crops up, there's trouble, Hugh thought. He must have come to the inn after he left me, and he wasn't in a good mood after our transaction. Maybe I could be a little to blame for what happened to Giles? He dismissed the idea as soon as he'd thought of it. Ivo Longspee was a nasty character, and there was no excuse for such violence.

"Why did he do that?"

"It was my fault, really. I shouldn't have screamed like I did."

"Steady on, Elizabeth. Start at the beginning, then I might follow your explanation."

"Sorry, Uncle Hugh. Giles was eating his dinner at a corner table. He had only had one mug of small ale, so he wasn't drunk."

Hugh nodded to encourage her to continue.

"Ivo Longspee came in and ordered food. That man is a pig! He always comes in on market day and has double portions of everything!" Her voice rose at the thought.

Maud put her head around the door from the public room and held up a finger to warn her daughter to be more discreet. "We can hear you in here." She hissed. "We do not openly criticise our paying customers."   She could have added, especially when they are of Norman descent and have influential family connections, but she was too busy to get involved in a long argument with her daughter.

"Don't tut at me, mother." Elizabeth whispered under her breath, making sure Maud could not actually hear her answer back. "He is a glutton, Uncle Hugh. He has the manners of one of his own pigs. He shovels in his food with both hands. He finished his meal and ate the bread trencher and demanded another fresh, rye bread, trencher. He does that regularly. He's never satisfied with just one, like every other customer."

"So? How did it happen?"

"I took the fresh bread to him and placed it in front of him. I smiled, in spite of my opinion of him. Father insists I must always smile at the customers." She shot another furtive glance towards the door in case her parents were listening. "He grabbed my wrist with one hand and pulled up my skirts with the other! I screamed! I couldn't help it. He wouldn't let me go even though I struggled."

Hugh nodded emphatically. He was beginning to understand.

"Giles ran over and grabbed him by the collar." She frowned at the memory of the next few seconds and seemed to lose her concentration.

"Go on. What happened next?"

"He threw Giles to the floor and hit him over the head with an oak stool..." The flow of words stopped abruptly. Once again Elizabeth broke down in tears as she relived the scene.

Hugh drew in his breath sharply and frowned at the thought. Oak was as hard as iron, and almost as heavy. Giles would certainly have felt that blow. He patted her on the shoulder and soothed her, as he used to when she was a small child. When she had regained her composure, he persuaded her to continue.

"Giles lay still on the floor. I thought that man had killed him! We carried him into the back room and I ran to get you. The rest you know."

"What about Longspee? Did he leave before someone fetched the bailiff?"

"Not him! He drank his drink, finished off his trencher and threatened my father he would report him for keeping an unruly house. He said it was wrong for innocent travellers to be attacked and threatened when they were only being playful."

"Did your father threaten him, then?"

"No, but Giles did! He shouted he would murder the man if he didn't leave me alone. It was all in the heat of the moment, you understand. Giles is not usually violent."

Hugh nodded thoughtfully. Certainly the short time he had been in Giles' company the lad had shown no tendency to violence.

"Did you send for the bailiff?"

"No. Everybody in the tavern had heard Giles threaten him; even those who didn't actually see what happened. Father thought it better to let things lie."

"Probably very wise. Anyway, Giles is recovering fast. There shouldn't be any permanent damage. He's young and healthy." Hugh gathered up his bag and handed it to John, who was still listening, silent and wide eyed, in the doorway. "Take this home, John. Put it safely in the chest in the solar until I get back."

"Father says, what do we owe you for your services?" Elizabeth asked.

"Nothing my girl. You're family."

"You will stay and eat with us?"

"I intended to have my meal here anyway, so why not. I can check on that young man again before I leave."

Chapter Five.

Next morning when Hugh awoke at first light, he was surprised to find the weather had turned very cold. A light frost covered the exposed cobblestones in the yard, a promise of a hard winter to come. When he ventured outside to fetch the water for his morning wash, he discovered a thin layer of ice on the surface of the water bucket. He pushed his fingers through the fragile coating and threw the disk of ice onto the yard, where it broke into a dozen pieces. Already the dawn sun was warming up the cold air and spreading dark patches of damp on the white frosty stones.

Hugh washed quickly, pulled on a clean shirt and stood in front of the turf fire to warm his stiff joints before he started the day. He was alone in the hall as John had already vacated his overnight place by the side of the fire, and was busy working in the stables. From the inviting smell emanating from the kitchen, Margaret was busy baking. A warm batch of fresh oatcakes stood on the table by the window.

Hugh helped himself to two and took them back to the hall to enjoy them by the fireside. He shivered. He was very aware of the cold now that he was getting older.

His fast broken, Hugh checked on the stables then unlocked the ground floor store room, opened one of the Spanish spice jars and poured some of the cloves into a linen bag. He intended visiting the priory kitchens that morning to offer some of the spices to the cook. On the way, he would walk up to the market stead to call on his patient at the tavern.

The market tavern appeared quiet. He thought at first they had not opened, but inside he found Erik van Driell and several of his crew, eating an early breakfast. Elizabeth and her mother were busy cleaning the room.

He greeted the ship's master then turned to his sister. "How's the casualty, this morning?"

"He's much better." Maud answered him without bothering to stop her dusting. Elizabeth turned her back on him and continued furiously polishing a table as if her life depended on the depth of the shine.

"Good…" He hesitated at their off-hand manner. "… Is there something I'm missing here? What's the matter?"

"Giles rose early, ate a hearty breakfast and dabbed himself with that monkshood ointment you left for him."

"Good. He must be feeling better. Let's have a look at him. Where is he then?"

"You're too late!" Elizabeth threw down her polishing cloth and stamped her foot, thrusting her hands on her hips. "You're much too late! Giles insisted you had cured him and he must get back to that precious boat of his father's. He's put to sea to go fishing. Nothing I could say would stop him." She picked up her cloth, turned her back on her uncle and continued furiously rubbing the oak table top, working out her frustration on the physical task of beeswax polishing.

Hugh shook his head and shrugged his shoulders. His niece had obviously hoped Giles would spend a few more days at the inn. Young people in love could never see enough of each other, but her plans had not worked out. Giles must be keen to catch more fish and shorten the time it would take to get a boat of his own. Hugh warmed to the lad. Love was grand but the practicalities of life must come first.

Elizabeth finished polishing the table. He could see her reflection in the mirror finish she had produced. She picked up her polishing cloth and flounced out of the room, without another word.

Maud straightened up from her work and smiled indulgently after her daughter.

"Here, you'd better have that poppy syrup back. He didn't need it. The boy's obviously tougher than he looks." She handed the unopened bottle to her brother and went back to her chores. Hugh was relieved the young fisherman was much better. Turning to the skipper of the Flemish merchant ship, he asked "Now then, Erik, how are you today? Have you managed to dock and unload?"

"I'm fine, but my temper is not so good!" Erik grumbled.

"Why, my young friend?"

"We have casks of wine and bolts of cloth for the priory but we can't get near the prior's wharf for all those barges unloading sandstone blocks."

"Ah! Our building prior keeps the river very busy with his masons' requirements."

"I have anchored the krugge in midstream. By the time we get near enough to the quay to unload, we will have missed the outgoing tide. We are stuck here until tomorrow morning."

"That may be lucky for me and for you." Hugh said philosophically.

"Lucky? I have to call at Boston on my way out to sea. All this delay costs money."

"I have some spices I want delivered to Amsterdam. I will make it worth your while if you will carry them and sell them at a good price for me."

"Bring them down to the wharf this afternoon. There's no hurry. We're going nowhere today. By then we may have found a place at the quay."

Hugh went over to his sister and asked her to serve the Flemish crew with another round of drinks, which he would pay for in due course. He left the inn and walked slowly up the busy market stead towards the priory. Tuesday was market day in Spalding. Already stalls were being erected and barrows pushed into position. He passed the time of day with the potter, stopping to admire some small earthenware containers, useful for storing salves and unguents, then he threaded his way between the peddlers and craftsmen towards the priory gates.

The priory gatehouse was almost deserted with one solitary guard standing on duty. The man at arms nodded Hugh through the entrance with a perfunctory glance. The lesson of the previous day had already been forgotten. It was only human nature, Hugh conceded, maybe the prior was at his retreat near Wykeham and with their master out of sight, the servants relaxed. In the kitchen the Brother in charge of the kitchens was tucking into a hearty breakfast. His eyes lit up at the sight of the bag of spice. He inspected the cloves closely, inhaling their aromatic perfume with obvious delight.

"They're best quality Spanish cloves. I bought them only yesterday."

"I'll take them all. The Lord Prior is very fond of the flavour of cloves. We have a brace of quail for his mid-day meal tomorrow. He'll enjoy a clove sauce with them." The cook wiped his hands on his apron and wrote out a receipt for Hugh to take to the steward's office for payment.

Hugh found Brother James in the library, instructing a young monk in the art of illuminating capital letters. James was a master of calligraphy. Many of the books he now cared for had been the fruits of his own labour. Hugh stood in the doorway and watched as the old monk narrowed his eyes and squinted between half closed eyelids at the parchment, holding the work at arm's length.

"It a sign of old age, when your arms get too short." Hugh quipped, interrupting the lesson.

"I can still see well enough to tell this young man where he's gone wrong." James said dryly. Then he relented and beamed at Hugh. "I have a new wine for you to try." He unlocked his store cupboard and took out a full container. "It's from Anjou. The cellarer tells me it's still a bit young, but he likes it." He poured out two full cups then, glancing at the novice calligrapher, poured a little into a small, cracked cup and grudgingly handed it to him.

"Here's health." Hugh sniffed the bouquet of the wine then sipped it. "Not bad. A bit sweet for me though. If you give it a chance it could age well." His eyes twinkled at the unlikely thought of Brother James storing any wine long enough to let it age.

"What can we do for you, Hugh? Do you wish to consult a herbal?"

"No, not today. I called on you on my way to find Brother Godfrey. I missed him yesterday. He was at Wykeham, I understand."

"That reminds me, talking of Anjou and herbals. At Chapter this morning we read out a letter from the abbot of Anjou. We have been sent a newly made copy of De Simplicibus Medicinis."

Hugh beamed with delight. That book was a rare and valuable treatise on medicines, written by the masters at Salerno University.

"I haven't yet seen it. The Lord Prior has it in his apartment at the moment."

Hugh nodded knowingly. He could understand the prior's interest in such a rare volume. He was disappointed, but he looked forward to consulting the book when it joined the other treasures in Brother James' care.

"Brother Godfrey will definitely be in the herb garden today. At chapter he was asking if any of the other brothers had experience of drying herbs for storage. You might well be the answer to his prayers. God moves in mysterious ways."

Hugh smiled indulgently. Brother James was a man with a simplistic belief in God's will. The vagaries of war and his experiences in the crusades had made Hugh much more circumspect.

"Another taste of this wine before you move on?"

Hugh hesitated, but only momentarily. "Oh! Go on then. But not a full measure, I have some work to do today."

Brother Godfrey was digging in the herb beds, his gown tied up at the waist. He stopped his work when Hugh came into sight.

Hugh recognised him immediately as the young cleric he had encountered at the Wykeham wharf, but his officious manner seemed to have changed.

The monk smiled affably. "It is Hugh Pinchbeck, isn't it? Brother James described you well. He told me you were a tall man with white hair. He also said you walked with a slight limp from an old battle wound. It doesn't seem to be bothering you much this morning." Godfrey held out a hand in greeting.

"I've learned to live with it." Hugh said. "Now, you need some advice on preparing your herbs, I understand."

"Brother Mark, God rest his soul, looked after all the priory's herbal preparation. I was starting to learn from him, but there wasn't enough time before he died."

"Show me your drying room. I'll see what I can suggest."

Godfrey gave instruction to his lay helpers to carry on turning the soil over and led Hugh to the drying area. He stopped inside the doorway to the new stone barn and pointed up into the rafters, where hundreds of bunches of herbs were hanging to dry. "What do you think?"

Hugh reached up and fingered some of the seed heads. "They're too damp. They will be mildewed unless you get more air through them."

Godfrey frowned and looked perplexed

"If anything, you've been too conscientious and hung too much in one room, in your effort not to waste your crops. If these were my plants, I'd thin the bunches out. Pick out the best and leave them hanging in here. The remainder you can lay out on the floor." Hugh glanced around the room. "What do you do for heat in here?"

"I tried a turf fire on the floor in the centre of the room, but the smoke affects everything. It coats the herbs in soot."

"Yes, it would. It would spoil most of them. You need a fire in one corner with a flue to the outside to take the smoke away. That's the kind of fire place I had the mason build in my outhouse at Eau Side."

Brother Godfrey beckoned Hugh further into his workshop and out of sight of the lay worker. He produced a jug of wine from under the bench.

"I get a generous allowance for making tinctures." He explained, with a smile.

"Not for me." Hugh shook his head vigorously. Normally he would have loved another cup of wine but Brother James had already persuaded him to drink too much at that time of the morning. "Is there anything else I can help with while I'm here?"

"We have two new casualties in the infirmary. One of the brothers and a lay worker fell off the scaffolding erected around the new tower. It happened only yesterday evening. I'd appreciate your opinion on their injuries."

Godfrey led Hugh through the priory grounds, past the mill, to the priory infirmary. This stone building was where the aged brothers, who were too old or infirm to work and take an active part in the life of the religious house, spent their days, and where they treated any monks who became sick. Hugh knew the hospitaler by sight but he had never been involved in the treatment of any of the priory inmates, only in the occasional blood letting. Brother

Mark had always managed the treatments very well on his own.

"I hear you have two badly injured men, Brother."

The hospitaler took them to the beds where the two men lay. He hovered in the background, anxious to hear their advice on what treatment to give them.

Godfrey explained. "The lay worker broke his leg when the scaffolding fell. Brother Ignatius fell on his back on a block of stone and has extensive bruising. As far as I can tell they have no other injuries."

Hugh checked the man with the broken leg. The broken limb had been set and splinted with a wooden staff. He measured the length of the broken leg against the good leg and made sure the ties were secure but not too tight to deaden the foot. He ran an expert hand down the skin, feeling for the break and the alignment of the bones. He smiled to himself and nodded his approval. Whoever had set the broken bone had experience of mending fractured limbs.

"Did you set this? If you did, you have done well."

Godfrey shook his head. "Not I. I haven't the experience. It was mended by one of the shepherds. He has set innumerable sheep's legs when they have injured themselves on the marshes. He says he could do it with his eyes closed."

"Get him to teach you. He's good."

The injured monk lay on his stomach. His bare back was a mass of broken skin and black bruises. His eyes were closed. He seemed to be asleep or barely conscious.

"We gave him poppy syrup to ease the pain. He couldn't bear to draw breath the pain was so intense."

"What have you applied to bring out the bruises?"

"Nothing yet. What would you suggest?"

"I find common dock is the best for such an extensive area. Boil the leaves in water and add some oats to thicken it. Apply this lotion when it has cooled. In this case I would soak clean linen pieces in the solution and lay them on the bruises, that way the application will dry out much slower. Change the dressing in the morning and in the evening, then you will not keep disturbing the poor fellow."

Godfrey looked at the hospitaler for reassurance, which was forthcoming. He promised. "I'll get the lotion made immediately. You will have it later today."

Several elderly monks were seated around the fire. Hugh knew that it had been Brother Mark's responsibility to check on them to make their old age more comfortable. "I presume your elderly patients have no new problems, hospitaler?"

"Nothing that a youth draught wouldn't cure." The monk laughed, then added more seriously. "Two of the brothers need a blood letting when you can do it. If you tell me when you can supervise it, I will prepare them."

Hugh had performed this surgical procedure for the monks many times. Brother Mark, like all the monks, was forbidden to cut into the human body by papal law, so blood letting was not in his repertoire.

"Good. Now I must go. I will call later in the week. But if you should need me before then, please send for me." Hugh left the infirmary and made his way to the steward's office to collect his payment for the package of cloves.

The steward's office was quiet. That morning there were no tenants waiting to pay their debts or to see Thomas Bohun on other business.

Hugh handed his receipt to the clerk in the outer office and waited while the man went into the inner room to get the payment authorised.

"Hugh, come in. I've been waiting for a chance moment to see you." Thomas bellowed from the other room.

The clerk held the door open, beckoning Hugh to go in.

"No one is to disturb us. That includes you." The steward shouted after his underling, as the man left the room.

"Now Hugh. I mentioned before that I wanted to consult you on a health matter." The portly lawyer rose from his chair and strode around the desk, pulling his clothes off as he spoke. With an obviously painful effort, he lifted the shirt off his weighty torso and over his head. Sitting on the edge of the desk in front of Hugh, he turned his back towards his visitor and said. "Take a look at my back."

Hugh did as he was bid and could immediately see the problem. The steward's back was covered in angry boils. From his shoulder blades to just above his buttocks was a mass of red, suppurating, lumps.

"Looks painful." Hugh sympathised. "By the number of old scars, it also looks to be long standing. You've had these for some time."

"Can you suggest anything to help?"

Hugh looked closely at the skin and noted there were a few deep-seated boils that were refusing to break and discharge.

"I think you'll have to clean it with a salt water lotion and apply a salve to draw out the poisons. It will heal, but it will take time and effort. One or two of the pustules are very deep. I may have to cut into them to let the poison out."

"As you are a surgeon, I expected you'd advise some cutting or bloodletting, but plain salt water? ... That seems a bit too simple a remedy. No ground-up saint's bones or dried dragon's blood? What about casting my horoscope?" The last suggestions were delivered with a note of sarcasm and were obviously the result of past, unfortunate experiences.

"You've taken some fancy advice before, by the sounds of those comment." Hugh laughed.

"That's as maybe, master surgeon. That advice cost me dearly but it did me no good, as you can see."

"In the Holy Land I've seen deep ulcers healed by the Arab physicians, with a simple salt solution and lots of perseverance. The king's own wound was bathed in salt solution for days after we cut the bad flesh from his arm."

"Right! I'll try anything. If it's good enough for the king it will do for me. Tell me what to do. Certainly, with all the salt pans the priory owns, I have no shortage of your simple medicine."

"Get your servants to boil some clean water, then dissolve about a mug of salt in a bucket of that water. Once it has cooled, keep it in a covered bucket and bathe your back with it twice a day. I will send you some ointment to apply after you have bathed and dried the area. I promise you should see an improvement in a week or so."

"You sound very confident, Hugh. Or is that to get me to pay you your fee now?"

"Pay me when the boils start healing. I'll send my boy over with a pot of salve as soon as I get home."

Thomas pulled on his shirt, grunting with the pain and effort He sank back gingerly in his chair. "If your treatment is a success, I'll willingly pay you. When do you want to cut into the deep pustules?"

"I'll wait a day or two to see if the drawing unguent has an effect. I am coming to bleed some of the brothers later in the week, I will decide then if your boils need incising." Hugh helped the steward replace his shirt then he continued. "I noticed you have had this problem for some time. There are many old scars."

"You could say that! I've been plagued for several years now."

"The king's surgeons taught me to recommend plenty of fresh green vegetables in the diet. They believe it cleans out the system and balances the humours."

Seeing Thomas grimace at this advice. Hugh smiled and sadly shook his head. It was just the reaction he had anticipated. He knew that wealthy men, like the priory steward, could afford to eat the best cuts of meat at every meal and most of them ate little else. Meat and sweetmeats were their staple diet. Vegetables and cereals were food for the poor.

"You have excellent watercress beds in the priory grounds. I would recommend an equal weight of fresh watercress be added to your meat, and that amount to be eaten at each meal."

Thomas looked unhappy at the suggestion, pulling a disgusted face at the very idea. Finally, he relented, shook his head, feigning disbelief, and grinned at Hugh. "If it can cure these eruptions, I'll eat a bucketful of watercress with every meal. But it does seem a rather simple regime." He unlocked his desk drawer and paid Hugh the money due for the cloves.

"Thank you, sir." Hugh put the payment in his purse and turned to go, but he had to have the last word. "Sometimes the simple remedies are the best. As the learned doctors would have it, you have an excess of some humour in your blood and the watercress will correct it for you. If not, we can try poultices and I will let some blood." He inclined his head in respect and left the steward mulling over the simple course of treatment he had been advised to follow.

Chapter Six.

The inhabitants of the fens woke up again to a hard frost on the Wednesday morning. Hugh stood in the doorway of the stable and watched the steam rising off the cobblestones as the slanting autumn sun warmed up the frozen yard. There was a slow moving, dark line of damp where the sunlight topped the buildings and moved slowly over the frozen cobbles, like the shadow on the sundial on the priory wall.

"I'll go to Wykeham as soon as you've saddled the horse." He shouted over his shoulder to John, who was busy inside the stable.

Hugh liked to visit his Wykeham holding at least once a week. Joseph, the reeve, did a good job, he was a trustworthy and loyal worker, but Hugh knew there was no fertiliser as good as the master's foot. If the workers on the farm anticipated him dropping by whenever he felt like it, they would always be on their toes.

"Your horse is a bit lively this morning, master. He hasn't been exercised for several days."

"Well, today's his lucky day. A visit to the holding and back, is all of ten miles. That will give him all the exercise he needs." Hugh stepped into the yard to let the groom walk the horse out into the sunshine. He climbed the stone steps by the stable door to help him mount his horse. His war injury didn't stop him doing many things but he found lifting his weight into the saddle from the ground was one of the few actions that did cause him problems.

"I will be back by this evening. You must take any messages for me, and make sure the fire stays in. Get some more logs chopped for the store and send for more turf. Judging by the frost this morning, we will soon be into the depths of winter."

Hugh's Wykeham holding consisted entirely of land that had been reclaimed from the sea. Centuries before, the Romans had built banks to contain the waters of the river Welland and to keep out the tides of the Wash. They had drained the surrounding fenland to produce good, fertile silt, which fed much of their vast empire

The priory kept the ancient drainage systems and sea banks in good order. Hugh was very grateful for the king's intervention when he returned from the crusade. The prior would have gladly kept the farm for himself as it ran down to the marshes and boasted a salt pan, but King Edward himself had put pressure on the prior to grant the lease of the holding to Hugh, in gratitude for his medical work on the battlefield.

Hugh trotted the horse along the riverside up to the great stone bridge, which spanned the Welland. There he crossed the river and turned into the morning sun, taking the road east, riding along the river to Fulney and out to Wykeham. Most of the town was now on the far side of the river. He glanced at his own house and yard across the water and smiled as he saw a puff of white smoke curl up from the brick chimney and over the thatch. He knew that John was already putting new turf on the fire. He settled his mount into a steady trot and followed the curve of the river along the old Roman bank.

Spalding was soon out of sight. There were few dwellings on that side of the river, only some tumbledown, turf and mud cottages, inhabited by landless men, who eked out a precarious existence selling a day's labour here and there to feed their families. A dog ran out of one of the tiny cottages and barked furiously at the passing horse. Hugh took a tight hold on the reins and dug his knees into the animal's flanks as it reared skittishly. John was right, the horse did need some exercise. A naked child, spattered with mud, ran out into the road and pulled the dog away. Hugh dug in his heels and galloped the horse to use up its excess energy.

At Fulney, he slowed the horse to a gentle trot as he passed by a herd of the priory cows being taken out to pasture. Further on, he cantered along the new road leading towards the grand house the prior had built near Wykeham,   and the wharf they had visited on the   journey back from Amsterdam. Finally, he turned off the prior's new road onto a track that led into the fen, towards his own holding.

By the time the thatched roofs of his farm buildings came into view, Hugh had slowed his sweating mount to a trot, and was enjoying the countryside. Ploughed fields belonging to the priory, stretched out to either side of the track. The light brown silt already showed the thin green lines of the autumn sown crops. In one small field where the seeds had been newly broadcast, a boy and his dog were scaring off the crows and seagulls, the lad slinging stones at the feathered thieves and sending his dog among them to scatter them into the air.

As Hugh passed the boundary stones between the priory land and his own, he paid more serious attention to the state of the land. From his high viewpoint on horseback, he could see a long way over the flat fen countryside. The first of his worker's he met on his way to the small group of houses near the creek, was Richard, the reeve's youngest boy, who looked after the sheep.

"Morning, sir." The boy recognised his master and respectfully bowed his head.

"Morning, Richard. How are the sheep?" He turned in his saddle to overlook the flock.

"We lost another one last night, master."

"From disease?"

The boy shook his head sullenly.

"Stolen, you mean?" This was becoming a regular problem. "Any idea who? Have we any beggars in the area?"

"My father says it's them across the creek."

Hugh looked towards the east, towards Ivo Longspee's holding, and frowned. Every time he had any kind of contact with that man there seemed to be trouble. "Have you found any traces of the thieves? Have you checked the mud flats along the edge of the creek? Maybe there's signs of a boat beaching, or footprints in the mud."

The boy nodded. "I'll walk back that way when I've finished here, sir."

Hugh thanked the lad and spurred his mount on towards the small knot of building by the side of the creek, where Joseph the reeve was already waiting anxiously to greet him.

"Morning, master. You've just arrived right. Betty has just baked a batch of fresh bread." He stepped forward and helped Hugh dismount.

Hugh followed his reeve into the largest of the houses, a timbered property with a reed thatched roof. He sat down by the turf fire and gratefully accepted a mug of ale, some goat's cheese and a small loaf, still warm from the fire.

"I've just spoken to your youngest. We lost yet another sheep last night, he tells me."

"Yes, master. That's three since the summer. All gone without trace. They're not straying. I'm certain they've been stolen."

"Richard suspects our neighbours again."

"Well he might. They are strange men that side of the creek. We see some questionable goings on."

"Like what?" Hugh raised his eyebrows.

"Like fishing boats putting to sea full of armed men. They wouldn't have room to catch fish with that number aboard, and they don't need swords and daggers to subdue herring."

"I see." Hugh had heard all this before but he didn't comment on that fact, as he knew Joseph worried about it. "Anything else suspicious?"

"They don't farm the land properly. There's no way that holding could feed ten or so men and their dependants. There's not a farmer among them."

Hugh nodded that he understood the comments. Even though he had only a handful of men and their dependants working his holding the land could hardly serve his table and fill all their mouths with food. A less able reeve would not have managed it.

"Anything else I need to know, Joseph?"

Joseph hesitated then decided to voice his concerns. "One of the men has taken in his widowed sister and her four babies. He's finding it a bit of a strain to manage...and er..."

Hugh, detecting the doubt in his reeve's voice, raised his eyebrows, inviting Joseph to complete what he had started to say.

"...I wonder how they'll manage. I don't want any more problems with stolen sheep."

"Are you saying one of our own men might be responsible?"

"No, of course not. There would be traces at his home."

"You've looked then?"

Joseph squirmed under Hugh's piercing gaze. "Well yes, I've looked. He lives a few miles to the west of here. I made an excuse to take some bread for his sister and her children. I looked for any traces of mutton joints, but of course I didn't find anything... nor did I really expect to."

Hugh smiled reassurance at the young man. "You are only looking after my affairs, Joseph. Don't be so hard on yourself. If there's nothing to hide, there's no problem. And it does well to let the men know you are vigilant." But he knew from his experience with fellow soldiers that often a thief is the least suspected man and often the closest to home. "Which man are you talking about?"

"Peter, the salt man."

"Is that it then? Nothing else to report?"

"Well...there was the business early this morning."

"Yes?"

"Peter, our man who looks after the salt pan down on the foreshore, came running up to the house to tell me there was a fight going on over there."

"Fighting among themselves?"

"I'm not sure. We could hear raised voices from over the water, but the high mud bank at the edge of the creek blocked our view. We climbed to the crest of the bank on this side but all we could make out was the top of a boat mast. It was moored just off the mud flats."

"Was it their boat or some other fishing boat?"

"We think it was another fishing boat because no one had seen them put to sea. Anyway, they shouted and yelled at the top of their voices as if they were being attacked, then it all went quiet and we heard no more."

Hugh drained his mug and sat by the fire, warming his damaged leg. It had been a chilly ride over that morning. The business of the Spanish cloves flitted through his mind again. The story told to him by Ivo Longspee, of a shipwreck and a failed rescue, seemed even more unlikely now that he had spoken to Joseph. The sooner those cloves were in Amsterdam, the happier he would feel. Seeing the reeve's wife hovering nearby, anxious to fill his every need, he dismissed the problem from his mind and threw the last dregs of his drink into the fire, where they spat on the hot turf. Hauling himself up from his comfortable seat he said wearily.

"Come on then, Joseph. I think we'd better walk the farm and take a look at the state of everything."

Hugh's holding was not a large one by priory standards, just four bovates of arable land, with an orchard, a small vineyard and a single salt pan. If the King hadn't granted Hugh a small pension as well as the holding, he would not have managed to keep himself and his workers in food and fuel. Their first stop was the vineyard, where Joseph pointed out the damage the early frosts had done to the tender vines.

"I will need all the clippings you can collect when you prune the vines, Joseph." Hugh used the juice for preparing a remedy for earache. Joseph then led his master over to the orchard where the swine were penned.

"The pigs look well." Hugh bent down and fondled the ears of a fat sow that had come grunting to the fence in the hope of a titbit. "Any problems with them?"

"No. They're as healthy as swine should be. We've had a good year. Lots of large litters and all healthy. They've done us proud."

Hugh leaned back on the fence around the pigs' enclosure and took the weight off his bad leg. "What about oats and barley? Do you think we should let the big field lay fallow again?"

"Must be time for it, master. We've spread plenty of muck on the smaller fields so they will crop well."

"Have you managed to keep back enough good seed this year?"

"Aye. Everything is under control." The reeve frowned. He was very experienced at managing the farm, and his master did not usually go into such detail about his plans.

Hugh read the doubt on Joseph's face. He slapped his reeve across his shoulder and smiled reassurance. "I'm only checking on these things because I can see problems looming, lad. The town bridge over the Welland is in a bad state of repair. It will take a lot of stone and a lot of the mason's skill to repair it properly. Then there's the drainage dykes; they need clearing. And the riverbanks need renewing. Our Lord Prior will expect the townspeople to pay for all these improvements. On top of these heavy tax burdens, financing the king's Scottish wars could prove the last straw for many of us. I'm just looking out for our survival." Hugh leaned over the gate and slapped a sow on its ample haunches. "We can well do without sheep being stolen. You'll have to put a constant guard on them, or bring them up to the yard every night."

"I know, master. Come the bad weather, certainly before lambing time, they'll be brought nearer the farm buildings anyway. I was hoping it could wait until then, but you're right of course."

Hugh completed his round of the farm and deliberately ended up at the salt pan, where a labourer was shovelling the newly formed layer of salt into sacks. "Is this Peter, the man who heard the disturbance this morning?"

"Aye, master." Joseph stopped the man from working and took him over to his master, to tell the story first hand

"It were at first light. I'd come down here to check on the state of the salt. I heard them over there." He pointed across the wide mouth of the salt-water creek to the raised bank on the other side. "They was making a great noise. You'd think they was being attacked, or something."

"You saw a boat, I understand?"

"No. I didn't see a boat, master. Just the top of the mast sticking up over yon bank."

"Any idea who's boat it was?"

"No. We get all the fishing boats by here on the early tide. Could have been a Boston boat or a Spalding boat. May even have been one from further down the coast. They all fish for the herring off this shore."

"Could you make out what they were shouting?"

"No, master."

Hugh decided on one last question to test the man. "We lost another sheep last night, Peter. Any ideas on where it could have gone?"

Peter shook his head and seemed genuinely concerned about the loss. "Unless its our neighbours" He nodded towards the far bank. "I can't think, master."

Hugh could detect nothing suspicious in Peter's manner. Realising he had learned all he could, he thanked the man, walked back to the main house with the reeve and took his leave of him. "I must get back to Spalding now. I have business on the docks to attend to. Let me know of any more problems with our neighbours or your work force. If there is more trouble from the next door holding, I'll have a word with the priory bailiff and the steward about it." With a small sack of freshly ground flour, some fresh goat fat for making salves and a bag of salt for his own use, slung over the horse's back, he left at a fast canter, anxious to be back in Spalding.

Chapter Seven

When Hugh finally rode across the great bridge at Spalding and turned down the towpath that skirted the docks, he was delighted to see the Flemish krugge had managed to dock at the priory quay and was being unloaded. Erik van Driell, was seated on a wine barrel supervising his crew. Hugh brought his horse to a halt beside the seaman.

"Glad to see you managed to get alongside, Erik. I would like to bring those spice jars down to you. Is that convenient?"

"Aye. Bring them in the next hour. We can put them at the stern for safety. I'm loading up with fleeces from Richard the skinner's warehouse, when we've got the priory goods unloaded. I'll put your jars among the sheep's fleeces. They'll travel safely there." Erik bent down, picked up the long bundle at his feet and handed Hugh the linen bag containing his bow and arrows. "Here, you might need these again."

Hugh took the bundle and smiled his thanks. He greatly valued his yew longbow. It was a fine example of the bowyer's craft and had cost him dearly. That bow had saved him in many a close scrape. He thought of it as a reliable old friend.

Erik patted the bow through the case and looked up at Hugh. "Thanks for your help the other day. I think your skill with this yew stave probably saved our lives."

Hugh was flattered at the compliment. "If you fancy a jug of ale, come up to the house. You know where it is." Then he dug in his heels and let his horse walk on towards home.

Erik van Driell left his men to complete the unloading and followed Hugh along the towpath on foot.

At Eau Side, young John was busy in the yard, chopping wood and stacking it under cover. He dropped his axe at the sound of the horse's hoofs on the cobblestones of the yard, and ran to help his master dismount.

"Is all well?" Hugh asked.

"Fine, master. You are back earlier than I expected."

"We need to move those Spanish spices from the store room to the docks. They're going to Amsterdam on one of the Flemish merchant ships." As Hugh spoke, the skipper of the krugge ambled up the yard towards them. "Here he is, the master of that merchant ship. Bring a jug of ale into the hall. We could both do with a drink."

When their thirst was quenched, Hugh took Erik to show him the Spanish spice jars.

"They are both full of best quality cloves."

"A Spanish seal I see. That quatity of cloves must be worth a king's ransom." The ship's master stroked his chin thoughtfully. He knew Hugh as a friend but he was still concerned for himself. "I suppose it's all above board? No chance they're stolen?"

Hugh smiled; Erik was no fool. "No. I bought and paid for them fair and square. In fact, the fellow who sold them to me is a kinsman of the Earl of Lincoln. I will admit I got a bargain, but that's because he's short of money."

The master chuckled; he was reassured. He was a shrewd trader and fully understood the lure of a bargain. "I find one man's loss is always another man's gain."

They loaded the spice jars onto a packhorse. John led the horse down the yard and along the towpath, while Hugh and Erik followed on foot. The group had just left the yard and was walking beside the river towards the quays, when they heard a horse galloping furiously along the Wykeham road, on the far side of the Welland. They all turned to look as the horseman drew level with them. The man was riding as if the devil himself was chasing him, his mount was wet with sweat and foaming at the mouth. Hugh thought he recognised the rider.

"John. Isn't that Ivo Longspee's groom? The man who came here with his master, when we bought the cloves from them?"

John nodded vigorous agreement. "Aye, master, and by the looks of that horse he's ridden it hard all the way from beyond Wykeham."

Whatever business had brought the man to Spalding, it must be very urgent. But Hugh didn't give the subject too much thought, for he knew his neighbours at Wykeham were unpredictable.

When they reached the docks with the cloves, the Flemish crew was still unloading the bolts of priory cloth. Erik shouted at his men, trying to hurry them along, but it made little difference for the problem was not of the crew's making. The prior's servants were checking every single barrel of wine and unwinding every bolt of cloth before they loaded it onto their wagons. Hugh smiled to himself. The prior was regularly checking on his men. It wouldn't do for them to accept delivery of a half-empty barrel of wine or a bolt of damaged cloth. Especially as my taxes are paying for some of it, he thought.

Time on the quayside passed slowly. The two men chatted as the crew unloaded the cargo. Ivo Longspee's groom rode back over the bridge accompanied by the bailiff and several of his men at arms. It was intriguing, but Hugh couldn't guess what was happening with his neighbours.

"Come sit by me." Erik made room on a barrel top. "Don't turn around and stare, but my crew tell me we are being watched by one of the prior's men at arms. He seems to be on the lookout from the bridge."

Hugh nonchalantly turned his head and glanced up at the bridge. He saw the bailiff's man leaning against the wall, trying to look inconspicuous. There was no doubt the man was watching the dock area. Something was obviously wrong.

"I think he has a companion concealed near the entrance to the market stead. I have just noticed another man at arms looking over this way."

The ship's master shrugged his shoulders. "Nothing to do with us, I'm sure. But I'll keep my eyes open to see what he gets up to. Now, tell me again how you came by all those spices?"

Hugh grinned to himself. Erik was a suspicious young man that was for certain. The sight of authority seemed to have brought back all his doubts.

Once the Flemish krugge was unloaded, the crew carried the spice jars on board and stowed them at the stern. The master got up from his seat and stretched his legs. Now it was time to board his ship and cross the river to Richard the skinners wharf.

"Wait a moment." Hugh whispered, holding Erik's arm to restrain him. "That man at arms is signalling his accomplice. Something is afoot."

Erik sat back on the barrel and glanced down river, towards the sea. "There's a fishing boat coming in to dock. Perhaps that's what he's been waiting for."

Hugh followed the young man's gaze and saw a local fishing boat manoeuvring along the middle of the river between the other moored craft. As the boat came nearer, he saw the white fish emblem on the prow and recognised it instantly as the Fisher's boat. Slowly it docked at the end of the quay. A boy jumped off and tied it fast, then things happened very quickly. The crew had no time to come ashore before the bailiff's man arrived at the dock with a group of men at arms.

"That looks like big trouble for some poor devil," Erik observed, quietly.

The men at arms surrounded the crew as they came ashore. Hugh stood up to get a better view but in the melee it was impossible to make out exactly what was happening. Suddenly he spotted a tall, slim, young man being detained by the guards. He frowned as he recognised the detainee by the dark bruise down one side of his face.

"They've got Giles! Giles Fisher!" He muttered to himself. It was indeed the young man Elizabeth had introduced to him only two days earlier.

The men at arms formed up with their prisoner in the centre of their rank and marched off towards the priory. The rest of the fishing boat's crew stood surprised and open mouthed as their young master was led away.

"Whatever he's done, it looks serious for him." Erik voiced both their thoughts aloud. "You appear to know him. Is he a local?"

"I met him only the other day. He seemed a pleasant enough young lad." Hugh said no more but his thoughts were racing, What would Elizabeth make of it all? He knew his niece would be devastated. "Look, I must go and have a word with the crew of that fishing boat. Someone I know could be involved in this business." He hurried down to the dockside and spoke to the crew who had now all jumped ashore.

"What's happened? Why has Giles been taken away?"

"We don't know." The young stripling spread his hands in a gesture of bewilderment.

"Hadn't one of you better run and tell his father. There must be some mistake. I'm sure he'll find out what's amiss."

The crew argued among themselves then agreed with Hugh's suggestion. An older seaman took charge and told the boy what to do. "You run to the master's house. You'd better call at the tavern and tell miss Elizabeth on your way back. We'll unload the catch and get it to the salting house."

The boy ran towards the market stead as fast as he could. Hugh walked home alongside the river, deeply troubled by the scene he had just witnessed. His niece seemed very taken with this young man. She would not be happy if he was gaoled.

Chapter Eight

Hugh and Will the fletcher sat in the market tavern drinking together and reminiscing about the crusades.

"It was a time I would not have missed for the world." Will said.

"Aye and me."

"Unlike me, you came out of it very well. I know you were wounded but when Edward was crowned, he did grant you a holding for your services to him."

Hugh nodded. He had a lot to be thankful for. He glanced at his sister, serving drinks to the other customers, and he thought about his niece, Elizabeth, and Giles, her young man. He had heard no more of the business at the quay and was sure it was just a simple misunderstanding. The young couple seemed very much in love and their eventual marriage would be advantageous to both families. An alliance between a tavern owner's family and a successful fishing family made good economic sense. That fact alone would have been enough to ensure the marriage took place, but these young people seemed to be very much in love. That was a bonus indeed.

Hugh had never married because he had spent his younger days soldiering and said he had never found the right woman. Most of his married friends had loveless marriages. He chuckled to himself when he recalled the old saying. 'A groom who does not regret marriage within the first year, deserves a golden bell.' He was sure Giles would get his golden bell, if he overcame this present difficulty and married Elizabeth.

"A coin for your thoughts." Will's voice broke into his reverie.

"Oh! Nothing really. I was just thinking we may soon be seeing my niece wed. She seems very taken with Giles Fisher. A happy marriage can be a blessing."

"Oh yes? Why have you never taken the wedding vows, then?" Will chuckled, he had been unhappily married but was now widowed.

"Never met the right woman. And it's too late now."

Hugh was just draining his second mug of small ale when he heard the sound of a distraught female voice shouting his name from the back room.

"Uncle Hugh! Uncle Hugh!"

He rushed to the door as fast as his limp would allow. Elizabeth was there.

"Giles has been... thrown in prison..." She collapsed onto a chair, out of breath from running.

"Steady on my girl. Get your breath back then tell me properly."

She leaned back and took several deep breaths until she was able to speak again. "I've just run all the way from the priory gaol...They've locked Giles up...We can't get in to see him."

The old man thought quickly. He had seen the prior's men march Giles away from the docks, but he had assumed the matter was to do with the argument in the tavern and it would soon be sorted out. Now Elizabeth was telling him Giles was being kept in confinement. Something was very wrong. He patted her on her back and asked, "What about his mother or father? Can they not see him?"

"No. His father was pleading with the gaoler when we got there. They won't let any of us see him. Can't you get in to see him. Uncle Hugh?"

He was very touched with her faith in him, but what could he do that Giles' parents couldn't?

"You're his surgeon. You were treating his injured face. Can't you visit him in gaol to do that?"

Hugh nodded thoughtfully. In her desperation his niece may have hit on a good idea. It was certainly worth a try. He didn't hesitate. He would do anything in his power to please Elizabeth.

"I'll go and get my bag, then we shall see. But don't expect miracles."

Hugh hurried back home, accompanied by his niece. He packed a pot of monkshood salve and a soothing ointment into a bag, and put two leeches into a jar for good measure, before they left the house. They walked together as far as the market tavern, where Elizabeth stayed, while Hugh went on alone to the priory.

At the priory, the gaoler was reluctant to let Hugh in to see Giles, even though he knew the old man was a healer and Hugh explained that Giles had a badly bruised face.

"Wait here in my room, while I send to the steward to see if you can attend to him." The gaoler sent a lad running to Thomas Bohun's rooms.

"I am treating his face." Hugh explained again. "He was attacked recently and badly bruised." Then he tried to extract more information from the man. "I believe there was some sort of fight in the market tavern with one of Henri de Lacey's kinsmen. Is that why Giles is held in here?"

"I don't know why he's here. They don't tell me the ins and outs. I do my work and I don't ask questions. You'd be wise to do the same."

Hugh shrugged his shoulders and hid his disappointment. The gaoler ushered him outside and locked the door behind him

The gaoler's lad was gone only a few minutes. When he returned, out of breath and hot, the news was good.

"The steward says you can go in to treat the prisoner's bruising. I'll be close by if you want me. Just shout." The gaoler said.

Hugh was let into the cell and heard the key rasp in the lock as the door was firmly locked behind him.

Giles looked up with a start for he had been told he would have no visitors. He rose with a smile, when he recognised Elizabeth's uncle. He would have greeted Hugh as a friend but the visitor shook his head quickly and held a silencing finger up to his lips warning him not to speak.

Giles understood the gesture and waited until the gaoler was well out of earshot before he spoke. "Good to see you, master. I've been allowed no other visitors."

Hugh opened his bag and took out the medicines. Uncapping the leeches, he reached into the jar and retrieved a single leech. "Right Mr Fisher, I've come to treat that bruising." He spoke in a voice loud enough for the gaoler to hear, if he was eavesdropping.

Giles nodded that he understood the situation and sat on the bed in silence.

When he was satisfied they were no longer being watched and the gaoler was out of earshot, Hugh put the unwanted leech back into its jar and patted the bruised area with a piece of linen dipped in monkshood salve. Leaning closer as he worked, he whispered in Giles ear. "Why are you in here? No one seems to understand what's happening."

"I don't know, sir, unless it's the fight I had with Ivo Longspee."

"But surely you were the only one hurt at the inn? You didn't land a blow, did you?"

"No, I didn't, but I can't think of any other reason for the bailiff to throw me in here..." He hesitated then added. "No... The prior knows of no other reason... as far as I'm aware."

"I see. It has to be something else more serious then, doesn't it?" Hugh continued to dab on the salve. "When was the last time you actually set eyes on Ivo Longspee?"

"At the inn, when he knocked me out with that stool."

"Have you been anywhere near him since?"

Giles hesitated before answering this direct question. He seemed to be choosing his words very carefully. Finally, he said. "I've not set eyes on the man since the fight at the inn."

Hugh realised immediately that this was not a straight answer to the question he had asked. He was suspicious of Giles, but even though he sensed something was being hidden, he decided to let it pass without comment. "Your bruise is healing well. Keep applying the monkshood salve I gave you."

"I can't, sir... I'm afraid I've lost it." Giles apologised lamely.

"Lost it? Where did you lose it? You know how poisonous that preparation is. If someone accidentally ate it, it could be fatal. I hope it's not anywhere to be found by some unsuspecting child!"

"That's not possible, sir. I lost it at sea. It was washed overboard when we were fishing in the Wash."

"Oh well, it's a good thing I brought more salve with me. I will leave it with you and call again tomorrow to check on your injury again."

Hugh was mystified. Those hesitations when Giles answered his questions had aroused his suspicions, but Giles was adamant that he was innocent of any crime. There had to be someone who could explain to him what was going on. He knew he couldn't return to his niece without some kind of explanation. It was then he thought of the priory steward. Thomas Bohun must surely know what was happening, and Thomas was now a patient of his. Maybe it was time to check on the steward's boils again. He wiped the excess salve from the bruising on Giles' face and applied a soothing ointment.

"Elizabeth is very worried about you, you know. It was her idea I came as your healer, to try to see you. Your father and mother have already been here but the gaoler has orders to let no one in to speak with you, so they were turned away. I suppose I don't count as he doesn't know we are acquainted as friends."

Giles smiled at the mention of his girl's name, but his expression changed at the mention that his father and mother had been denied access to him. He looked very worried as the seriousness of his situation began to dawn on him. His imprisonment could not be for some simple breaking of the prior's rules, it had to be much more serious than that. If only he knew what he was accused of, he might be able to refute it.

Hugh shouted to the gaoler to unlock the cell door, as he was finished with the prisoner. The man soon came and let Hugh out. On the way to the main door, Hugh tried to engage the man in conversation again, digging for information with a discreet question or two. He got nowhere with his queries and decided, as the gaoler seemed amiable enough, that the man probably knew no more than Giles or himself.

At the door, the gaoler put his hand on Hugh's arm to stop him leaving, and said. "The steward wants to see you in his quarters, sir. He asked me to request you call on him on your way out. He sent his personal servant with the message only a few minutes ago."

Hugh thanked the gaoler. That unexpected invitation fitted into his plans perfectly. He turned to the man and assured him he would be back the following day to check the prisoner's wound, then he made his way through the priory grounds to the steward's rooms.

When Hugh entered the steward's office, Thomas Bohun was waiting for him.

"I hope I haven't inconvenienced you, asking you to call."

"No. I was here to see the new prisoner. I have been treating him for a badly bruised face. I called to check on his progress. What can I do for you, sir?"

Thomas peeled off his linen shirt and turned his back on his healer. "Well, what do you think?"

Hugh was extremely pleased with what he saw. The drawing ointment had brought most of the boils to a head. The saltwater applications had cleaned the area and many of the burst boils were already healing. "I think it's time to change from the drawing ointment to one which soothes and heals. You have done well."

"I've even eaten that disgusting watercress with every meal!" Thomas grunted in disgust.

"Good. I am pleased with the results."

"I will carry on eating watercress. I can see it will be worth it." His tone of voice belied his words.

Hugh tried to bring the conversation around to Giles. "Your prisoner is in a bad way. I understand he was hit over the head with an oak stool. He's lucky it didn't break his skull. I found him not a happy man."

Thomas nodded. "He will be much more unhappy when he's tried for murder."

"Murder!" Hugh was astonished. "Who's been murdered?"

"Ivo Longspee. His groom reported the death this morning."

Hugh was lost for words. He realised that was why the groom had come galloping into Spalding, but his mind was full of unanswered questions. How could Giles have murdered the Norman? How did Giles come into contact with the victim when he was fishing in the Wash? Maybe they had clashed over some piracy incident at sea? He realised he must find out the truth of it. He tried to sound casual and disinterested.

"Sounds a strange business. How was Ivo Longspee murdered?"

"Poison." The steward answered with that one chilling word.

Hugh could not believe his ears. "Poison?" He repeated the word but couldn't grasp the implications of it. "Is there clear evidence of this poisoning?"

"Longspee's groom was positive his master died at home after a meal, showing all the known signs of poisoning. He accused the prisoner. If there is enough good reason for us to hold the prisoner, he'll go for trial at de Lacy's court in Lincoln. Meanwhile we must hold him here and gather the evidence."

Hugh drew in his breath sharply, but tried to let no concern show on his face. He considered Giles' position and didn't like what he knew. Ivo Longspee was always bragging he was a kinsman of Henri de Lacy. The Earl would not be lenient to anyone who had harmed a member of his family; no matter how minor a member he happened to be. If Giles was proven guilty the penalty had to be the death sentence.

Thomas, unaware of Hugh's dark thoughts, smiled benignly at his healer and abruptly changed the subject. "I like the smell of that new healing ointment."

"Yes. It's pleasant. It's based on violets." Hugh continued applying the preparation to the man's back. "I'll leave the jar with you."

When he had finished the dressing of Thomas's back, Hugh helped him on with his shirt.

"Have you been asked to become a member of the new Guild of Saint Mary?" Thomas asked, casually.

"A bit above me, I'm afraid." Hugh could not afford to mix with the rich merchants and officials who would form the new guild.

"We are having a feast next week. I will see to it that you are invited as my guest. You might even find some prospective customers for your healing skills among the richer members."

Hugh smiled his thanks, packed his bag and left the Steward's office in a daze. The news of the poisoning overshadowed everything else. What could he tell Elizabeth when he saw her? His instincts were to tell her only what he had heard from Giles himself. There was no need to mention poison, no need to upset her any more today. He limped slowly out of the priory grounds and down to the market place, visibly dragging his bad leg more than usual.

Elizabeth was at the door when Hugh arrived. She had been waiting there all the time he was gone.

"Did you see him?"

"Yes. It was a good idea of yours to visit him as his healer. They let me in for a short time."

"Well? What did he say?" She asked impatiently.

"Giles doesn't know why he's being kept in gaol. He can only think it was the fight at the tavern with Ivo Longspee, but he can't understand how that incident is so serious a matter to keep you and his parents away from him."

Elizabeth bit her lip and fought back her tears. She couldn't understand it either. Hugh continued. "You have no idea what he's been doing, have you?"

Before Elizabeth could answer, Maud, the girl's mother, joined them from the back room. "Any news, brother? Did you find out why Giles is imprisoned?"

Hugh hesitated. He had learned the real reason for Giles' imprisonment from the prior's steward, but no one outside of the priory seemed to be privy to the information. He decided to keep the knowledge to himself for the time being, that way he would not break a confidence, and he might get more information out of Thomas Bohun. Besides, he realised it would break Elizabeth's heart, and he couldn't bring himself to bring her such bad news. When he did reply to his sister's question, he chose his words extremely carefully.

"Giles has no idea why he's there. I was just telling Elizabeth, he can only think it is to do with the incident here, when he attacked Ivo Longspee and was knocked unconscious."

"That doesn't seem fair to me. That Norman butcher has too much influence."

Hugh nodded agreement then took his leave of them, glad to be making for home. Seated once more by his own fireside, Hugh mulled over all he had learned from his visit to the priory. Ivo Longspee was dead from poisoning. His experience told him it must have been a virulent poison to kill a large healthy man like that. The medical knowledge he had gained made him well aware of all the dangerous substances usually found in his native fens. He went through the list in his mind, considering the possibilities, trying to understand how Giles could have obtained such a poison, and how he could have administered it. There were many poisonous wild plants available in the fens. Hugh counted the possibilities on his fingers. There was nightshade, foxglove, yew, henbane, bryony and hemlock. There were several sorts of poisonous toadstools and even the common crowsfoot and of course, there was always monkshood.

"My God! I'm a fool. The answer is staring me in the face!" Hugh exclaimed aloud to the empty hall. "Monkshood is the most poisonous one of them all and Giles had a pot of my monkshood salve with him. There was enough in that pot to kill several men!" He thumped his chair arm hard with his fist. "He could have used my salve. He had the necessary poison." Hugh jumped up from his chair and paced the floor, wrestling with his thoughts. "He had the means to kill, but did he have the opportunity?" Hugh limped up and down room getting more and more agitated as he thought about the circumstances of the murder.

"No. It can't be! Giles was fishing at sea. How could he have been at Wykeham at the Longspee holding?" That thought consoled him. Obviously, the bailiff had heard of the fight at the tavern and had assumed Giles was getting his revenge. Maybe someone had reported how the young man had threatened to kill the Norman. When the death was investigated properly they would realise Giles was nowhere near the victim. There had been no opportunity for him to administer poison. He was obviously innocent of the crime.

Chapter Nine

As the evening closed in and the rush lights were lit, Hugh sat in front of the fire drinking beer and going over the day's events. The news of Ivo Longspee's death and the way it had affected his niece, had upset him greatly, but he was confident it would all work out right in the end. His relaxation was interrupted by a shout from young John, his yard boy.

"Sir. There's a man asking to see you." The lad's youthful face appeared in the flickering light in the hall doorway.

"Who is it, John? Anyone you know?"

"No sir. He's just standing at the bottom of the yard. He refused to come up to the house and asked me to get you. He wouldn't say what it was about, but he was most insistent."

Reluctantly, Hugh slipped on his sheepskin jerkin, left the comforting warmth of the fireside and followed the lad down the yard. In the twilight he could just make out the figure of a man holding a sack in his arms. As they got nearer, he realised there was something familiar about him. Suddenly he recognised the profile and realised it was one of the seamen who had been on the Fisher's boat when the bailiff had arrested Giles. Hugh's curiosity was by then thoroughly aroused

The man stepped forward at his approach and asked in a low, gruff voice. "You Hugh Pinchbeck?"

"Yes. Who wants to know?"

The man ignored Hugh's question and dropped his heavy sack onto the cobblestones. "Here. Giles asked me to deliver this to you." Without offering further explanation he turned to walk away.

"Wait!" Hugh grabbed the man's sleeve. "Giles never mentioned this when I saw him earlier."

The man stopped in his tracks and turned back to face Hugh. "You've been to see Giles? I understood no one could get to see him."

"Yes, I saw him. I went to the priory gaol to treat his bruises. Now what's this all about?" As he spoke, Hugh bent down and opened up the sack. He was startled to find a huge piece of fish inside it.

The seaman looked sheepishly down at his feet and said nothing.

Hugh stroked his chin thoughtfully. He recognised the flesh as whale meat; an expensive delicacy he enjoyed when he could get it, but a luxury that seldom came his way as the Lord Prior had the rights to all whales washed up on the nearby coast.

"Come up to the hall and have a drink of ale with me. You and I have some serious talking to do."

The seaman considered the offer for several seconds before he shrugged his shoulders and reluctantly nodded his agreement. Dragging his feet, he followed the old man back to the house.

Hugh carried the sack to the kitchen where John's mother was baking and left the fish with her for salting. Once in the hall, standing with his back to the fire beside his guest, each of them with a full mug of ale in his hand, Hugh continued his probing questions.

"That has to be whale meat, surely? A piece of fish that size can't be anything else"

The man nodded.

"Your nets are for herrings; they would never hold a fish of that size. Where did you get it?"

"It was beached near the mouth of the estuary."

Hugh waited for more information but his companion remained stubbornly silent. He turned to face the fisherman and asked sharply. "Look, I need to know all Giles' movements on your last fishing trip. Are you going to help me?"

There was still no reply, only sullen silence

Hugh was fast losing patience. "Heavens, man! Giles is going to marry my niece. He is in gaol, accused of a serious crime. If only for his sake, you must tell me what you know."

The man cleared his throat noisily and shuffled his feet. At last he asked in a barely audible voice. "What do you want to know?"

"I want to know where you got this whale meat. I know whales are very valuable and I know the Lord Prior lays claim to every one beached on the shores locally. They'd have you behind bars if they knew you had it."

The man half turned as if he was preparing to run off.

Hugh placed a restraining hand on his arm and hastened to reassure him "I'm not going to tell anyone about it, don't worry. In fact, I am very pleased with the gift. It's most welcome."

The fisherman relaxed and started to explain. "We spotted the whale on the shoreline past Wykeham as we left the Welland estuary. We were on our way to the herring grounds."

"Ah! On the foreshore of Ivo Longspee's holding was it?"

"Aye."

Hugh had feared as much. He thought carefully before he asked. "You were there? You saw all that happened? Tell me every detail."

"We ran the boat close into the shore and two of us waded inland to the whale carcass."

"Two of you? Who exactly would that be?"

"Giles and me, we are the tallest. We checked the meat was fresh. It was only recently dead and fit to eat. We cut several large pieces from the fish and took them to the boat."

"Did anyone see you there?"

"Aye, unfortunately they did. As we returned for a third time, some of Ivo Longspee's men arrived from inland. They were armed to the teeth, waving swords and spears and threatening us. We had to run for it. We pushed our boat out to deeper water and made our getaway."

Hugh let this new information sink in. Ivo Longspee's men would certainly have fought them for the meat because whale meat was a very valuable commodity. A whole whale was ten times more valuable than a day's catch of herrings was ever likely to be. He went on with his probing.

"Did anyone go near the farm? Did Giles or you go near the buildings?"

"No, sir! We ran for our lives as fast as we could, back to the boat."

"So, there is no way Giles came into contact with Ivo Longspee or his home?"

"Why these questions? All I know is that on our way back to Spalding, I was told a list of a few friends that Giles wanted the whale meat delivered to. You were on the list. That's why I came tonight after dark." The man sounded suspicious of Hugh's motives and all the questions.

"Did you know Ivo Longspee is dead?"

"Yes. I heard that rumour from someone in town."

Hugh was not entirely surprised by this answer; bad news always travelled fast in small towns. The groom probably made no secret of his master's death. He'd probably called at one of the town's taverns before he returned home."

"Did you hear how he died?"

"No."

Hugh reasoned that as the town gossips knew about Ivo Longspee's death, the manner of his death would also soon be common knowledge. He decided to break his silence and try shock tactics. He said gruffly. "The man was poisoned. Giles is suspected of the crime." Then he watched the man closely to gauge his reaction.

"Poisoned! By'r Lady!" The fisherman shook his head in disbelief and seemed genuinely shocked by this revelation. "Who would poison him? Is that really why Giles is in gaol?"

Hugh nodded, reasonably satisfied from his reaction that the man had no prior knowledge of the poisoning.

"Well, it certainly wasn't Giles. I was with him all that day until he was arrested at the dockside. I will testify that to any court in his defence."

"I would expect no less from a loyal servant. But you see, that's the problem. You are Giles' man. Would any court believe your word?"

The man looked away and frowned. "The Lord Prior will know I am no thief or liar."

"But you are a thief for taking the whale meat and I'm sure Ivo Longspee's men could identify you. Anyway, the Lord Prior won't be interested in your testimony. Giles will be tried at Henri de Lacy's court in Lincoln because Ivo Longspee was the earl's kinsman and the prior most probably wants to wash his hands of the whole affair. There's sure to be some family loyalties tied up with his verdict."

"What can we do?" Deep concern showed in the man's voice at this new worrying information.

Hugh didn't answer. The conversation had confirmed his worst fears. Because of the fight in the tavern, it could be argued that Giles had a strong motive to get even with the Norman. To make matters worse, Giles had threatened to kill him, in front of several witnesses, and he also had the means to do it, because of the monkshood preparation, which Hugh himself had provided. Now it seemed he had had the opportunity to commit the crime, for Giles had been on Ivo Longspee's land the very day the Norman died of the poison. Innocent men had been hanged on much less evidence. At the back of Hugh's mind was the growing doubt that he had misjudged the young fisherman, and Giles had indeed sought his revenge on Ivo Longspee. It was an unpalatable thought, especially as Elizabeth was so fond of the lad, but a possibility that had to be considered.

Hugh had another sudden thought. He asked. "Tell me, did Giles take a face salve with him, the one I gave him for the bruising?"

The man nodded. "I saw him apply it before we left the docks."

"Do you know where it is now?"

"No. I haven't seen it since."

Hugh frowned. Another possible way to prove Giles innocence had closed.

"If he needs it, I'll search the boat for it."

"Yes, you do that. Pray to God you find it."

The two men lapsed into silence watching the flames and white smoke curl up towards the chimney opening. As they stood side by side in front of the turf fire, each considering Giles plight, there was a loud knock on the front door of the house. Hugh put down his empty mug, took up the rush light, and went to see who was calling on him at that late hour. He found a young man at the door with a note addressed to him. He took the folded parchment and walk back to the fireside, but by the time he reached it, the fisherman had gone.

"Well, I suppose I've learned all he can tell me." High muttered to himself as he opened the message and held it up to the light. It proved to be his invitation to the guild feast, signed by Richard the skinner, the master of the new guild and by far the richest man in Spalding. Thomas Bohun had been as good as his word. Hugh would ordinarily have been delighted to receive such an invitation but the thoughts of his niece's unhappiness and the plight of her young man overshadowed any pleasure he felt.

Hugh refilled his mug with beer and sat by the fire contemplating all he had learned that evening. In his mind there were all kinds of questions raised by these latest revelations. Had Giles lied about the monkshood salve or had he genuinely forgotten he had it with him on the boat? How far was the beached whale from the houses on Ivo Longspee farm? How easy would it have been to go unseen into one of those homesteads and add a poison to the food or drink? Without actually seeing the layout of the farm, Hugh knew all this was mere speculation. There may be only one way to answer these questions. He'd have to visit the scene of the Norman's death.

The Longspee holding lay next to Hugh's own land in the fen beyond Wykeham. The two farms were separated only by a tidal creek, which opened into the Wash near the entrance to the Welland. Hugh had never had reason to set foot on the Norman's holding, but it seemed a visit to his late neighbour's holding was now overdue. He would cross the creek and offer his condolences to the family. That Christian act would give him an ideal excuse to take a look around.

"That's what I'll do!" Hugh muttered to himself. "Tomorrow, when I've finished my business here in Spalding, I'll go visiting my neighbours."

Chapter Ten

It was still early when Hugh called into the market tavern next morning, on his way to the priory gaol. Elizabeth was on her hands and knees, scrubbing the floor of the main room. Her father had removed the covering of old reeds and was preparing to spread some fresh ones in their place. She sat on her haunches and stopped for a minute to talk to Hugh

"Please tell Giles that I miss him. Tell him I'm sorry I was angry when he got up from his sick bed to go fishing at sea. If he comes back to me safe and sound, I will never be angry with him again."

Hugh smiled reassurance. She was making desperate attempts to come to terms with the awful events of the last few days. She seemed to sense how bad things were for her beloved Giles.

"I have prayed at the Priory Church four times since he was imprisoned. If there is a God, he will listen to me and set Giles free."

"I'm sure you're right, Elizabeth. Let's hope he'll soon be home." Hugh tried to say the right words to comfort her, but he did not like the weight of evidence building up against the young man. "I'll go now to dress his bruises. I'll give him your message. It's sure to lift his spirits."

She jumped up and threw her arms around Hugh, hugging him tightly in an uninhibited show of gratitude. He patted her shoulder and smoothed her hair, feeling very protective and fatherly toward her, but he took care to hide his doubts from her. She trusted him to put things right but he knew what a predicament Giles was in.

At the gaol, Hugh was greeted cheerily by the gaoler and accepted openly as a healer visiting his patient. No obstacles were put in his way because the man was aware the steward trusted this healer. Once they were left together in the locked cell, the gaoler went back to his meat and ale. "Shout for me when you want to go," he called over his shoulder.

Giles was standing against the far wall of his cell. He turned and smiled wanly at his visitor

"How are you feeling today?" Hugh asked, as he turned Giles' bruised face to the light and examined the effects of his treatment. Checking the gaoler was already out of earshot, Hugh whispered urgently. "I will soon have no excuse to visit you. The bruising is clearing up well. We must think of another excuse to carry on the treatment... Maybe if you feign a pain in your jawbone, I could come and treat that? When the gaoler is about, hold your face in your hands as if it aches. Don't overdo it. I don't want him to be suspicious of me."

"Very well." Giles agreed readily. "But, do tell me what's happening out in the world."

"Well... Elizabeth sends her love. You are a lucky man, Giles. She obviously loves you deeply. She is praying daily for your release."

Giles flushed with pleasure at this remark and smiled to himself at some secret memory.

"But other things are coming to light that we must discuss. Sit down near the window and I will bathe your face as we talk. We mustn't look suspicious if the gaoler looks in on us."

They moved to other side of the room where there was a bed and a small, crude table. Giles sat on the edge of the bed. Hugh took a piece of linen and gently dabbed his bruised face.

"One of your men delivered some whale meat to me last night."

"Good. I asked him to do that."

"Yes, but he also told me where it came from. You were at Ivo Longspee's holding that morning, weren't you?"

"Yes, but I didn't see Ivo Longspee there."

"So you say. But you wouldn't have to set eyes on the man to poison him."

Giles pulled Hugh's hand away from his bruise and turned towards him, his face ashen with shock. "Poison, did you say?"

"Hush!" Hugh held a finger up to silence his patient. He smiled to himself with satisfaction; Giles' reaction to the news was some kind of proof that he was not aware of the manner of the Norman's death. It was either proof of his innocence or the man was an accomplished actor.

"Poison." Hugh repeated the word quietly. "Dead from poisoning. And you are the only suspect." He whispered the last words into Giles' ear and the young fisherman was left in no doubt about the gravity of his own situation. "Now, I expect you to tell me everything. No more keeping things back. If I am to try to help you, I must know all."

Giles lapsed into sullen silence; his arms crossed tightly over his body, his shoulders hunched protectively, his chin on his chest and his head bowed in despair.

Hugh pressed on with his questions. "You had the monkshood salve with you on the boat. Your fisherman confirmed that to me when he delivered the whale meat. Do you know where it is now?"

Giles shook his head and looked puzzled.

"Think hard Giles. What happened to it? Did you use it all?"

The prisoner scratched his head and considered. "He's right. I had it in my pocket. I used some before we set off. The wind was cold and my face was burning over the bruising...I remember putting it down on the side of the boat...I don't remember seeing it again after that."

"Could someone else have taken it?"

"No...I think, if anything, it would have toppled over the side. We had a difficult journey down the river and I was busy manning the tiller."

Hugh considered this explanation. It was hardly convincing, but it could well have happened like that. Giles would have been very occupied with the boat as the river was so busy. He decided to ask a direct question. "Tell me honestly, did you administer poison to that man?"

"No." Giles shook his head emphatically.

"Do you know who did?"

"No, honestly. When you just explained that poison was involved, that was the first I knew of it."

"Good. I believe you." Hugh tried to sound positive and cheerful but the facts looked grim. Felons were hung every day on far less evidence. He hesitated while he considered what next to tell Giles.

"I can't pretend there is no case against you. The circumstances speak for themselves. You were heard to threaten to murder Ivo Longspee when you fought in the inn."

Giles nodded glumly.

"You were heard by many witnesses. And you were on the man's land the morning he died...Tell me, were you seen there?"

"Yes alas! Some of his men saw us at the whale carcass and shouted at us to go away."

Hugh was already aware of these facts but he shook his head sadly for he was certain the prior had already been informed of all of it. The groom would have related it all when he reported his master's death. He voiced his fears aloud. "We must assume your accuser has passed this information on to the Lord Prior."

"But, I didn't do anything!" Giles protested.

"So you keep saying. Put yourself in the place of the bailiff. What would you think? There's something else. The man was poisoned and there are few more potent poisons that monkshood."

"I told you. I think I lost it overboard."

"It could be argued you used it to kill Ivo Longspee, then disposed of the evidence."

"Oh God!" Giles buried his head in his hands and let out a single sob.

"Don't fret. I'll try and clear your name. Now I must go. I have to see the priory steward. I may even find out something of use to you."

Hugh left the prisoner deep in despair. He had not intended to upset Giles but confronting him and seeing his reactions was the only way to convince himself of his innocence or guilt. Giles was not guilty, of that Hugh was now sure, but how was he ever going to prove it to the authorities?

Thomas Bohun was dictating accounts to his clerk when Hugh was shown into the room. He turned to face his visitor.

"Ah! Hugh, why are you here today?"

"I called to give you the healing ointment and to see how you are progressing with your treatment, sir."

"Good man!" Thomas pulled his shirt up over his head to bare his torso. There was no break in his dictation and the clerk never once looked up from the table.

Hugh smiled. The man's quill scratched noisily over the parchment as if his life depended on it. Knowing the steward's uncertain temper, it probably did.

When Thomas turned his ample back towards the light, Hugh was delighted to see a further marked improvement in his skin condition.

"Good." Hugh muttered, more to himself than to the patient, but Thomas jumped on the comment.

"Good? You can see more of an improvement?"

"Yes, definitely. Already some of the boils are showing signs of healing. Your back does not look as raw as it was. You have been following my instructions well."

"I don't take informed advice then ignore it!" Thomas snorted. "You are not the first physician I've used, but you seem to be the best."

"If you continue the treatment for a few weeks, maybe it will all heal."

"Do you really think so? I have had these eruptions of the skin for years. If I could rid myself of this scourge, I could even sleep on my back again. It would be a miracle."

"I'm sure the prior would claim God has performed bigger miracles." Hugh smiled.

"Not for me, he hasn't!" Thomas grinned wickedly. "But, in the past when these boils have abated, they have always returned. Will I have to use your treatment for ever?"

"No. I've been thinking about that. I think the learned doctors would say your humours must be out of balance. I could suggest a way to balance them."

Thomas stopped his dictation and eased his shirt back on. He tied the collar loosely about his thick neck and gave Hugh his whole attention.

"You will have to continue using the salt lotion. Maybe twice a week will suffice."

"That's no problem. The priory has several salt pans. I have a plentiful supply of free salt. But is that all?"

"No. On the crusades the king's physicians always taught that diet was a very important thing to aid healing. Much fresh fruit and vegetables are needed, to complement the spiced meats. We soldiers tended to eat meat exclusively if we could get it. God intended us to eat the fruits that grow in the fields and orchards, as we are taught Adam did in the Garden of Eden."

The steward scowled. "I do not like fruit or vegetables, especially that watercress. I am a rich man and can afford the best meat on my table for every meal. Green stuff! It is all animal fodder as far as I'm concerned!"

Hugh smiled broadly. He had fully expected that reaction. The steward obviously enjoyed indulging in the best cuts of meat and in honeyed sweetmeats, as befitted a man of his rank and prosperity.

"I, as your healer, am telling you to continue eating the watercress as a daily addition to your food. It must be fresh and it must be eaten in equal amounts to your meats. And you must eat other vegetables as they come into season."

Thomas scowled again, but then his face broke into a relieved grin. "Is that all? As I said before. No ground up saint's bones or dragon's blood? Your remedies are too simple, master Hugh. And far too inexpensive I'm thinking!"

"You could be right. But they are all God given, nevertheless."

"Enough of this banter. I will eat a bucketful of freshly picked watercress from the priory beds, every day of my life, if it will keep this affliction away."

"Good. Now, if I may mention it, sir. I have just come from the gaol and my patient there is in despair."

"He might well be. The signs are not good for him."

"Has nothing come to light in his favour?"

"Nothing. Nothing except a stay of execution because Henri de Lacy will not be in Lincoln for some time. The king and his nobles are kept in the North by the continued unrest on the borders with Scotland."

"How long before he returns?"

"Could be Christmas before we send our felon to Lincoln for his trial. Meanwhile he will remain here in our safe keeping until then."

Hugh shrugged his shoulders as if it was of no account, but secretly he was very pleased with this gift of time. It would give him the space he needed to find out what really happened at Longspee's holding.

When Hugh returned home to Eau Side he found young John pacing up and down the hall, waiting for him.

"Yes John? You seem anxious to speak with me."

"There was a man asking for you, sir. I told him you was at the priory."

"Who was it this time, a patient? Was it someone ill again?"

"No sir. It were a master Fisher. He wanted to speak to you about his son, Giles."

Hugh shook his head and grunted. He should have anticipated this visit. It had to be Gilbert Fisher, Giles' father. He must have heard about the gravity of his son's predicament from the fisherman who delivered the whale meat. Hugh had put off seeing Giles' parents for much the same reason he had not told Elizabeth the whole story, because there seemedlittle encouraging news he could tell any of them

Now he realised Giles' parents might be aware that Ivo Longspee was dead from poisoning, and that their son was held in the priory gaol for that crime.

Almost to himself, Hugh said "I'd suppose I'd better go and see Gilbert Fisher and tell him all I know. He and his wife must be beside themselves with worry about their son."

John didn't answer. He understood little of what was going on.

Chapter Eleven

Hugh put his medical bag in the Solar and went to the market stead hoping to find Gile's parents. It was market day and they usually had a fish stall near the market tavern, where they sold their catch of fresh fish and salted herrings.

The market was well underway when he threaded his way between the stalls and booths. People were busy buying food and utensils. He hesitated at the butcher's stall and noticed that there was an unusually crowd around the next stall, which was a baker's. The baker, a man from Crowland, a village a few miles upriver from Spalding, was loudly shouting his wares. His banter had drawn a large audience, but many of them seemed angry. Hugh pushed his way through the people, who were standing several deep, and made straight for the fish stall.

"Ah! Thanks for coming, Hugh. We need to talk with you." Gilbert Fisher greeted Hugh as soon as he stepped clear of the crowd around the bakery stall.

Hugh grinned sheepishly at the man and nodded politely to his wife, a large lady who stood at his side. "I should have come before this, but there really was little I could tell you."

"You seem to have found out more than we managed to do. We are his mother and father but no one tells us anything, except he's held in prison and we can't see him." Mistress Fisher raised her voice angrily. Her husband smiled apologetically at the visitor as if his wife was blaming Hugh for the lack of information.

"I can only apologise to you both. I found the truth out only yesterday and I have been trying to decide what I can do to remedy things."

"We don't blame you, Hugh. In fact, we are indebted to you for finding a way in to see the boy. Tell us, exactly what is he accused of?"

Hugh stepped around to the back of the fish stall and stood between the anxious parents. He patted Mistress Fisher's hand and gave her a reassuring smile. "I know how you must feel, but now I've spoken to your son, I'm convinced there's been a mistake."

"Of course there's been a mistake! My Giles is a good lad. He wouldn't hurt anyone. When we are allowed to see the bailiff, I'm going to tell him

Gilbert interrupted his wife's indignant speech. "Of course, dear. But let the man explain everything first."

Hugh spoke in a low voice and told them all he had learned. He explained how Ivo Longspee had died of suspected poisoning. He reminded them how Giles had threatened the man in the tavern, in front of witnesses, and how his fishing boat had landed on Ivo Longspee's shoreline the very morning the man had died.

"Poison!" Giles mother snorted. "How do you think our son had access to poison?"

"I treated his bruising with wolfsbane salve. And I left a pot of it with him."

Gilbert let out his breath like a punctured bladder. "I see. It begins to look bad for the lad."

Mistress Fisher would have none of it. She protested loudly. "I'm his mother and I know he wouldn't harm anyone."

"I agree." Hugh assured her. "I've talked to Giles in gaol and I'm convinced he is innocent, but Ivo Longspee is a relative of the Earl of Lincoln and the prior will send your son to Henri de Lacy's court in Lincoln for his trial. Unfortunately, circumstances do not bode well for him

Giles' mother opened her mouth to protest again, but her husband silenced her with a stern look.

Hugh continued. "...I can see that Giles had a motive, because of the fight in the tavern. He had opportunity when he went ashore at the Longspee holding to carve up that whale, and he had the means to carry out the poisoning with the monkshood I gave him. It looks bad for him."

The mother burst into tears. Gilbert Fisher shook his head helplessly. "What do you think, Hugh? What can anyone do?"

"I am going to visit the Longspee holding; it's next to mine in the fen. There is only a wide salt water creek separating our two parcels of land."

"Of course."

"I want to see where it happened and I will talk to anyone who witnessed it. I strongly suspect Ivo Longspee was up to no good with the bad company he kept around him. I may be able to find out what really befell him. It may even have been a falling out among thieves."

Giles' parents fell silent. Now they understood the extent of the case against their son, they were fearful for him. Gilbert stroked his chin and said quietly. "I've known felons convicted on less evidence than this. It looks bad for my boy."

"I'll do what I can. Don't give up hope yet," Hugh said lamely. He could think of nothing else to say to reassure them.

"Does Elizabeth know all this?" Gilbert asked suddenly.

"No, not yet. I only found out by chance from the prior's steward and I think that was told to me in confidence. I suppose I'd better go and explain to the girl, right now."

Hugh turned to walk to the tavern but events in the market stead overtook him. While they had been talking quietly behind the fishmonger's stall, a troupe of travelling acrobats had started their act in front of the market tavern. They had reached the climax of their performance, forming a colourful pyramid with one man held high above the rest on his fellows' shoulders. Hugh was surprised by the spectacle. He had been so engrossed in his conversation with the fishmongers he had missed entirely the first part of the act. A small dwarf of a man in a red suit turned somersaults in the front of the pyramid and held out his hat to collect money from the appreciative crowd. Suddenly a loud disturbance broke out among the crowd beside the show.

An old woman's voice shrieked from the nearby bread stall. "You are a thief! You have sold me a lightweight loaf!" Pandemonium broke out in the crowd. The baker ran to hide behind his stall but the crowd pushed forward to get at him.

Another voice shouted accusingly, "You Croyland folk are all the same. You'd sell your own mother for a groat!"

"It's not the first time he's done it! He was fined only last month for selling his bread against the assizes. The prior sets these standards and he's bound to abide by them, like every other tradesman."

The crowd pressed forward, pushing the baker's stall over, tipping all his wares onto the cobbled ground. The baker vanished under a heap of bodies, kicking and screaming, protesting his innocence. The crowd surged back and pushed into the pyramid of tumblers.

Hugh limped forward instinctively to try and help the acrobats, but it was too late. The topmost man hurtled to the ground and fell awkwardly on his back. It was obvious he must have hurt himself badly. Hugh rushed to the man's side and kneeled down beside him.

"Can you hear me?" He shouted above the noise of the crowd. The acrobat only groaned in agony.

Can you walk into the tavern?" Hugh felt the man's legs, checking for broken bones. Satisfied there were no obvious breaks he asked the fallen acrobat again if he could walk to the tavern. "I can't do much out here in this crowd. Things are getting ugly." He looked up and saw the priory bailiff and three men at arms had arrived on the scene and were trying to calm the fight that had developed around the baker. Fists were waved at the bailiff. Dozens of frantic women scrambled over the cart, clawing up the fallen loaves and hiding them under their clothes.

The tumbler rose shakily to his feet, grasped his right shoulder with his other hand to support it, and limped into the tavern.

"Sit down, man. Let me see the damage." Hugh guided him to the nearest stool.

"My shoulder... out of joint...done it before." The young man spoke with a broad foreign accent, wincing in pain between each short statement.

Hugh gently lifted the protective hand from the damaged joint and felt the extent of the injury. He could feel the dislocation but he was relieved to find no broken bones. "You're right. Your arm is well out of the socket. I'll have to put it back again."

"Can you do it?"

"I think so. I've mended a few displaced shoulders after battles...Now, what's your name...let your body relax and I'll push the joint back"

"My name's Leonardo. Call me Leo, master." The man, an Italian by the way he spoke, clenched his good hand into a fist, closed his eyes and gritted his teeth. "I'm ready."

Hugh pushed against Leo's body with one hand and pulled on the limp arm with the other. There was a loud click and a scream of pain from the patient.

"Your shoulder's back in joint. Now we must bind it up to hold it in place and you must rest it."

Leo nodded vigorously that he understood. That final movement shook off the ribbon of red material that had held back his blond hair. A mass of blond curls fell across his face. Hugh smiled; it was a fitting mane for a young Leo. He would remember the man's name for that reason alone. By this time the rest of the troupe of acrobats had joined them in the inn. They surrounded Hugh and their leader. The room was full of the gabble of foreign voices as they all tried to speak at the same time.

"What's going on here then?" Jack, Elizabeth's father, parted the crowd to see what was happening in his bar. "Ah! I might have known you'd be involved." He grinned when he saw Hugh. "Whenever there's an accident you seem to be at the centre of it."

"It's my profession." Hugh protested with a smile. "I am a healer, after all."

"And so good. So good." Leo, who had recovered remarkably well, spoke up.

Hugh turned on his patient. "You sit still until I've bound up that shoulder. You will need to rest that joint for a week or two."

"No. I need to rest it until the Guild Feast, then we must entertain the guests."

Hugh shook his head in disbelief for the feast was that very evening. But the tumbler had had similar injuries before, so presumably he knew what to expect from this one.

"Hugh, do you want a drink?" The innkeeper shouted above the babble of voices.

It was then Hugh remembered what he had intended to tell Elizabeth and her parents. "I'd better have one. Then I need to speak to you and my sister, in private."

Leaving his patient surrounded by the other acrobats, Hugh went through to the back room.

"That sounded serious, Hugh. What's the matter?" Jack followed him into the private quarters.

"Is Elizabeth here?"

"No, I sent her out to get fresh food from the market."

"Good. I'm pleased in some ways. What I must tell you concerns her, but she would probably panic if she was here to hear it from me."

"Who is going to panic?" Maud, Hugh's sister had overheard the comment as she came into the room.

Hugh explained. "I have seen Thomas Bohun, the priory steward, and I know why they are holding Giles in prison"

The publican and his wife nodded for him to continue.

"Ivo Longspee died of poison and they think Giles murdered him." Hugh hesitated a few seconds to let his message sink in.

"Murder?"

"Giles assures me he had nothing to do with it, and I want to believe him, but that does not alter the facts."

"What facts?" Jack asked indignantly

"The fact that Giles threatened to kill the man, here in your tavern..."

"That was only temper and a hot-headed youth speaking, surely you can't..."

Hugh held up his finger for silence, then continued "... The fact that he was on Ivo Longspee's land the morning it happened. The fact that he had the necessary poison, because I gave him that monkshood preparation."

Hugh's sister and her husband were dumbfounded. They stared at each other in disbelief.

Hugh continued. "To make matters worse, Giles will be tried at Henri de Lacey's court in Lincoln, because Ivo Longspee was a kinsman of the earl." He held out his hands in a gesture of helplessness and waited for this new information to sink in.

"Oh Dieu! Poor Giles...Poor Elizabeth." Hugh's sister voiced all their feelings.

At this point, Elizabeth walked into the kitchen carrying several large loaves of bread and some fresh vegetables. "That baker has been caught again selling underweight loaves. He's for the tumbrel this time." She laughed at the prospect of a public humiliation for the man. "The crowd turned over his cart and took his bread. I managed to grab these."

Hugh looked from Jack to his sister and raised his eyebrows in question. His sister patted him on the shoulder and dismissed him.

"You go about your business, brother. We'll explain to Elizabeth what you told us."

Chapter Twelve

Hugh realised he would learn nothing new in Spalding to help Giles clear his name. Even though he was unsure of the boy's innocence, he felt bound to find out what had really happened, for his niece's sake. Besides, he was very curious about his neighbours in the fen. If Ivo Longspee was dead, who was looking after the farm? What effect would a leaderless bunch of pirates have on his own Wykeham holding, on his livestock, his men and their families? He had much to gain by visiting Longspee's holding to see it for himself.

"John, get my horse ready. I'm going to Wykeham. Tell your mother I will be over at the holding most of the day. Don't bother to prepare any food for my return, I'll probably eat at my sisters." Hugh trotted his horse out of the yard and hurried to his farm, anxious to see for himself what was happening.

There was no sign of any of his workers when he cantered over the boundary of his holding. The shepherd boy, who made it his business to check on any newcomer to the farm, was nowhere to be seen, neither was anyone else. Hugh spurred on his horse, a deep feeling of anxiety growing within him.

No one came to greet him when he rode into the yard, although there was a reassuring plume of white smoke rising from the reeve's cottage. Hugh dismounted and pushed open the door to Joseph' house.

"Oh Sir! You had me worried then. Do come in and sit down." Joseph's wife looked shocked at the unexpected visitor. She left the cooking pot she was tending and rushed to clear the table.

Hugh glanced around the single room. There were signs of a hastily eaten meal still on the table. A hunk of bread and some cold meat had been left uneaten on a wooden charger; a wooden mug still contained half of its fill of ale.

"Where is everyone?" He ignored her invitation and stayed silhouetted in the open doorway.

"Down at the creek. There's trouble with our neighbours."

Hugh turned on his heels and hurried back to his horse. The creek was on the far side of his holding but only a matter of minutes away on horseback. Once there he found all his workers standing at the water's edge. All eyes were looking across the dividing tidal inlet. Joseph turned as the sound of a horse approached them and looked relieved to see it was his master. He ran up the bank to help Hugh down from his mount.

"Trouble?" Hugh asked.

"Could be, master. There's been a lot of noise and disturbance all morning but now it's gone very quiet."

Hugh looked over to the opposite bank of the tidal creek, but could see no one because the far holding was completely hidden by the high mud banks alongside the water. The only sign of life was a plume of smoke and the smell of burning hay.

"There was fighting and shouting. We think they have fallen out among themselves. I got my men together in case some of them decided to come this way."

Hugh nodded. With their leader dead, that was exactly what he had feared. He listened intently but there was no sound from across the water.

"Sound peaceful enough now, Joseph. I think they've gone, probably taking anything of value and all the food with them. Were there any women and children among them?"

"Longspee definitely had a woman there. She had a young son. We've seen her walking with him on top of the bank when the men were out at sea. Can't say about any others."

"How long since you heard any movement from over there?"

Joseph looked questioningly at his workers. After a few words were exchanged among the group he turned to Hugh. "About an hour."

"Good. Get the small boat I'm going over to see what's going on."

Joseph looked doubtful at this suggestion. "Is that wise, sir? What if they are still about and looking for trouble?"

Hugh grinned broadly. "They'll find it, if they tangle with me." He slapped the short sword at his side to emphasise the remark, but Joseph still looked doubtful.

"Right man, you and two others can come with me. How's that suit you?"

It was obvious from the reeve's manner that he was not entirely convinced of the wisdom of his master's plans but he picked his two biggest men. He chose Peter the salt man and the swineherd, made sure they were fully armed then sent his son to bring the small boat to them. They rowed across the narrow creek and beached the boat on the far shore.

Hugh led his small party to the top of the bank from where they could overlook the neighbouring farm and buildings. Everywhere looked deserted. Everywhere there were signs of the fighting his men had reported hearing; carts were overturned, fences broken down and hay lay smouldering in the barn. The body of a man lay against the side of one small hut. From the strange angle of his neck and the lack of any movement, it was obvious he was dead. Hugh walked over and checked the man.

"That one's dead." He turned the man's body over with his foot to reveal a deep, gaping, sword wound across the back of his neck.

"There's no beasts left in the pen or the yard." Joseph shouted. "They've taken them all."

"If they had any left to take!" Hugh shook his head at sight of the devastation.

"Over here, sir. Look here. There's one piglet in this sty, master." Hugh's swineherd called him over.

"That one must have hidden itself well." Hugh bent down to tickle the small pig's back and was surprised to see its tail was missing. He examined the stump and the wound where it had been severed. "What do you make of this?"

"Looks like frostbite, master."

"Frostbite! We've not had it that cold surely? Do any of our pigs have frostbite?"

"No master. I just thought it looked that way." The man shrugged his shoulders.

Hugh patted the piglet's back and straightened up. This was a mystery. The piglet did look as if its tail had been lost to frostbite. But what frost? Hugh turned to his swineherd and told him to take the pig back to their holding, when he returned.

The reeve interrupted them with an urgent message. "There's a wisp of smoke rising from the main house, master"

Hugh glanced up and saw there was indeed a thin plume of white smoke drifting up from the hole in the ridge of the largest building. "You're right. It looks as if we've found signs of life. Follow me."

At the house all seemed deserted. There was no sound from within and no one answered Hugh's insistent knocking at the door. He shouted to tell the occupants who he was and why he had come. There was still no reply. Finally, his patience ran out. Putting his shoulder to the door he forced it open.

Hugh hesitated in the doorway, letting his eyes get used to the dark interior. There was a small fire smouldering in the centre of the earthen floor. It appeared to be only recently lit from the new turf piled on it. He turned his head and let his eyes take in the entire scene. Suddenly from the far corner of the room, from behind a small curtain, he heard a snuffling sound.

"Come out. We mean you no harm. We are your neighbours from across the creek. We've come to check if you need help."

At first there was no movement or sound, then a woman's tear stained face peered out at them through the gap in the curtain and a small child stepped nervously out into the room.

Hugh smiled reassurance. "We heard fighting. We've found one casualty already."

The woman grabbed the boy and hugged him close to her. Hugh could see the poor wretches were filthy. The woman was in a particularly bad state; dirty rags hung off her thin body and recent tears had left light lines in the dirt on her face. Her cheekbones shone through her skin, testifying to her starvation.

Hugh stepped into the centre of the room followed by his three men

"They've all gone." She said, in a flat voice, devoid of any emotion. "They wouldn't take us. We would have been a burden to them."

Hugh turned to Peter the saltman, and ordered. "Row back to our shore and fetch some food and drink. We can't let a woman and child starve to death."

The woman collapsed onto the floor in front of the fire, buried her head in her hands and sobbed.

Hugh knelt down beside her and spoke reassuringly to her, finally persuading her to sit up and dry her tears.

"When he died, the rest of them fought among themselves for anything worth taking. We hid until they went." She explained in a low voice.

"Who are you? Were you related to the dead man?"

"No. I was just his woman. I am Lucy Moulton and this is my son." She patted the child lovingly.

"Were you here when he died?"

"Yes."

"Would you tell me how it happened, please."

Lucy sighed deeply as if everything was too much trouble but she tried to comply with Hugh's request. "He had just eaten his meal and lay down in there." She nodded towards the curtained area. "He's still in there."

Hugh stood up and drew back the curtain. In the dim light he could just make out the still figure of Ivo Longspee, lying on the low bed. The dead man was fully dressed and wore a chain mail vest and steel helmet. Hugh took a close look at the corpse and knew, without any doubt, that this was the man who had attacked the krugge when he returned from Amsterdam. There was no mistaking those strong, weather beaten features. This Norman had undoubtedly been a pirate and thieves' creek had deserved its notoriety.

Hugh turned back to the main room and asked the woman. "Who will bury him?"

She hesitated, then seemed to resign herself to the situation. "He has left sufficient funds for a funeral. He told me he had dictated his instructions to a clerk in Spalding and has left that document with the money."

Hugh was mildly surprised at this. If the dead man had left money and instructions in case of his death, he must have led a precarious life, expecting death to come to him at any time. It reminded him of the preparations some old soldiers made before each battle. The facts fitted well with the pirate existence that he suspected Ivo of leading. Remembering why he had come to the holding, he asked "How did he die?"

"He was poisoned."

"Poisoned! How can you be so sure?"

"He ate his meal as usual, then went to bed to sleep it off. I heard him scream and when I went to him, he was vomiting and holding his stomach. The bile was green and blood streaked. It had to be poison, surely?" She closed her eyes and swayed.

Hugh held her firmly by her shoulders and waited for the faintness to pass. He looked around the hut. "Is there any drinking water here?"

The woman reached towards a jug, which stood in a dark corner. Hugh took it up and held it to her lips.

"Had he been ill before today?"

"He had complained of stomach pains all this week, but he was always strong and fit. I think he sometimes just ate too much."

Hugh remembered his niece's description of the man's appetite when he ate at the tavern. She had told how he always demanded an extra bread trencher with his meal.

"Tell me the exact symptoms he suffered before he died; describe his last hours to me in detail."

Lucy shifted her weight and pulled the child closer to her. "He ate his meal as usual. He ate all the bread I had just baked. I had ground the last of the grain. There was none left for us." She pointed to a wooden meal chest standing in the corner of the room, as if to back up her words. "After about two hours, he complained he was tired and he felt sick, but I took no notice as he always drank too much strong beer with his meals."

"Anything else? Did he complain of numbness or losing the use of his limbs? Did he have visions?"

She considered her answer carefully. "He said nothing about numbness, but he did stagger to his bed like a drunken man."

"What about visions? Did he report seeing anything peculiar?"

"Yes. He did scream about monsters in his bed. That was just before he died. He shouted that his belly was on fire, then he complained it had spread to his arms and legs." She crossed herself religiously. "Maybe it was a devil come for his soul. Up until then he was fully in charge of his senses. He had even threatened to beat me when he recovered from my bad cooking."

"Bad cooking? Did you cook badly?"

"No, not I. If he'd not eaten it all, the boy and I would have gladly finished it." She hesitated, then shrugged her shoulders. "I think the grain could have been off. The flour smelled fusty to me, as if the mice had fouled it. But he insisted it was good Spanish rye and it couldn't be wasted."

Hugh decided on a direct approach, just as he had with Giles. "Tell me, woman, did you poison him?"

Lucy crossed herself religiously and vigorously shook her head. "That would be a mortal sin. I wished him no ill. We had been happy together in the beginning. This is our child." She instinctively gathered the boy to her skirt, where he hid his face from the strangers, sucking his thumb for comfort.

Hugh's ears pricked up at that mention of Spanish rye. The cloves he had bought from the Norman were from Spain; the crests on the jars proved it. He lifted up the lid of the meal chest, took out the sack and inspected it. It was a coarse weave with a round, blue crest stamped onto it. Even though the impression was faint, he recognised the design as identical to the one impressed in the wax seals on the clove jars. So, the grain was part of the same wreck. He held it close to his nose and sniffed at the contents. It did indeed smell a bit damp.

"Has this bag been wet?" Hugh held the sack out to the woman.

"He brought it back from a wrecked merchant ship. It was dry when he brought it in to me. There were two other sacks that had been thoroughly wet by the sea. They were spoiled and no good for us to eat. I was feeding them to the swine rather than waste them."

Hugh put his hand inside the sack and pulled out a few grains, which had lodged in one corner. He looked at the rye, sniffed it again, then let it drop onto the fire. Having learned nothing new, he threw the empty bag back into the corner of the room. He was about to ask another question when they were interrupted by the arrival of Peter with some freshly baked bread and a jug of fresh milk.

"Here. You and the boy eat something before we speak further." Hugh handed her the food and stood aside to give them time to eat. While they enjoyed the simple meal, he pulled aside the curtain and inspected the body of her master more thoroughly. The eyes were closed and the face washed. The arms were crossed on the chest in a restful pose. She had laid him out with due reverence. It looked as if she really had cared for the man in spite of his ill treatment of her.

In death, Ivo Longspee looked almost noble, the air of restless energy and all signs of his fiery temper had gone. Hugh checked the body for any signs of what had caused his death, but found no trace of violence. He bent over and sniffed at the mouth hoping the poison, if indeed poison had killed the man, had left a trace of an odour, but he detected nothing unusual. Reverently he covered the body over and bowed his head in a short prayer for the man's soul. As an old soldier Hugh had met death in many guises. After a battle he had often performed that simple last right, whatever the dead man's race, colour or religion. Ivo Longspee, whatever his faults on earth, must now meet his maker. Like every man who ever lived, he would be judged and pay for his sins. A short prayer would not go amiss.

"What's to become of the body?" Hugh's reeve asked.

Hugh looked questioningly at the woman.

Lucy, who had eaten most of her food and seemed sufficiently recovered, pointed to the curtained annexe. "There is money and a parchment detailing how he wanted to be buried. It's hidden in there in his money chest."

Hugh raised his eyebrows at this revelation. "Money chest? How did that little treasure escape his men's attention?"

"Only I know where it's hidden."

"And you will turn this money over to the church for his burial?"

"As any God-fearing Christian would!" She was indignant at Hugh's question. "What kind of person would rob a man of a Christian burial and his place in heaven?"

Hugh nodded his approval. To do otherwise would surely jeopardise one's own immortal soul. He was beginning to trust Lucy Moulton. He doubted she could have had a hand in the Norman's untimely death.

"Where is this money chest?"

Lucy eyed her neighbours thoughtfully, then made a decision. "You have been good to me and my son. I'm sure you can be trusted to carry out a dead man's last wishes. The chest is hidden beneath the body." She pointed again to the side room where the dead Norman lay.

Hugh nodded approvingly. That was the last place Ivo Longspee's men would have looked, even if they suspected that their leader had made provision for his end.

"Joseph. Go and fetch the chest in here."

The reeve reluctantly did his master's bidding and returned carrying a small oak box, bound in iron, with a decorative lock set in the lid. He placed it on the ground at Hugh's feet.

"The key?" Hugh asked Lucy.

She put her hand under her dress and pulled out a string on which hung an iron key. Hugh took it from her and opened the chest. Inside he found a bag of silver coins and a document sealed with a wax seal. It was addressed to the Lord Prior of Spalding.

"Your master was surely expecting to die at any time, from the elaborate preparations he has made." Hugh looked down at the woman. "Living the kind of life I suspect he led, I am not entirely surprised at this. I will take this to the prior and see it is acted on. No doubt Ivo Longspee made adequate arrangements for his funeral and for mass to be said for his immortal soul, as befits a man of his family and breeding." He turned to one of his other farm hands "You had better bury that body we found in the yard; that's the least we can do. Then we are finished here."

The woman, who had been sitting on the floor, hungrily finishing the last remains of the bread and milk, stopped eating at Hugh's remarks. She looked up sharply. "What will happen to us? With him gone we have no money and nowhere to go."

Hugh scratched his head and considered their plight. "You have little choice. You must go to the priory at Spalding and ask for their charity. No house of God will turn away a destitute traveller. " He stood and watched as the boy and his mother finished their meal.

The boy spoke for the first time. "Thank you, sir. That's all we've eaten in three days."

"Didn't your master feed you?"

"Only sometimes, sir. Only when there was enough left over from his meal."

Hugh shook his head in disbelief. Ivo Longspee was a wicked and greedy man. That much was becoming all too obvious.

The woman seemed revived by her small repast. She rose shakily to her feet and pulled her shawl around her shoulders. Hugh looked at her and the boy and felt very sorry for them. He considered what he could do to help them.

"Well, boy do you think you could ride a pony as far as Spalding?"

Lucy answered for her son. "He could try, sir. If we had a pony."

"I am going back to Spalding when I've finished here. I could accompany you both to the priory."

For the first time the woman smiled. "I would be greatly indebted to you, sir." She grabbed his hand and kissed it.

"Right." He turned to his men. "Let's get them back over to my holding. It will be a slow journey to the priory, so we'd better set out immediately."

An hour later, the small party left for Spalding. The woman rode behind Hugh, the boy was set astride a piebald pony. Joseph followed on his horse leading the boys mount by a rope. They made good time getting to Spalding, where Hugh took them to the priory to lodge them in the pilgrims' quarters before he visited the prior's steward to deposit the money chest with him and to ask him to arrange the burial.

Chapter Thirteen

Richard the skinner, who was the town fellmonger, and several of the other wealthy men in the Spalding area were minded to form a guild of Saint Mary, to worship at the new parish church, that was being built across the river from the priory. Religious guilds, such as the one they proposed, were being formed at many local churches to pay for a priest and to purchase candles and vestments to the glory of God and their patron saint, as well as provide for their members' burials. It was their pious hopes that being in a guild would guarantee their place in heaven. Hugh had been invited to the inaugural feast, at which Richard hoped to convince his fellows of the wisdom of forming a new guild and to persuade them to lend their financial support.

Hugh threw the dregs of his beer onto the fire and went to his bedchamber to get himself ready for the feast. He had little enthusiasm for the event but felt obliged to accept Thomas's invitation and put in an appearance. He changed from his dusty daytime clothes into something more suited to the evening's entertainment, knowing full well that the richer members of the guild would be advertising their wealth with an obvious show of finery. He felt out of place with the local gentry, so he took his time getting ready, aiming to arrive when the feast was underway and the room was crowded, so that he might slip in unnoticed.

When Hugh finally arrived at the hall, the evening was well advanced. He found a place to sit near the entrance and surveyed the room, which had been set out with long tables along each of three walls. By the light of the numerous rush lights set on the walls he could see the high table. Richard the skinner and the more important guests were seated at this table, which was raised so that it could be seen from anywhere in the room. Unlike the lower tables, this one was spread with a white linen cloth. The men and their wives at the top table were dressed in their fine clothes and furs. Richard was very conspicuous in a blue robe with a fox fur trim. Hugh glanced at the top table and saw that Thomas Bohun, the priory steward, was among those honoured guests.

As Hugh arrived, servants were bringing the fish dishes to the tables. Great pike and herrings were being served, along with freshly baked bread and wine. A group of musicians provided the entertainment at this early stage of the banquet. This motley orchestra, composed of a dulcimer, a harp, a lute and handbells, was finding it difficult to make itself heard above the noise of the servants and the loud conversation of the diners.

"Pass the wine." The man on Hugh's left shouted, raising his voice above the general din.

As Hugh handed the flagon over to his neighbour, he realised it was Giles father. "Ah Gilbert. Good to see you here."

Mistress Fisher, who was sitting the other side of her husband, leaned forward and smiled at Hugh. Her husband rested the wine flagon on the table and seemed to want to talk.

"Those herrings are part of our catch." He pointed proudly at the wooden dish set between them.

Hugh nodded that he understood and chewed on his bread.

"I understand you are friendly with the priory steward. Can't you use your influence to help my son?"

Hugh swallowed the mouthful of food and shook his head. "I have no more influence with the priory than you. They just use me for my healing skills. If I could help, I would, but I can assure you, no amount of pleading by me will make any difference in a suspected murder."

Gilbert Fisher shrugged his shoulders and turned to explain to his wife what Hugh had said.

Hugh feigned an intense interest in his meal, inspecting every piece before he ate it, trying to avoid any unpleasantness.

"Master Pinchbeck?" A young servant came over to the table and spoke to Hugh.

"Yes?"

"Master Bohun wishes to have a word with you at the top table." The boy directed Hugh's attention to the steward, who raised a hand and beckoned Hugh to go to him.

Hugh wiped his mouth and took a swig of the wine before he went to see what was wanted of him.

"Hugh, I want to introduce you to Richard the skinner, our host for the night." Thomas waved a hand at the richly dressed man sitting beside him, then leaned over to his neighbour and said. "This is Hugh Pinchbeck. The man I was telling you about."

The fellmonger inclined his head, smiled, and said something in a voice so low Hugh couldn't hear him above the music. It was all very polite and proper.

Thomas Bohun leaned closer and whispered in Hugh's ear, "Richard will be contacting you. He needs to discuss a health matter with you. I have told him how much I value your advice."

Hugh smiled his thanks and threaded his way back to his seat at the far table. The steward was as good as his word; he would prove a useful introduction to Spalding's wealthier inhabitants. He sat down with a satisfied smile on his face.

"There. I told you. You have influence." Gilbert Fisher wagged a finger at him.

Hugh ignored the comments and busied himself eating his meal.

After the fish dishes, came duck and game birds with peas pottage, then the cooked meats were served: succulent pork, roasted on the spit, and mutton, liberally basted with spices and herbs. The final course was composed of various comfits. Hugh immersed himself completely in the business of eating and drinking to avoid further conversation with his neighbour and his wife. He also drank rather too much wine in his efforts to keep himself occupied and unapproachable.

The master of the feast clapped his hands for silence and shouted to the guests, announcing the troupe of acrobats who were already tumbling onto the floor.

Hugh was pleased to see the group of performers he had helped in the market tavern. His eyes searched the troupe to see how the man with the dislocated shoulder was recovering, but he couldn't see him. Suddenly, from nowhere, the familiar figure of Leo appeared in front of him and shook a hat at him, begging for coins.

"Alms for a poor man with a broken shoulder." The acrobat said jokingly and grinned broadly at Hugh.

"I didn't expect to see you here tonight." Hugh said.

"I'm resting as you suggested. I'm doing the dwarf's job. He's going to top the pyramid in my place." Leo bowed low to Hugh, put his hood back on his head and ran to join the rest of the troupe, where he picked up a bladder on a stick and played the fool, pretending to chase the other performers as they tumbled around the centre of the room.

Hugh poured himself another large drink and sat back to enjoy the performance. The travelling troupe was very good. Every member was an accomplished juggler as well as a versatile acrobat. Even the dwarf played his new and difficult part to perfection. The audience roared their appreciation at the end of the performance and threw a shower of coins into the centre of the room. Leo and his men gathered up the offerings and retired outside for their suppers.

After the acrobats' performance, Richard the skinner rose from his seat and banged his pewter mug on the table to get everyone's attention. The entertainment was over and the serious business of raising interest in the proposed new Guild of Saint Mary, got underway. Already he had the support of all the people at the top table, but the expense of a ful- time priest and the upkeep of a chapel, with the cost of regular candles and offerings, required still more money. The majority of the guests seemed impressed with the aims of the new guild and shouted their support for it. Hugh, who was already worse for drink, but not enough to lose all caution, wondered how much of that enthusiasm was the wine speaking and how many of his neighbours would deny their support in the light of a sober dawn.

It was well after midnight before the gathering broke up. Hugh threaded his way unsteadily through the beggars at the door, who were already fighting for the table scraps that the servants were throwing amongst them. The Fishers followed him out into the night air, clinging together to keep upright and singing a drunken duet. He staggered along the riverside path, stopping every few steps to regain his balance. At the quay, he leaned heavily on a bollard and watched the moon reflected in the dark water, rippling past him on the incoming tide, moving the boats against their mooring ropes and disturbing the waterfowl sleeping on the muddy banks. Two frightened ducks broke cover and took wing at his approach, protesting loudly at being disturbed. Hugh was surprised by the sudden noise and tripped on his lame leg. He sat down heavily on the towpath and rolled onto his back, where he would probably have remained until morning, if two friends hadn't come along and found him there.

"I thought you looked in need of help, master." Leo and one of the other acrobats lifted him up by his arms and dragged him along the towpath to his home on Eau Side.

Hugh was awoken next morning by shouts from the yard. John's distant voice broke into his dreams.

"Oh! By St Hugh! Never again." Hugh groaned as the daylight burnt into his eye and his head thumped with each heartbeat, as if it would split in two.

John shouted again. "Master! Master! The tide has come into the yard in the night. It must have been an extra high one."

Hugh turned over to reach for the jug of water he kept by his bedside, intending to refresh his mouth, but his hand fell on a warm body. He realised, with a start, that someone was in bed beside him!

"What the devil...!" Hugh sat upright but immediately saw dancing lights and had to stop any sudden movements. Holding the top of his head with both hands, he turned to face his companion and slowly opened his eyes again. There in his bed, smiling back at him, he saw the rosy face of his housekeeper, Margaret!

Chapter Fourteen.

After breakfast, which he took alone at the table in the hall, Hugh sat and tried to recall what had actually happened the night before. He remembered the feast and drinking rather a lot of wine to avoid speaking to Giles' parents. He remembered Thomas Bohun introducing him to Richard the skinner and he recalled watching the acrobats. He knew he had started to walk home alone but only faintly recalled falling on the riverbank and someone helping him. The rest of the night was a blank. Somehow he had arrived home and managed to undress and get into his bed.

Hugh remembered all too clearly, the shock of waking up to find his housekeeper snuggled up to him in his bed. How she got there was a complete mystery to him. Presumably she had undressed him and put him to bed, but why had she got in with him? Try as he would, there was no recollection of what happened between falling on the towpath and waking up with Margaret at his side. Judging by the sideways glances she kept giving him as she served breakfast, and the secret little smile she had permanently on her face, the sooner he found out exactly what had occurred between them, the better.

"Are you in today for meals, master?" Margaret asked.

"I'm not sure…maybe…I'll have to see." Hugh found it hard to look her in the eyes. Even though he had never married, he was not a stranger to women. As a soldier he had sometimes taken advantage of the willing camp followers that were always available, but bedding his housekeeper, and doing it when he was so drunk, he didn't recall exactly what had happened, was not what he had intended. He was aware she was an attractive woman, much younger than he was, and a good housekeeper, but he did not intend to break the habit of lifetime and marry at his time of life. Tentatively he asked. "What happened last night, Margaret?"

"What do you mean, sir?" She pretended innocence.

"How come you were in my bed this morning?"

"Don't you remember, sir?"

He thought he detected a sly smile on her face and felt colour rising to his cheeks. "By St Hugh, woman! I don't even remember getting home!" He thumped the table in his frustration.

"Don't worry, master. Nothing happened." She smiled at him, as if she wouldn't have minded if it had. "You were drunk. John and I undressed you and got you ready for bed. Those performers carried you up to your room, where you collapsed. After we'd undressed you, you were holding so tightly to me, I couldn't get away, so I snuggled up to you, and we both fell asleep."

Hugh sighed with relief. "God be praised!...I mean... That was good of you."

She added coquettishly. "It really was my pleasure, sir. I'm sorry if you were upset"

Hugh, taken aback at her forward manner, but nevertheless slightly flattered by it, tried to reassure her. "I mean, I'm sorry I was so drunk..." He hesitated, not satisfied that he was making himself clear "...If I'd been sober, I would probably have enjoyed your company even more, I'm sure."

Margaret broke into a broad smile and practically skipped back to her kitchen.

Hugh wished he hadn't uttered that last remark; he realised he had already said too much. Margaret was a good worker, but in his haste to reassure her he had compromised himself. Now life would be more complicated than ever. He lingered over his oatcakes and drank another mug of water to wash the taste of stale wine from his mouth.

"Master! Master!" John came running into the hall from the yard. "There's a barge with a coffin on it coming up the river. They say it's Ivo Longspee's funeral"

Hugh pulled on his jerkin and followed the lad down the yard to the riverside, arriving there just as the barge sailed past. He watched the boatman manoeuvre the small craft, with the coffin and an escort and a priest on board. It moored alongside the priory quay, where there was a crane to remove the stone blocks from the barges. As soon as they came alongside the quay, several monks and a crowd of locals moved to greet them.

"It looks like being a big funeral, master." John voiced Hugh's thoughts aloud.

"Aye lad. Twelve pence will buy a priest to say mass over your coffin. Plenty of food and ale at the church will ensure all the mourners you could wish for. He's bought himself a good send off with his plunder."

They watched as the coffin was swung ashore by one of the cranes on the prior's wharf, and loaded onto a wagon, which stood on the dockside in a shallow pool of river water, left from the night's high tide. The hired mourners lined up behind the coffin and the whole procession made its way towards the market place and the entrance to the parish church. Hugh was surprised to see Lucy Moulton and her young son were among the mourners. He made a quick decision to join the ceremony, as he wanted to speak with her again. Turning to limp up the yard to the house, he told John.

"I am going to the funeral service. Tell your mother I will be back for lunch."

In the church, which was overflowing with mourners, the wooden coffin stood before the high altar. Several candles in tall stands burned around it, their yellow flames flickering in the slight draft, their smoke curling upwards towards the dark oak beamed roof. Six hired priests knelt at the altar, dutifully reciting mass for the Norman's soul. A motley crowd of mourners filled the aisles. Hugh slipped through the main entrance and joined the congregation. After a few minutes, to get his bearings, he moved to stand next to the woman and her son.

She turned to see who had joined her, and smiled when she recognised Hugh.

"I need to speak with you urgently." Hugh whispered. "I'll see you back at the priory in the pilgrim's quarters after the service."

She kept her head bowed but nodded she understood.

Once he was sure she had understood their arrangement.

Hugh said a brief prayer for the dead man's soul then left the church as quietly as he had come. He knew the funeral would take some time.

The mass took long enough, but the distribution of alms and food to the mourners would take even longer. He walked up the market stead to the priory where he hoped to find Brother James in the library.

The priory grounds were even busier than usual. Apart from lay workers cleaning up the mud the high tide had left on the areas nearest the river, several shipments of new stone were being dressed by the masons to complete the prior's new quarters. Hugh threaded his way through the bustle, deliberately avoiding the steward's office, and made for the hospital, where he checked on the progress of the two casualties that he and Godfrey had treated. Once he had assured himself that they were progressing well, he entered the cloisters and made his way to the priory library.

In the library, Brother James was instructing a young brother in the art of grinding soot to make black ink. The young monk was covered to his elbows in the black pigment. James looked up as soon as Hugh entered the room.

"Ah Hugh! Just in time to try a new vintage from our mother house." He unlocked the wine cupboard and lined up two cups. "You had better go and wash your arms." He waved the young monk away.

"Thank you" Hugh never refused a good wine.

"You are welcome. What can we do for you?"

"I want to consult the herbals to check on a poison."

James raise his eyebrows but nodded he understood the request. "I suppose this has to do with the poor soul who is being buried today?"

"Yes. Ivo Longspee was poisoned, of that I have no doubt. But how and with what is a mystery."

"I heard it rumoured monkshood was involved."

"That's what is being said. But I am not so sure. Please, may I check the new copy of De Simplicibus Medicinis?"

Reverently, James reached the volume down from the shelf and opened it on the table.

"Monkshood...let me see...monkshood..." The old monk leafed through the thick pages until he found the appropriate entry.

He turned the book towards his guest. "Here you are, Hugh. You have adequate Latin, read it for yourself."

Hugh checked the details of the plant on the beautifully illustrated pages. The text, which described the effects a large dose would have on a human, pleased him, when he saw that he had remembered the symptoms correctly. Numbness of limbs and body were always found in cases of monkshood poisoning. He nodded and smiled to himself.

James was watching him closely. "Does that satisfy you, Hugh?"

"Yes and no. There was a witness to the man's death. She stated there was no numbness, but she could be mistaken of course. How would she know what the victim was feeling? She did mention he complained of a burning sensation in body and limbs. I myself checked the corpse but could neither see nor smell a sign of monkshood about his mouth. I am not convinced he died from that poison."

"From what I hear, it was indeed some lethal substance that killed him, there seems no argument with that. What else could it have done it?" James asked.

"I know of very few poisons available in these fens, that would produce such a quick effect. Monkshood must still be the prime candidate, in spite of my misgivings." Hugh lapsed into silence and sipped his wine. He turned over the pages of the herbal and admired the fine writing and the beautiful coloured illustrations. As he read the text, he was aware that a nagging doubt, at the back of his mind, was worrying him. He felt there was something he had overlooked, something vital to understanding how Ivo Longspee met his end. He thought over his visit to the Wykeham holding, trying to grasp the elusive feeling, knowing it could be important, but not quite managing to bring it to mind. He frowned at the effort.

"You look preoccupied." James interrupted his thoughts.

"Yes. I visited the scene of the murder. It was next to my holding at Wykeham. I am still turning over the events in my mind trying to understand what could have happened."

"Tell me about it, Hugh. Often, talking to someone can crystallise your thoughts." Brother James smiled encouragingly at his friend. "Indulge me, and have another drink."

Hugh refused this offer of a refill and marshalled his thoughts. "There really was little to see at the farm, it was in a mess because his men had ransacked the place before they left. Once he was dead, they fought among themselves and fled with anything they could steal."

James sipped his wine, nodded he was following the description and waved his hand to bid him to continue.

"Everything of value they could find, was gone. All the livestock was gone. No. I tell a lie…there was one small runt of a piglet hiding in the corner of a sty. The poor creature had lost its tail from frost bite." Hugh immersed himself in thoughts of his visit to the Longspee holding.

"Ah! Saint Anthony's piglet; the runt of the litter. In my youth on the family farm we always called such a runt the Tantony piglet." James lined face broke into a smile as he remembered that scrap of information from his past.

Hugh scratched his head. "Ivo was already dead when we found him. His woman, Lucy Moulton, the one you have lodging in the priory pilgrim quarters with her boy, had already prepared his body. I took a look at him then, but there was nothing to see. There were no wounds on him nor any outward sign of how he died."

"A typical poison case, I would say." James drained his cup and reached again for the wine bottle.

Mention of the word poison brought Hugh's attention back from his ruminations. He looked blankly at his friend and asked. "What did you just say about Saint Anthony?"

"The runt of a litter of pigs is often referred to as Saint Anthony's piglet. My family were farmers. They kept many pigs. I helped them before I joined the priory, you know."

Hugh nodded vaguely. The information was interesting but he was too engrossed in his own thoughts. Abruptly he put down his empty mug. "I think I must go and speak with Lucy Moulton. She may be able to help me."

At the pilgrims' quarters in the priory, Hugh found Lucy and her son.

"I see you are already back. Is the funeral over?"

"No. We came away after the service was finished, before the food and wine was distributed to the mourners."

"I was a little surprised to see you at the church. Especially as Ivo Longspee treated you so badly."

"He is dead now. Every departing soul deserves our prayers."

Hugh was surprised again by the woman's piety. He changed the subject abruptly to what he had been considering. "You remember at the holding, you mentioned they had fed damp rye to the pigs? Tell me, where could I find any of that grain that remains uneaten?"

"That's simple. I used to feed the pigs. The sacks are tucked under the thatch of the pigsty, on a beam right above the doorway." She seemed about to question why he should want the remains of a sack of spoiled rye grain but changed her mind. Instead she confided in him. "The boy really is Ivo's son, you know."

Hugh was taken completely by surprise at this admission. He didn't know what to say.

Lucy continued. "He said he would never acknowledge a bastard child, but I think that's why he tolerated us there."

"What will you do now?"

"I am thinking of travelling to Henri de Lacy's court in Lincoln and throwing myself and the boy on his mercy."

"Ah yes! Ivo Longspee was a kinsman of the Earl's, I believe."

"He was only a cousin of Lady Margaret de Lacy, she was a Lungspee and daughter of the Earl of Salisbury before she married, but I am desperate. There's nothing else for me to do. Maybe she'll take pity on us and I can find employment and a roof over our heads.

We can't pose as pilgrims forever."

Hugh thanked her for her help and took his leave of her. He was surprised how quiet and dignified the woman had become now she had her freedom and was no longer starving. His reminded himself that his first priority was to help Elizabeth and Giles. He had been back to the holding at Wykeham and had searched for any clues to the cause of the Norman's death but to no avail. He felt in his bones that the answer to the riddle of the poisoning could be in that last meal that Ivo

Longspee had eaten, but there was no way of proving how the poison was administered or who had done it. There had been many men at the holding at the time, maybe he would never find out who had administered the lethal dose.

As Hugh limped across the market stead the hearse bearing the dead Norman's coffin left the church on its final journey over the stone bridge to the new burial ground at the church of St Mary and St Thomas on the other side of the river. The sounds of revelry filled the air, from the mourners who had enjoyed the free food and wine. He wondered if God would want to hear mass paid for by the spoils of piracy and murder.

Chapter Fifteen.

On his next visit to Wykeham, Hugh found other problems awaiting him. The night's high tide had breached part of the earth bank that was their only defence against the sea. His men were working hard to repair the damage before nightfall and the return of the next high tide. Bundles of faggots were being used to fill in the gap. Clay was shovelled over them and stamped into place.

"Trouble, Joseph?"

"Aye, master. Tonight's tide is expected to be bigger still. If we don't strengthen the sea defences we could be inundated."

"Anything I can do to help?"

"No. We've moved the livestock to the higher ground and we've almost finished the work here. What did you come for?"

"I need to cross the creek again to visit the far holding."

Joseph frowned.

"Is there a difficulty?"

"They never did look to the maintenance of their sea wall, even though it's part of their agreement with the priory, the same as us. Last night it broke in two places and the tide got into the holding."

Hugh considered this setback but he was still determined to look for the rye sacks.

"I must go over, Joseph. It could mean life or death to Giles Fisher. Can you spare a man and a boat?"

"I'll take you myself, Master. I'd like to see for myself what state their sea defences are in. The water could spread inland and may affect us."

"Good. When I get back to town, I'll let the priory know the state of the land. They will not want to lose one of their farms to the sea."

Hugh and the reeve crossed over to the deserted holding. Where the tide had overrun the ground nearest the sea, pools of salt water had turned the land to mud, strands of brown seaweed lay everywhere. The going was very slow as their feet sank deep in the black mud, but they eventually managed to reach the pigsties. There was no sign of any life except for a rat or two, which scurried away from them as they moved about. Hugh climbed into the sty and felt above the door for the rye sacks, but to no avail, there were no sacks there. Lucy had told him where to look but she must have been mistaken.

A complete search of the area yielded no sign of the rye. Turning to Joseph he said. "I've one more place to search, Joseph. Follow me." He trudged through the mud to the higher ground surrounding the homestead.

Inside the hut, Hugh found all as they had left it, apart from the dead man's body. The remains of the turf fire lay in the centre of the floor, the empty water jug was standing where he had placed it and the empty grain sack lay discarded in a corner. He turned the sack over with his foot and found it eaten away, most certainly by the rats. Turning to Joseph, Hugh said. "Nothing here. There's nothing here!"

The reeve raised his eyebrows questioningly.

"I know it must seem strange to you, Joseph, but I needed to come back here in case I'd missed something that would help me understand how Ivo Longspee met his death."

Back at his own holding Hugh sat by the turf fire and devoured a small warm loaf and enjoyed a mug of small beer, while the reeve's wife found some straw to clean the mud off his shoes.

"Did you have any problems in Spalding with the high tide last night?" Joseph asked.

"The yard boy told me the water just managed to top the river bank and wet the yard."

"That's bad. Tonight there will be a full moon and the wind is getting up from the east. The high tide will be blown into the Wash, and water will back up the Welland. Spalding could flood tonight, master. Will you need any help there?"

Hugh considered this advice. He knew full well that Joseph was right, but he had been too preoccupied with thoughts of Ivo Longspee's death and Giles' trial, to give much thought to the tides. He realised now he would have to move the goods from the dry store below his house to the upper floor where they would be safe. He had corn and flour stored there as well as some of his dried herbs and spices. He'd better return home as quickly as possible. "I could do with another man to help move the stores from the lower floor. What time is tonight's tide expected to peak?"

"In the early hours of tomorrow morning; soon after midnight. Shall I come and help?"

"No need, Joseph. Just spare me one of the younger workers for the night."

Once Hugh had arrived back on Eau Side he set the men to clearing the downstairs storeroom, stacking the sacks and barrels upstairs in the main hall. When everything was neatly piled against the walls, he asked John to make sure there was enough dry wood and turf stored above the yard for cooking and heating the household.

It was getting dark by the time all these tasks were completed, so the man from the Wykeham holding curled up beside John in front of the fire, to spend the night in Spalding. Hugh arranged for two men with lanterns to stay awake all night and watch for the high tide. Thoughts of Giles and proving his innocence had to wait for another day. But then, Giles was going nowhere, so that matter could safely be left. The chance of flooding and the damage to the town and to his home, was the most pressing thing. He was feeling very tired from his busy day at Wykeham so he went to his bedroom and lay on the top of the bed, fully dressed, leaving instructions he was to be woken up at midnight or before, if the water rose to a dangerous level.

It was just before midnight when John called Hugh from his bed.

"The water is close to the top of the bank, sir. What should we do?"

"I'm coming, John. Give me a few minutes." Hugh hauled himself off the bed and limped down the yard to where a small group of men stood with lanterns. He found several of his neighbours there, looking out anxiously over the swollen river. Lanterns and rush lights were dotted along both banks of the river, forming small pools of light that reflected on the racing tide. The water rushed through the town, carrying tree branches and debris with it. The wind was blowing a gale from the direction of the sea. A small boat spun past them, from down river, it's frayed mooring rope floating uselessly behind it. Out of control, it could be heard crashing against the other boats in the darkness. Hugh looked out over the surging water and knew a difficult night lay ahead.

Just after midnight the water rose level with the top of the Welland banks, then breached the defences near the stone bridge, the lowest part of the town. Almost immediately the reinforced bank gave way and a gaping hole appeared in it. Dark, muddy, seawater poured into the priory grounds. Within a short time, the tide had pushed the water level over the bank at Eau Side and Hugh found his home threatened by water on two sides. The water from the original break had flooded the low-lying parts of the town and was rising rapidly along Eau Side at the front of his property, while the river was spilling into his yard and creeping towards the foundations of the house at the back. He said a silent prayer and told his men to retreat to the upper floor where a turf fire still burned in the hall. There was nothing any man could do now, it was all in the hands of God. Judging by the volume of water and the ferocity of the wind, which had increased as the river level rose, most of the Lincolnshire fens would be inundated that night.

Hugh and his men sat up all night, watching, waiting for the tide to turn and the water levels to return to normal. With the dawn came more pressing problems for the town. When the tide turned, all the water that had gone inland started to flow back to the sea carrying even more debris with it from upriver.

At first light, Hugh took off his shoes and waded barefoot through the muddy water down the yard to the riverbank. He was relieved to find the bank at the bottom of his property had held firm. The only flooding they had suffered, was caused by the tide topping the defences. In past winters there had been some high tides but they had not experienced one that high for several years. The combination of tide and the driving wind had been the town's undoing.

"Man the bridge!" A cry went up from the direction of the stone bridge. Hugh looked upriver and realised the arches under the bridge were becoming blocked with debris. Men could be seen running along the parapet with long poles in their hands, their cries carried as far as his yard. He limped back to the house and shouted for his men.

"No rest for us yet. We are needed at the bridge." Hugh realised if the debris stuck under the arches, the force of the water could damage the structure of the old bridge If that happened, Spalding's strategic importance and its prosperity as a major crossing place in the fens, would be jeopardised.

At the bridge, scores of men were working frantically with ropes and poles, trying to free the trees and branches that were damming the flow of the river. The water level was building up beyond the bridge, flooding once again into the priory and the town.

"Push over here," a boy shouted for help on his side of the river.

Hugh stood on the top of the bridge and looked out over the chaos. Huge trees had been uprooted and carried along by the retreating tide. Dead livestock floated among the debris. The bodies of two bloated pigs floated down the river and slammed against the wall of wood beneath the bridge. Every so often a branch would crack and give way, which seemed to make the very foundations of the bridge shudder under the strain.

"Free that large willow in the middle. That will allow the smaller stuff to escape." Hugh cupped his hand and shouted this to the men who were standing at the riverside near the bridge.

To Hugh's dismay, John, who had followed his master to the bridge, took a long pole and jumped down onto the tree trunk, he was soon joined by several other lads as they tried to prise the logjam apart. Ropes were fixed to some of the willow branches and harnessed to two packhorses on the bank. With the combined effort of men and horses, the willow tree was slowly turned in the water and began to follow the receding tide under the bridge.

Hugh was proud of the lad but fearful for him and well aware that Margaret would never forgive him if anything happened to her only son. He watched the huge tree trunk glide slowly under the bridge with John still standing on it. He limped quickly across the bridge to see the tree come out the other side, but it did not appear because the upper branches were wedged firmly under the arch.

"Chop them off." A man threw an axe to the boy.

John, who was balanced precariously on the tree trunk, swung the blade and cut through the offending branches. With a final loud crack, the tree broke free of the bridge and swirled around in midstream. Hugh watched horrified as the boy toppled off the tree into the swirling water.

"John!" He shouted as he raced along the towpath, following the floating debris. After some minutes, that passed so slowly they felt like hours, Hugh saw the boy come spluttering to the surface and cling onto some of the smaller branches that were dragging in the water in the wake of the main trunk. He followed helplessly as the willow floated swiftly downstream, past his house and on towards the sea.

Hugh was desperate. He felt responsible for the boy's predicament. He ran to the riverbank and untied a small boat from the flooded quay. Without stopping to think, he pushed it into the centre of the river and paddled furiously after the retreating tree.

"John! John! Hang on." He yelled at the top of his voice as he rowed and steered the small boat towards the mass of floating branches. He could no longer see John's head but he prayed he was not too late and the boy was still hanging on. As he guided the prow of the boat into the mass of small twigs, forming the topmost part of the tree, he caught sight of the bedraggled figure of the boy, clinging on for his life. John was obviously exhausted but still alive. Holding out a paddle and leaning over the side of the boat, Hugh shouted for the lad to swim and grab hold of it, but John was too weak. He clung grimly onto the thin branches with a precarious finger hold. In desperation Hugh tied the prow rope of the boat onto his belt, stripped to the waist and lowered himself into the freezing cold water. A few strong strokes and he was alongside the boy. He grabbed the lad's coat and dragged himself and his burden back to the boat. The cold river water seemed to freeze him to his very bones but he struggled hard to push the boy up into the boat and to get himself out of the torrent. John was little help in this endeavour for he was barely conscious. With one stupendous effort, Hugh pushed the boy's limp body into the boat and hauled himself in afterwards. Once in the boat, Hugh wrapped John in his dry jerkin and struck out for the bank.

At the riverside, strong arms helped them ashore. Their plight had been noticed by Hugh's other men, who had followed the boat along the flooded towpath on horseback. In no time at all Hugh and John were back in the hall, stripped of their wet clothing and wrapped in blankets, warming themselves in front of the roaring fire. The boy was none the worse for his ordeal, but Hugh was feeling his age and the effects of the superhuman efforts he had made in the river.

"It's bad news for all of the Lincolnshire fens, master." One of the workers, who had just returned from the bridge, told Hugh. "They think the sea must have covered thousands of bovates of low-lying land. Much stock and human life has been lost this night."

Hugh shivered and drew the blanket closer to him. He reflected on his own experiences and worried for his own staff and property. "Most of Spalding has been under water tonight. There will be a lot of clearing up to do in the next few weeks. What about the Wykeham holding? Do you think they will have escaped unharmed?"

The man shook his head. "I don't know, Master. I can only hope and pray my father and mother have survived the night there."

Hugh looked at the circle of tired and mud flecked faces around the fire. He smiled sadly. "We have nothing to reproach ourselves with." He looked at young John who was sitting in his mother's arms, a blanket wrapped around him. "We have saved at least one life tonight."

Margaret looked up at Hugh with large, thankful eyes. He looked away, too embarrassed at the feelings he saw there.

Chapter Sixteen

On the morning after the flood, the few inhabitants of Spalding who had managed to get some sleep, awoke to a wet and dismal world. The entire town had been invaded by the murky water. Banks of thick, stinking mud spread over the market stead and every roadway. The cellars and ground floor of the houses and buildings told the same story. Lay workers at the priory were washing the mud from the stone flooring of the parish church. Everywhere people were cleaning up the debris of the night before and praying the floods would not return.

Hugh slept only a few hours in his chair before the fire. He was so tired he had fallen asleep there, still wrapped in a blanket. Margaret looked after the fire, a job usually performed by her son, letting the exhausted lad sleep soundly on the floor with the other men. At first light Hugh woke up with a start and stretched himself.

"By'r our Lady! But I'm getting old." He ached all over from his exertions and from sleeping in an oak chair. He looked about the room, saw the exhausted men still snoring in front of the glowing turves and immediately recalled the traumatic events of the night. He looked apprehensively over at John, but relaxed when he saw the lad was sleeping as sweetly as a baby.

Margaret got up from her vigil beside her son and tiptoed over to her master. "Would you like some breakfast, master?"

"What have we? Did the river get into your kitchen?"

"Yes, but not too much. I've already cleaned up and lit the fire in there. I've some oatcakes on the baking stone, if you could fancy some."

Hugh nodded his thanks and made to rise from his chair. "Oh! The devil! But my leg aches!" He fell back wincing with pain.

Margaret looked very concerned for him. "Can I do anything, sir?"

Hugh rubbed his painful knee and shook his head. "A dip in the cold river hasn't helped my stiff old joints, Margaret. Leave me in peace. I'll be moving in a minute or two." He continued rubbing his knee to warm it and get the feeling back.

Eventually everyone was awake, fed and dressed. John was none the worse for his ordeal and very proud of himself for freeing the tree from under the bridge. The man from Wykeham set out immediately after breakfast, hoping to ride back to his family at the holding. Margaret set about swilling the floors to clean the stinking river mud from the house. Hugh crawled slowly up the stairs to the solar to rest on his bed, but sleep didn't come easily to him. With the emergency over, thoughts of Giles' plight came flooding back to him. He was left with the same nagging question. What did cause the Norman's sudden death?

If Ivo was poisoned, why didn't Lucy or the child get symptoms as well? Hugh asked himself that question over and over again. For a time he considered the possibility that she had poisoned her tormentor but from his dealings with her, he was sure she wasn't capable of such a heinous crime. He had to admit he was lost for an answer. Hugh did however come to the conclusion that Ivo's woman, Lucy Moulton, could be his key witness. Thank goodness she was still lodging at the priory. She could confirm that she had never seen Giles near the house at Wykeham. Having tried in vain to make sense of the circumstances of the Norman's death, Hugh gave in to his exhaustion and shouted for a mug of beer. All that thinking was very thirsty work.

John carried the jug of beer to his master. "Mother tells me I am to thank you properly for saving my life, master."

Hugh was embarrassed. He would have done as much for any child in danger, but he realised he was growing very fond of the lad. He searched for something to say to change the subject.

"Your mother wants me to teach you to shoot in the bow, boy. What do you think about that?"

John's eyes lit up. "I know you were a bowman in the king's army, sir. I would learn properly from you."

"Have you ever shot in a bow, lad?"

"Only a few times, sir. I have made a bow out of green wood but it wouldn't shoot very far. I've never owned a proper one."

"Right, that's the first thing we must do. I'll get a small bow made for you, and some practice arrows, then we will put a straw target at the bottom of the yard and shoot together."

The boy was overjoyed at this offer. He ran down the stairs shouting the news to his mother. Hugh poured himself a drink and returned to considering the problem of proving Giles' innocence. As the day unfolded, he limped several times down the yard to view the water level in the Welland. By midmorning it was obvious the incoming tide would not be quite as high as the one the previous night.

The yard and downstairs rooms at Eau Side were swilled down and cleaned. The goods that Hugh had had moved to the hall upstairs, were left on that upper floor, just in case the river overflowed its banks again. With everything under control and back to some kind of normality, Hugh thought it was time to see Giles and explain what progress he had made with the evidence for his defence.

"Margaret, I'll be out the rest of this morning but back to eat at mid-day. I'm going up to the gaol. It's two days since I saw my patient there." He picked up his bag, limped to the stables and rode to the priory gaol.

The town was in a very sorry state that morning. Hugh realised just how lucky they had been when he skirted the bridge and saw the priory workers repairing the gaping hole in the riverbank where the tide had rushed through. It was obvious from the thick mud and slime everywhere that the priory grounds, which lay alongside the river, had been badly flooded. Bundles of small branches were being hastily stacked into the gap. Clay was pushed into the bundles to hold them down and waterproof them, sandstone blocks diverted from the priory building were stacked on top of this repair to compress it and add stability. Looking at the size of the gap in the bank and the lowness of the land at that point, Hugh feared the defences were unlikely to keep out the next high tide, which would peak just after mid-day. He stopped on the bridge and surveyed the chaos the high tide had left in the river. Boats were pushed together in a muddled mass. Many of the smaller vessels had broken away from their moorings and were now stranded high on the mud banks. Fishermen and sailors were working hard to repair the night's damage and prepare for the inevitable return of the next high tide. Hugh turned his horse from the bridge and slowly trotted up the market stead.

In the market place, still more people were clearing up the mess. The tide had reached right into that part of the town, depositing silt, tree branches and debris everywhere. At the market tavern, his sister and her family where clearing out the last of the wet, rush, floor covering. He stopped to speak to her husband who was forking the tangled mess into an orderly heap, so that it could be taken away and burned. Maud, who was scraping the mud from the floor, stood up and straightened her aching back. She nodded to her brother as he looked in at the doorway.

"Bad night. Did it do much damaged?"

"Spoiled our new floor covering, but apart from that and one barrel of ale spoiled, we got off very lightly. What about you? Did it flood badly, right next to the river?"

"Thanks to my reeve's warning I managed to move the foodstuffs upstairs. Apart from the stinking mess, we got off very lightly. Have you heard much news about the rest of the town?"

"Two poor families at Fulney have lost lives. I hear one couple managed to cling onto the remains of their hut but their three children were washed into the river and drowned. They've asked the river men to keep an eye out for the bodies."

Hugh shook his head. He always passed those turf huts when he rode to Wykeham. He didn't know the people who scratched a living there but he knew it was on a particularly low stretch of the road. "That's bad. Well I must get on. Tell Elizabeth I'm going to see Giles. I'll call on my way back."

At the priory prison the gaoler met Hugh at the gate and greeted him. "Ah! Master Hugh. You weren't washed away by the river, then? I heard Eau Side was badly flooded again."

Hugh nodded. "We had a sleepless night, but it could have been worse. I see the priory didn't escape completely."

"That was the low-lying land, down by the river. We had no problems up here." The gaol was on slightly higher ground and had escaped the worst of the deluge. Seeing Hugh was waiting to enter the building he asked. "What can we do for you now?"

"I've come to see my patient. I couldn't manage it yesterday because of the flood, but his face will still need attention."

"Then he'll have to get his attention in Lincoln."

"Lincoln? Surely he's not been sent there already?"

"Aye. News came that the earl is at his manor at Pontefract. He is due in Lincoln in the next few days. I think the prior was glad to be rid of your patient."

Hugh was shocked. He had expected to have more time to gather evidence in support of Giles. "When did he go?"

"The bailiff's men took him from here first thing this morning."

"I see. I suppose he's on his way by boat via Boston?"

"No. The river here is choked up with boats because of the flooding. The bailiff thought the river Witham, from Boston to Lincoln, would be in a similar state so he opted to send him by road."

Hugh knew the road to Lincoln had to cross several rivers. The river Trent in particular, could be a problem at any time of the year, but with the rivers of the area flooded, it might prove to be impassable. "How did they go? Were they all on horseback?"

"No. The prisoner was tied hand and foot, and carried on a cart. He's a young fit lad and they wouldn't trust him not to escape if he was unfettered."

Hugh thanked the gaoler and rode slowly home. His mind was now in turmoil. He knew the bailiff's party would be much slower travelling with a cart than with everyone on horseback. The journey from Spalding to Lincoln by road would take three or four days under normal circumstances, but there were serious doubts in his mind if they would reach the Trent before the water rose and blocked the route. It seemed highly likely that Giles and his escort would be delayed on their way to Lincoln.

I have no choice, he thought despairingly. If I am to intervene on the lad's behalf, I'll have to follow him and get there before he stands trial. But what can I say in his defence when I get there? Hugh was sure in his own mind that Giles wasn't capable of murdering Ivo Longspee, but that was only his personal feelings, he had no solid facts to back up that conclusion. At best he could speak up for Giles as a character witness, but who would listen to him?

Chapter Seventeen

Hugh spent a restless night wrestling with the problem of how to prove Giles innocent. He paced the bedroom, going over and over the events of the past few days in a vain attempt to make sense of it all. In the small hours of the morning he crept downstairs to the kitchen to quench his thirst with a mug of small beer. John who had fallen asleep in front of the fire in the hall, was disturbed by the creaking of the oak floor. He followed Hugh into the kitchen.

"Are you well, master?"

"I'm fine, John. Just couldn't sleep."

The boy wandered back to his warm place by the fire and went immediately back to sleep.

Hugh smiled, in spite of his anxieties. "Oh to be that young and have no worries!" he sighed.

Back upstairs he lay on his bed and went over the evidence against Giles for the hundredth time that night. No matter how he looked at it, he had to face the fact that Giles appeared to be the prime suspect. Things did not look good for the boy.

As the dawn approached, Hugh fell into an exhausted sleep, punctuated by vivid nightmares about Elizabeth and her young man. Ivo Longspee figured in every one of these dreams. By the time the sunlight crept into the yard, Hugh was sound asleep and snoring.

"Master! Master!" John ran up the stairs shouting for Hugh's attention.

Hugh woke up with a start, not really knowing where he was. He sat bolt upright in his bed and blinked at the daylight as John burst into the room.

"Master, come quickly, There's trouble at the Wykeham holding!"

Hugh stared at the lad in disbelief. How could he know so early in the morning that there was trouble at Wykeham?

As if to answer the unspoken question, John said. "Robert, the reeve's son, is here. He's ridden over with an urgent message for you."

Hugh dressed hurriedly and went downstairs to the hall. Standing in front of the newly lit fire was Robert, with a mug in his hand.

"Robert. You're about early. What's happened?"

The shepherd boy bent his head in deference to his master then delivered his message.

"Dad says come at once, master. Peter's family are sick. The youngest is very ill."

Hugh knew his reeve would never have sent the boy all the way to Spalding so early in the morning, unless things were very serious indeed. He wasted no time on breakfast. He gathered a selection of his nostrums and threw them into a bag. John was already saddling his horse.

In the kitchen, Margaret was busy cooking. She was surprised when Hugh hurried in and grabbed a handful of warm oatcakes.

"Can't stop, Margaret. Got to get to the Wykeham holding. Someone's very ill there." Without further explanation, he stuffed an oatcake into his mouth, mounted his horse and galloped to the town bridge. Young Robert, on a fresh mount, followed close behind him.

As they galloped to Wykeham, Hugh managed to get more details from the young shepherd boy.

"How did this happen, Robert?" Hugh shouted above the thud of the horses' hooves.

"I don't know, master...Peter came to the house before dawn. He was shouting for my dad to come and help him."

Hugh nodded that he understood.

"He said his family were ill and the youngest looked as if he was dying... Dad sent me at once to get you...That's all I know."

Hugh knew that Peter, the saltman, was unmarried but he did remember Joseph telling him that Peter had his sister and her children living with him. Maybe the children had contracted some pestilence. Many children died of the ague in the fens.

As they approached the Wykeham farm, Roberts began to lag behind; he was exhausted by the double journey at such a fast pace. Hugh waved his hand at the boy, signalling he could slow down, then he dug his heels into his mount and left the lad far behind.

Joseph had a horse already saddled in the yard, awaiting Hugh's arrival. He mounted as soon as he heard the clatter of hooves and signalled Hugh to follow him. In a matter of minutes, they were at Peter's hut in the fen.

"Do you... know what's... happened, Joseph?" Hugh asked, breathlessly.

"Only what Peter told me. They've had a bad night. The woman and her children have been up all night vomiting and holding their stomachs with pain. It looks like they have eaten something that's not agreed with them."

Hugh dismounted, took his bag of remedies from the saddle and followed Joseph into the house.

Peter met them at the door and took them over to the patients. "My sister is feeling a bit better, master. She's not vomited for two hours but the youngest is unconscious..."

"Are you alright, Peter?"

"I'm fine."

"Good. Now we must get to the bottom of this mystery illness. Tell me, yesterday, did you eat the same food as the rest of your family?"

Peter frowned. He had been working at the saltpan all day so was not aware of what they could have eaten. "As far as I know we all had the same, but I wasn't here until nightfall."

"Were they all well then?" Hugh pressed on with his questions, determined to find out what the problem was. He did not voice his fears aloud but he knew a virulent sickness could spread to the rest of his workers and more lives could be lost. On the crusades he had seen fevers go through a camp of men, like a fire through a field of ripe barley.

"My sister complained of stomach ache after she had put the children down to sleep."

"What exactly did you eat yesterday?" Hugh was still convinced the sickness was due to bad food.

"I had cold pie. Rabbit, that one of the boy's trapped. I ate it at the saltpan."

"And the family?"

"As far as I know they ate the same."

Hugh was still curious. He walked over to the wooden meal bin, where they stored the grain and flour to protect it from rodents. He lifted the oak lid to check the contents. "Ah! This looks familiar." He held up the remains of a sack of grain and pointed to the circular blue crest imprinted on the sacking. "Spanish rye from the Longspee holding, I'll be bound."

Peter looked away, guilt written all over his face.

"So, Peter, you took the remains of the pig food from the Norman's holding."

Peter turned on Hugh, his eyes flashing and his demeanour challenging. "Yes. It was of no use to anyone. The rats would have had it. My sister and her children were starving. So I went back after dark and I took it...Why not?"

Hugh smiled disarmingly. "I see no reason why not. As you say, it was going to waste. But that is the same batch of rye that Ivo Longspee ate immediately before he died."

Peter slumped against the hut wall, completely deflated, all the anger and defiance drained out of him. He buried his head in his hands and sobbed. "Oh, Holy Mother! What have I done?"

Hugh asked the reeve to take the man outside and comfort him while he had a closer look at the woman and her sick children. The small boy was stretched out on the earthen floor on a blanket. He could see the child was sweating profusely and deathly pale. Hugh placed his hand on the child's skin and felt how cold and clammy it had become. He placed his fingers gently on child's neck, feeling for a pulse then he bent down and placed his ear against the child's chest.

After some minutes of trying to find signs of life, Hugh straightened up and sadly shook his head. Reverently he bent down and covered the child's body with part of the blanket then pressed his hands together and offered up a silent prayer for the boy's soul.

The woman let out a shriek and broke down in sobs, burying her face in her hands.

"He's gone." Hugh shook his head sadly. "Whatever was wrong with him, it was swift to take his life. He didn't suffer for long."

Peter, who had heard his sister's cry, rushed back into the hut and broke down in tears. The reeve tried to comfort them both.

Hugh examined the other members of family. They all seemed to be suffering from the same symptoms, but they were not as sick as the boy who had lost his life. Turning to the woman again he asked. "Tell me, what was different in the food you ate and the pie you baked for Peter?"

She dried her eyes and answered him. "Peter had the last piece of yesterday's pie as he left the house early. When he had gone, I ground some new grain and baked fresh bread for the rest of us."

Hugh nodded. That was the answer he had expected. "I presume you used the flour you ground from the rye in this sack?" He held up the sack with the Spanish seal imprinted in the weave. "I don't know what we are dealing with here, but it has to be a particularly strong poison of some sort. I can only recommend rest and plenty of small beer to drink for those of you stricken with it. Drink plenty, rest and pray to God you recover."

The woman went over to the dead child and hugged him to her breast. Gently, Peter pulled her away and put his arms around her. She buried her face against his chest and started to weep again.

Hugh patted Peter on the shoulder, then turning to Joseph, he said. "This rye must be the culprit in both deaths. It must contain something very poisonous." He dipped his hand into the bottom of the sack and pulled out a handful of the seeds. Letting them fall back through his fingers, looking for some sign of a contaminant, but there was nothing obvious to be seen.

"We have a mystery here, Joseph." Hugh shook his head glumly. "How would poison get into a sack of grain? Who would do such a thing?" He didn't voice all his thoughts but he considered the implications. How could Giles have found time at the holding to add monkshood to the two sacks of grain, especially as they were stored in different places? Why would he bother to contaminate pig feed if he only intended to take his revenge on Ivo Longspee? None of it made any sense.

Hugh dipped his hand into the sack a second time and held the grain up to his nose. "There is definitely a fusty smell about this rye." He held his hand out to let Joseph smell the contents.

"Smells damp to me." The reeve turned up his nose at the odour. "Could be mouse droppings."

"Well, it has been in the sea." Hugh stroked his chin with his free hand. "But that's not the only answer I'm sure." Turning to Peter, he added. "I will take this grain with me and try to find out what it contains that is so dangerous."

Joseph followed his master out of the turf hut into the yard where the two men talked quietly together.

"What shall I do about the theft, master?"

"Nothing. They have had enough tragedy from a simple mistake. I can't blame him for taking what he thought was only going to waste. After all, he didn't steal from me, as he could so easily have done."

"What about the dead boy?"

"Get the local priest to arrange a burial. I will pay for it."

"What happens now, master?"

"Nothing. We must get on with our work. I have to return to Spalding and you have my holding to run."

Joseph turned to look back at the hut. "I'll see what food we can spare for those wretched children."

"Good man. I knew you would." Hugh rolled up the part sack of grain and tied it firmly to his saddle. "Now I must return home. Let me know if there are any further problems. They may yet all recover from this pestilence if they rest and drink plenty."

Hugh returned to Spalding and the problems he had left there but in his heart he knew he would have to follow Giles to Lincoln if he had any hope of influencing the court hearing.

Chapter Eighteen

Having made up his mind to follow Giles to Henri de Lacy's court at Lincoln castle, Hugh quickened his pace and hurried back to the priory. He knew he would have to speak with Lucy Moulton and persuade her to accompany him to Lincoln to bear witness to how her master had died.

Lucy was resting in the pilgrims' lodgings of the priory when Hugh found her.

"Lucy. I have to go to Lincoln to try to save Giles from the gallows. I will need you to testify for him."

Lucy looked excited at the prospect of going to Lincoln. She had decided already that that was her only chance of a good life for herself and her son. "Good. We will do all we can."

"We? Must you bring the boy now?" Hugh had hoped to get to de Lacy's court quickly. If the young boy came, he would slow them down."

"I will go nowhere without my son. He has had enough problems in his short life. I will not abandon him now."

"Oh! No one is suggesting you abandon him. I was hoping you and I could travel quickly and he could follow."

"No. There is no way I will go without him." She was adamant.

In spite of his frustration, Hugh had to admire her concern for the boy. He realised he must make the best of the situation. It was obvious they could not travel to Lincoln by boat via Boston and the river Witham, because of the chaos left by the floods. "Forgive me for suggesting we leave your boy behind. We, all three of us, will ride to Lincoln, but we must leave as soon as possible. I must get there very soon after Giles and his escort. If I can have an audience with the earl, a trial may not be necessary."

"I have no horses but I will leave as soon as you are ready. I have nothing to keep me here at this priory."

Hugh considered his options. "We must set out tomorrow without fail. Be ready, lady."

Lucy smiled at the prospect and started to get together her meagre belongings in preparation for the journey.

"I will bring food and drink for us. We can discuss the audience with Henri de Lacy as we ride."

Hugh hurried from the priory and called at the market tavern to explain to his sister and her husband what was happening.

"I can provide food and beer for the journey." His sister volunteered. "We have pies and drink made for our customers." She hesitated. "Don't you think you'd better call on the Fishers before you go?

Lucy Moulton and her son were waiting early the next morning at the priory gate for Hugh to arrive. On his way to the priory he called on Giles parents who insisted that two of their young fishermen accompanied the party to Lincoln as robbery on the highways was common and Lincoln was a good fifty miles journey through some lonely countryside. It was mid-morning before the three horsemen picked up the woman and boy and set out. Hugh sat astride his strongest horse with Lucy seated behind him, the boy rode a small pony and their escort followed, leading a spare mount for Hugh.

Hugh had prepared hastily but thoroughly, for the journey. As well as the food that Margaret had packed for him, his sister had insisted on supplying them with even more. The spare mount carried the provisions, a change of clothes, his long bow, a sheaf of arrows and his short sword. He knew the trip would be arduous and the weather changeable. Although the rain had stopped that very morning, he knew it would be a miracle if they managed the whole journey in the dry.

Robert, the fisherman who had given Hugh the whale meat, was the older of the two accompanying them. He already knew of Hugh's efforts to save Giles, and was quite talkative.

"Do you think the boy and woman will make it all that way?"

"They have to. She is a vital witness to help free Giles."

Robert nodded, then asked. "What about the rivers? We have to make three river crossings between here and Donnington, then there's the Hammond beck between Donnington and Sleaford. They're not wide rivers but they're sure to be in spate, just like the Welland."

"There are fords. We shall have to wait until we get there to see if we can cross safely." Hugh tried to sound positive, keeping his doubts to himself.

"I suppose we must hurry to get to Lincoln before Giles is sentenced?"

"No. There's no immediate hurry. The Earl is not yet at Lincoln. He's travelling from his castle at Pontefract and is expected there in the next few days. They'll be too busy with preparations to hold a court at the castle before he gets there. There are sure to be other pressing legal cases awaiting his arrival. I'm praying for a week to prove Giles is innocent." Hugh spurred his horse to a trot. Looking over his shoulder he shouted, "The sooner we get moving, the sooner we'll be there."

The party left Spalding on the Pinchbeck road, bound for Lincoln. Hugh let Robert take the lead and dropped back to ride beside Lucy's young son, anxious that he kept up with the group and came to no harm. The road was muddy, so progress was slow. In some areas the streams and brooks had overflowed their banks leaving the land soaking wet. Sheep huddled together in the fields, staying on the raised ridges between the water filled furrows. It was a wet, cold and miserable world, which exactly matched Hugh's mood.

Once or twice the boy's pony slipped on the mud and he almost overbalanced. Hugh halted the group and tied the boy onto his saddle with a length of rope, then he took the animal's halter rope and led it behind his own mount. After that simple precaution, they made much better time and soon left Spalding far behind them.

During the ride, Hugh chatted to his passenger to make the journey pass quicker. "Do you know anyone at Henri de Lacy's court?"

"No. Although I did once meet his wife, when Ivo took me to a family gathering."

"Will she recognise you, do you think?"

"That's very doubtful. I only saw her for a moment as she passed by. She didn't even acknowledge Ivo, and he was supposed to be a kinsman."

Hugh shook his head. He realised that Lucy's welcome at Lincoln castle was by no means certain, that meant he could not rely on her to get him an audience with the Earl. Things looked uncertain for him, and doubly so for Giles.

Hugh had brought the half-empty rye sacks with him. Absentmindedly, he fingered the bundle under his coat. He felt certain that the key to Ivo Longspee's death was his last meal and that food, as Lucy had confirmed, was prepared with the fusty Spanish rye. At the back of his mind he had the vague feeling that he should know what had caused the poisoning, but he felt he was grasping at shadows. On the journey he had plenty of time to consider all the virulent poisons that were available in the fens, but that exercise proved futile. He realised there had to be something he was overlooking. Hugh prayed to God that he was right and some divine inspiration would reveal the truth to him, for he knew he had only a limited time to find the answer. Within a week Giles could be tried for murder and taken to the gallows. That gave him too little time to think out his strategy.

The road to Pinchbeck had been muddy but passable. Once through Pinchbeck, the village where Hugh had been born, they waded through the river Glean, the stream that separated that village from Surfleet. They found the roads in a bad state but not bad enough to turn them back. At midday they crossed the second stream and halted at Gosberton to rest and eat a little of the food they had brought with them. Margaret had cooked a batch of oatcakes and a meat pie, which Hugh shared with Lucy and the boy. By late afternoon the group had forded the third tributary that emptied into the Welland estuary at the coast.

During the afternoon they stopped at a wayside inn for a rest and for a warm meal. Hugh had brought what little money he had left and Giles' parents had helped out with a generous donation. The party drank their ale and ate their meal in silence. The arduous journey was taking its toll on the travellers. Lucy and her son were already exhausted. Robert and the other fisherman were saddle sore, being unused to spending hours on horseback. Hugh, although the oldest by far, was probably the fittest for the journey. He sat apart from the others, quietly preoccupied with the forthcoming task of persuading the Lincoln court that Giles was innocent, but having little solid evidence to prove it.

Finally, they arrived at the bank of the swollen Hammond beck. That stream was much wider than usual and the water was faster flowing. Hugh went to the very edge of the torrent and stared across the swirling muddy water. Judging by the solitary willow tree standing in midstream, the swollen brook was at least four times its usual width. The reed beds, which flanked the beck, were almost totally submerged, with only a few of the tallest reeds and the occasional bullrush just showing above the surface. The track they had come along disappeared at the water's edge. It could be seen reappearing at the other side, but there was no way of telling how deep the ford was, or exactly where it was safest to attempt a crossing as the water was so murky. They stopped and drank some of the small beer they had brought from the inn while they decided what to do next.

Hugh voiced his fears. "If we miss the solid pathway, we could be swept downstream. The horses will probably manage to swim to the bank but we may not be so lucky."

"I fear for my son and myself." Lucy was in tears. "We should turn back."

"No." Hugh was adamant. "There has to be a way over."

It was then they heard the sounds of a horse trotting towards them. A young man came into view on the other bank of the river. He looked to be travelling light with no provisions, and his mount was clean compared with the mud spattered, Spalding horses.

Hugh watched carefully. From his appearance he guessed the man must be local and would have a good idea where it was safest to attempt to cross.

The rider hesitated for a few seconds, checking his bearings, then plunged his horse into the beck. He did not use the crossing area that lay exactly between the two tracks, but directed his horse a little downstream of the ford.

Hugh watched as the man and horse made their way slowly across the swollen stream. The water level rose steadily as they reached the middle of the waterway, but it did not cover the horse's back. He breathed a sigh of relief when horse and rider emerged wet but safe, on their side of the water. Hugh greeted him. "Well done, lad. I notice you took a line to the side of the old ford. Is that the secret of getting over safely?"

The youth nodded and grinned. "You'll get your legs wet but you can cross safely if you take it carefully. The surface of the old ford has been churned to deep mud by horses' hooves and wagon wheels. It's like quicksand in parts." He dismounted and peeled off some of his clothes to wring the water from them.

Hugh went back to talk to the rest of his party. He explained that there was a way across the Hammond beck, but it was precarious. After some discussion, they reluctantly decided to try to cross. He took his sword and cut himself a long branch from one of the Willows to use as a depth stick, then he organised his party into the best order for their safety. He and Lucy would cross first, feeling his way with the willow wand. Robert would bring up the rear. The other three would cross between them.

Hugh realised that the boy's pony was the shortest of the group and would probably lose its footing and swim, with dire consequences for the rider. He untied the lad from his saddle and transferred him to the spare mount. The younger fisherman followed Hugh with a rope joining his mount to the boy's horse. Robert would cross last, leading the pony by its halter rope.

Slowly and painstakingly they entered the muddy waters. Hugh probed the bed of the stream with the stick in his right hand and controlled his mount with his knees, which proved painful because of his damaged leg. The cold water rose steadily up the flanks of his horse, filling his boots and wetting his clothes but he chose to ignore the discomfort. Inch by inch, he eased his way across the swollen brook, stopping at every step to feel for soft mud, obstacles or deep depressions in the river bed. It took them several minutes to negotiate the crossing. At one stage all five horses were strung across the stream and struggling to make headway.

Hugh gritted his teeth and ignored the searing pain in his knee. Suddenly his horse felt firm sand beneath its hooves. It lurched out of the water and up onto the far bank. Slowly but surely all five horses and riders made the safety of the other side.

The local youth who had shown them where to cross, shouted encouragement to them as he put on his damp clothes. "You did better than a party of men at arms we had here earlier. Their wagon got stuck and they couldn't get across. I don't know what did happen to them."

The Spalding party waved their thanks and dug their heels into their horses' flanks to get up some speed to help dry their clothes. They stopped at the very next wayside inn they came to, in the village of Heckington, and dried their clothes as they drank hot mulled ale in front of a roaring fire.

It took two more days to complete the ride to Lincoln. The low fen land was still recovering from the disastrous floods but as they journeyed north, the higher country had more of an air of normality about it. The rain stopped but the east wind, blowing from the Low Countries and the North Sea, was cold and cutting.

Hugh pulled his coat about him and tied it with a spare bowstring. He looked across the countryside towards Lincoln, which was many miles ahead of them, and saw the cathedral, with its high central tower and two smaller turrets at one end. The imposing stone edifice rose from the Lincolnshire plain like a huge, man-made, cliff. Travellers always knew the way to take to find Lincoln because the cathedral beckoned them like a beacon across the flat lands surrounding the city. Hugh had been that way before and knew that it would still take them two days to reach the church on its mound, even though it appeared to be so deceptively close to them. He didn't tell Lucy or the boy of this aberration, for the sight of their goal seemed to have given them hope and renewed their energy to carry on.

Slowly and imperceptibly the cathedral grew in size as the travellers drew closer to the city. As they approached Lincoln, the roads became much busier. They passed farmers, tradesmen and merchants bringing their wares and provisions to de Lacy's market and court. News of the Earl's imminent return had spread rapidly through the surrounding villages. New supplies of food and drink would be needed to feed the multitude of followers that always accompanied Henri de Lacy. Hugh passed the time of day with one of the farmers, pushing a small cart laden with baskets of live chickens.

"Good day. The roads are crowded."

"Aye. The Earl will be at the castle within the next day or so."

"Lincoln will be full. Any suggestions where we can stay a night or two?"

"That could be tricky. Rumour has it the King has business with the Earl at Lincoln. Their combined courts will number hundreds. That means every available bed will be taken."

Hugh shrugged his shoulders at this news. The King was always to be found in the centre of a whirlpool of activity. It would make his task more difficult. Henri de Lacy would have no time for petitions like his. Mind you, there could be a silver lining to that cloud, Giles was likely to languish in gaol for some time to come. It could be months before the court had time to try him for murder. He returned to his request for accommodation.

"Surely a local like you has good contacts in the city? Can't you suggest anywhere for us to stay?"

The man shook his head.

Hugh decided to try again, this time telling a small lie. "The lady we have with us is kin to Henri de Lacy. She would be greatly in your debt if you could think again."

The man looked around at Lucy and her son and doffed his cap to them. "Maybe there will be room at the Tabard Inn. Tell the innkeeper that Will

Ancaster recommended you. Tell him I have his chickens on my cart."

Hugh thanked the man and spurred his horse to a trot, leading his small party towards Lincoln, leaving the farmer and his laden cart struggling in the centre of the track.

It was late on the afternoon of the third day before the Spalding group rode the straight Roman road into the city. By then the Norman cathedral was towering over them, its high stone walls dominating the landscape like a colossus, a tangible reminder of the Christian religion that dominated men's minds and lives. Hugh crossed himself and offered up a silent prayer for the happy outcome of his mission and for the safety of Giles Fisher. He glanced across at the towers and walls, which surrounded the castle. Somewhere within those walls Giles was imprisoned. His mind went back to Spalding and to his niece, who was praying for him to get Giles freed. He sighed at the thought of the difficult task ahead of him and set his mouth in a determined line.

Lincoln was a fast-growing city. Outside the stone walls and the ramparts of the defences, buildings of all shapes and sizes had sprung up, lining the road. Single storey buildings jostled with small churches and new, imposing, two storey houses. The wide street leading up to the arched gateway in the wall, was filled with travellers all making for the city within. To most of the visitors from Spalding it was a new and awe inspiring experience. The sights, sounds and smells of a busy city were foreign to them. Hugh was not so easily impressed. He had seen many such towns and cities on his travels on the crusade. He shepherded his companions into a tighter group, all too aware that cutpurses and pickpockets thrived in the bustling atmosphere of such places.

Chapter Nineteen.

Lincoln was alive with activity, like a damaged ants' nest. The cobbled streets were seething with visitors. Street vendors called at every corner offering to sell the travellers food and drink. Eels and pickled herrings; meat pies and game; wine and beer; all were offered for sale. Entertainers vied with each other and jostled the pilgrims and visitors, begging for money. The smell of meat roasting and of bread baking mingled with the stale odours of people and animals living in close proximity. In some places the streets stank for they were open sewers.

Without a doubt cutpurses and pickpockets mingled among the legitimate crowds. Hugh, who knew what dangers city life held, kept his eyes peeled for trouble, warily threading his way through the throng, leading his small, tired, band to the Tabard Inn, a small hostelry in the narrow streets behind the cathedral.

The innkeeper met them at the door, his arms folded and his ample frame barring their way.

"Sorry, but we are full. I have no more room. I am running out of food. Lincoln is too crowded."

Hugh leaned forward and whispered in his ear. The mention of Will of Ancaster and the imminent arrival of a fresh supply of chickens, visibly cheered the man up. His attitude softened. He unfolded his arms and spread his hands in a gesture of helplessness.

"I wish I could help but..."

"Surely you can manage one small lady and her son?" Hugh interrupted him, pulling several coins from his money belt.

The innkeeper stroked his chin, eyed the coins greedily, hesitated only momentarily them made his decision. "I can accommodate the lady and the boy in a small sleeping chamber but you others will have to sleep in front of the fire in the public room or in the stables." He stated his price, which was rather high, and held out his hand for the money.

Hugh counted out the coins onto the outstretched palm and thanked the man, realising that Lincoln was far too busy for him to argue about the price. With so many visitors converging on the city at the news of the earl's return, places to sleep and eat were hard to find. Rumours that King Edward would meet with the earl had only swelled the number of travellers. Hugh knew they would be warm and dry, and they would be fed. There was fodder and stabling for their horses; no one could ask for more. He grinned to himself when he recalled some of the places he had rested during the crusades, but a sudden sharp pain in his damaged leg reminded him he had been much younger and fitter in those days. He rubbed his knee ruefully. That river crossing at the Hammond beck was taking its toll.

As soon as they had eaten and rested, Hugh ordered the two fishermen to look after the horses. With Lucy and her son resting after the arduous journey, he left the Tabard inn in search of the city gaol.

Lincoln gaol was part of the vast, castle complex. The city was of great strategic importance. When William of Normandy first conquered the English in 1066 he had erected fortifications in the most important areas. So important was Lincoln, the castle had been built by him only two years after the conquest on the site of an old Roman garrison. That wooden structure was soon replaced by a permanent stone building. The importance of Lincoln, with its great cathedral and its position as a centre of government, was reflected in the present imposing castle with its thick stone walls.

Hugh approached the castle gateway in the throng of people delivering food and drink for the forthcoming banquets. Lost in such a crowd, no one stopped him at the gate. He was soon inside the outer courtyard and heading for the gaol. Although he had met no problems entering the castle grounds, he found the gaol was well guarded.

"Halt! Show your authority." A man at arms barred his way at the entrance to the gaol.

Hugh smiled and tried to explain he was asking after Giles Fisher, who was being held there.

"You will learn nothing without permission from the bailiff. So don't waste my time, old man."

Hugh was not pleased with this reception, but he knew the young guard was only acting under orders. "Where can I get permission? I must see one of your prisoners."

The guard shook his head and sighed. "You and hundreds of others. The cells are full, awaiting the earl's arrival. We have more important things to be doing than holding courts for robbers and murderers. I doubt if you'll find the bailiff today."

Hugh could see he would get nowhere. He turned on his heel and made his way out of the castle and into the busy streets of Lincoln.

Chapter Twenty

Lincoln was buzzing with rumour and counter rumour. Some said that the earl had arrived, others argued that the king was expected first, that very afternoon. General opinion split between the news that the earl had arrived but the king was not due for several days, or maybe that the king was already in the castle awaiting Henri de Lacy's appearance. All of this conjecture ceased when the earl and King Edward rode side by side through the gate of the city followed by hundreds of retainers and a long baggage train, which trailed behind them into the distance.

Hugh heard the roar of the crowd and managed to scramble to a high point to see the procession pass by. He was pleased. Now he knew that Henri de Lacy was in Lincoln, he could ask for an audience with him and plead for Giles. He followed the baggage train into the castle grounds, getting through the gate with no problem, but entering the castle building was more difficult. With both the king and the earl in residence, security was heavy. The guards had been doubled on all the doors, even the one to the kitchens. Try as he might, Hugh could get nowhere near Henri de Lacy or his bailiff. After three unsuccessful attempts, Hugh realised that the men at arms at the doors were beginning to recognise him and were eyeing him suspiciously. He left the castle to reconsider his strategy and decided to visit the nearby cathedral in the hope of finding a quiet place to reflect on his problems.

The cathedral was indeed quiet that afternoon. Hugh entered at the main door and knelt before a side altar to ask God for help in his quest to free Giles. From afar he could hear the sound of a choir practising plainsong, otherwise the church was almost silent. Occasionally footsteps could be heard crossing the stone floor as a priest or lay worker went about church business. Hugh bent his head and redoubled his prayers for help.

After half an hour of fervent praying and no inspiration to show for it, Hugh opened his eyes and straightened his back. He recalled how he had always prayed before a battle, even before the skirmish at Acre, when he had been speared through his leg. Sometimes he was sure God had heard him, but his prayers had fallen on deaf ears on that occasion. Maybe this time was to be the same. Hugh bowed his head and crossed himself and was about to renew his prayers when a studded oak side door opened and a group of people spilled noisily into the main aisle of the cathedral. The door closed behind them with a resounding bang. He hesitated and waited for the men to pass, as they were breaking his concentration.

At the head of this unruly group was a lone priest, closely followed by a portly man carrying a banner. Behind these two figures filed a dozen or so other men. They were a motley crowd. From their appearance it was obvious the majority were local tradesmen. In some cases their clothes gave a clue to their occupations. One man was definitely a miller from the dusting of flour on his smock and in his hair, another obviously a mason for he had traces of stone dust in the folds of his leather jerkin. The group stopped just in front of Hugh and fell to their knees. The priest led them in a noisy gabble of prayer.

Hugh watched them, mildly curious at what they could be doing at that time of day, when he would have expected them to be about their work. They all appeared to take the praying very seriously, making frequent signs of the cross and other demonstrations of devotion. Some voices seemed to be raised louder just to drown out others. At last they fell silent with their heads still bowed. Hugh was about to settle back to his own prayers when the man holding the banner rotated the pole in his hand, allowing the embroidered flag it bore, to be seen from where Hugh was kneeling.

Hugh glanced at the inscription then read it again in surprise and disbelief. He whispered the words aloud to himself. "The Guild of St Anthony!" This was indeed a coincidence. Once again Saint Anthony had crossed his path. Brother James, the librarian at Spalding priory, had mentioned Saint Anthony's piglet when he had first told him of the runt with the frost-bitten tail. Now he was reminded of that particular saint in Lincoln cathedral. Could this be an answer to his prayers? In the priory library the saint's name had stirred distant memories for him, but nothing had come of it. Suddenly his mind leapt to the significance of the name.

"Of course! Saint Anthony's fire!" He almost shouted the words, and was embarrassed when one of the praying tradesmen lifted his head and turned around to look directly at him. Hugh ignored the man, bent his head, and thanked God for the inspiration he had just received.

When he left the cathedral, he found the streets of the city were busier than ever. He hurried through an inn yard, taking a short cut back to the Tabard. He was amazed when a familiar voice shouted his name as he walked under the archway into the yard.

"Master Hugh, sir!"

He turned to find Leonardo and his troupe of acrobats had taken up residence in the hayloft above the horses.

"Leo? What the devil are you doing here?"

"I could well ask you the same thing. We are here to make a crust. What brings you so far from Spalding?"

"I have business here."

"We hope to have business here, as you put it. We have been working the streets for alms but we have been asked to entertain at the banquet when the Earl of Lincoln entertains your King Edward."

Hugh could not believe his ears. He was unable to get past the outer courtyard of the castle but these tumblers had actually been invited inside. Of course, here was the answer to his prayers. Leo and his troupe of acrobats could walk into the castle unhindered. Entertainers were always welcome at a feast. Now he had to find a way to become one of them. With that in mind, he invited Leo to join him in the tavern for a drink and a talk.

At the Tabard inn he found Lucy and her son had rested and eaten when he returned there from his visit to the cathedral and his meeting with Leo. He was in a much more positive frame of mind and was pleased to find she was still determined to present her son to the Lady Margaret de Lacy. He had persuaded Leo to let him join the troupe of acrobats when they entertained at the earl's banquet; that way he was sure of getting into the hall. Now he had a more pressing problem. How was he going to persuade the earl that Giles was innocent of the murder of Ivo Longspee?

"Did you see the prisoner?" Lucy asked as soon as he entered her room.

"No. Unfortunately the castle is so well guarded and so busy, with both the earl and the king in residence. I got nowhere with my questions."

"What will you do now?" She sounded genuinely interested in his problems.

"I have devised a way to get into the banquet tomorrow night. Of course, that doesn't get me an audience with Henri de Lacy, but it is a start, I suppose...I wish to talk to you about what I may ask you to tell the earl...if we ever get a chance."

"I can only tell the truth."

"That's all I ask. I will try and smuggle us both into the hall tomorrow night. I will try to petition the earl and you must do what you can to speak with his lady. Can you do that?

"Indeed I will, but I must take my son with me."

Hugh frowned. It would be touch and go for him and Lucy to get into the hall. The boy was really one person too many. The doubts showed on his face

"No boy, no mother!" Lucy said flatly.

Hugh smiled through his gritted teeth. In some ways he admired her loyalty to her son, but that didn't make his life any easier. He relaxed and smiled again. "Of course. I'll do what I can." Then he went to the stables and retrieved the Spanish grain sack from his saddlebag.

His meeting with the Guild of Saint Anthony had given him a clue about the possible cause of Ivo Longspee's death. The manner of that death, the things leading up to it and even the fusty smell of the grain, all fitted well this new theory. This time Hugh was sure he had the answer, but convincing the earl would not be easy. He lifted the neck of one of the sacks and sniffed at the stale odour inside. He was relieved to find that same fusty smell was present and as strong as ever. There was definitely a fungal infestation of the bag or its contents. He delved his hand into the bottom, took out a handful of the flour and held it up to the light. Sure enough, there were a few coarse, pink and black particles intermingled with the rye grain; particles that should not be there.

"If only I had a full bag of it." Hugh voiced his thoughts.

"A full bag of what?" Robert, the fisherman who had accompanied him to Lincoln, had come quietly into the stable.

"A full bag of this." Hugh held out his hand and showed the grain to his companion "What do you make of these small discoloured bits?"

Robert came closer and inspected the rye. He shook his head. "What bits? It looks a bit dusty, but then it's the very bottom of the sack. What am I supposed to see?"

Hugh tilted his hand and let the grains run back into the sack. "Nothing, Robert. If you can't see it then perhaps no one else will." He realised that he had to find a much better way of presenting his evidence. He may have found a way to gain access to the earl but it would do him no good if his story was unconvincing.

Hugh rolled up the sack and pushed it back in his saddlebag. Here was yet another problem for him to solve. His thoughts turned to Spalding and his niece, Elizabeth. She had such faith in him. He felt he must live up to her expectations and get Giles free. His house at Eau Side also crossed his mind. He was missing his home already, his own chair and bed, his own fireside, the fresh food and home brewed ale.

Hugh wondered what his workers were doing in his absence. Margaret would see that the house at Spalding was run properly and Joseph, his reeve at Wykeham, would be working the holding as usual. The neighbouring holding, which was deserted with Ivo Longspee's death, would still be in a sorry state.

Maybe some landless beggars had moved into it. There were always lawless men on the roads. That could present a problem to Joseph, with more sheep stealing and worse. Hugh shrugged his shoulders. Ivo Longspee's holding was   problem for the landlord, and Spalding priory was not slow to look after its own interests. He was sure the empty holding would not present a problem for much longer. The prior would soon put someone into it to look after it.

Shrugging off his concerns for home, he concentrated on his problems in Lincoln. There had to be a way to convince the earl that Ivo Longspee's death was not caused by Giles. He mused over the problem as he sat in the tavern and sipped a mug of small beer.

Chapter Twenty One.

At last the afternoon of the banquet arrived. Hugh had spent most of the intervening time with the troupe of Italian tumblers, watching them prepare their act and working out his own role in it.

"You are too old and crippled to do any tumbling." Leo was brutally honest in his assessment.

Hugh grinned in spite of the bluntness of that comment.

"We must find an easy job for you. Could you do the midget's job of collecting the coins that are thrown to us?"

Hugh nodded. That was within his capabilities, he was sure.

"You will have to dress like the rest of us or you will be refused entry to the castle."

Again, Hugh nodded agreement. He didn't like the idea but needs must.

"The midget's clothes will not fit you. We must make some for you. I have a little cloth left over that we use for repairs. I think the important thing will be a fool's hat for you. You can get away with wearing coloured hose and a jacket if you have the correct hat."

Hugh looked doubtful.

"If you will get some highly coloured hose and a jacket, I will make the hat."

Hugh nodded agreement. He had no idea where he was going to obtain the necessary costume but he knew that Leo was doing the best he could, which was probably far more than he could have asked. He left the troupe of Italian tumblers and made his way back to the Tabard to share his news with Lucy and enlist her help in getting costumes for himself, for her and for her boy.

Later that day the tumblers joined the throng of servants and men at arms crowding into the castle gates. Hugh, Lucy and her son, tried to hide themselves in the ranks of the entertainers, as they went into the outer baillie.

"We are come to entertain the king." Leo announced his intention with an exaggerated sweep of his hand and a few backward somersaults. The guard eyed the group in silence. Hugh, feeling the man's eyes linger on his poorly dressed figure, waved the collecting bag under his nose and begged him for alms.

"Get in, and mind you behave." The guard stepped aside and let them through.

Hugh sighed with relief and kept himself well hidden in the crowd.

Leo found the steward who had hired them, and let the man know they had arrived then returned to his troupe with news.

"We will be performing after the main meal, when the fruit and sweetmeats are served. We must practice out here to warm up, but there is plenty of time. After the performance we may go to the kitchen and ask for any leftovers."

Hugh patted the grain sack, which he had tied around his waist under his costume, and found somewhere to sit down and rest. The injured knee was giving him much pain. Getting wet at the Hammond beck and the constant strain of riding a horse, had caused the joint to become swollen and red. He cursed to himself for not bringing his nostrums with him. In his hurry to follow Giles to Lincoln he had left Spalding unprepared.

Leo and his acrobats started loosening up exercises and practised a few tumbles and juggling moves to prepare themselves. The midget went through his new routine. He usually somersaulted around the edges of the room between collecting the offerings from the crowd.

Hugh felt conspicuous and out of place, just sitting watching. He glanced around to see what Lucy and the boy were doing but they were nowhere to be seen. He realised they must be trying to contact Ivo Longspee's kinswoman, the Lady Margaret de Lacy. He wished them as much luck as he wished himself.

With little to do to pass the time, Hugh drifted towards the entrance to the banqueting hall. He leaned against a convenient wall and watched the preparations.

Inside the hall, trestle tables had been set on three sides of the huge room. Guests would sit on forms behind these tables. Behind the guests, keeping a discreet watch on everything, Henri de Lacy's men at arms would patrol the perimeters of the room. At the far end of the room was the top table, set with pewter and silver dishes and goblets. The important guests and their ladies would be seated on oak chairs. In the centre of this table, Hugh noticed the most imposing chair and guessed that the king would occupy that central position. Next to Edward would be the earl, and next to him his lady. To the king's left would be another important nobleman or maybe the Bishop of Lincoln. The whole group would be splendid in their finery.

Gradually guests filled the room. A group of musicians in the gallery above the top table started to play their music. The banquet soon got under way. Between the tables an army of servants rushed to serve the meal. Trays of meats, fowl and fish were carried aloft and placed before the honoured guests. The people at the top table ate from the splendid pewter plates. The lower orders had their food served on bread trenchers. The meal was substantial. Venison, pork and lamb were served in a variety of dishes. Duck and wildfowl were brought from the kitchen, with dressed swan for the top table. Great Pike were carried in, on oval dishes. A Sturgeon was presented to the noble guests. Everyone ate heartily, breaking their food with their fingers and with the knives they had brought with them. Between courses, ordinary guests scrambled for finger bowls of water left at intervals along the centre of their tables. Squires carried pewter bowls of water and white napkins for the diners at the top table to cleanse their hands.

Hugh glanced into the hall as servants came and went. He noticed that Edward was engrossed in conversation with the Bishop. Henri de Lacy nodded agreement between mouthfuls of food and smiled occasionally at his wife. Food and drink flowed freely. Everyone was relaxed, enjoying the banquet.

As they cleared away the main courses and brought on dishes of apple snow and custard tarts, a servant was sent to usher in the entertainers.

Hugh and the Italian troupe of tumblers had been waiting patiently in an anteroom. Now they sprang into life, somersaulting into the room and occupying the floor in front of the top table. Hugh joined them as they tumbled into the centre of the hall.

King Edward refilled his wine goblet and broke off his conversation with Bishop Sutton to look at the tumblers. He looked tired from his travels and seemed in a mood to be entertained. Hugh looked at the grey-haired old man and saw that the young prince he had supported on the crusade had grown old and weighed down by the passage of time and the worries of kingship.

Leo and his men excelled themselves, juggling with long knives and lighted torches. They tumbled and somersaulted with lightning speed. Finally, they formed a human pyramid that stretched up into smoky the rafters of the hall and waited while the midget clambered up to the very top.

While this was going on Hugh kept his head down and mingled with the performers, taking care to position himself near the top table. He waved his hands in time to the tricks the acrobats performed, trying to look as if he was directing them. No one took any notice of the old man.

Finally, the performance came to an end. The pyramid unfolded as each layer of tumblers somersaulted onto the oak floor and held up their hands for applause. Leo lined them up and led them out of the hall towards the kitchens, where they hoped to get paid and served with food scraps from the feast. Everyone except Hugh left the hall. He remained behind.

He made his way to a spot directly in front of the king and addressed him. "Sir. I beg ..." He had only just begun to raise his voice to attract the attention of the guests at the top table, when a sergeant at arms noticed him and rushed to drag him away.

"Away man. You have finished here. Don't bother the honoured guests." The young man grabbed Hugh by the arm and attempted to hustle him away.

Hugh may have been old and in pain but he was an old soldier and used to looking after himself. One quick movement and the guard crashed to the floor in a clatter of fallen weapons. The sudden noise silenced the whole room. Armed men, swords drawn ready, rushed to overpower the interloper. Hugh ripped off his fool's hat and knelt in front of the king.

Edward, who had unsheathed his own dagger at the first sign of trouble, pushed the knife back into his belt and looked at the shabby figure in amazement. "Sir Hugh? Hugh Pinchbeck? My surgeon? It is you, isn't it?"

Hugh nodded.

The king threw back his head and roared with laughter. The other men at arms held back as soon as they saw that the king recognised the man, and was actually addressing the bedraggled figure.

Edward turned to Henri de Lacy, at his side and said aloud, so that all the room could hear him. "This man saved my life at Acre." Turning to Hugh he asked. "Did I not arrange for the Spalding priory to lease you a holding for the service you rendered me? Why are you dressed like a fool and entertaining us at a banquet?"

Hugh stepped forward and began to explain why he was disguised and what he was doing at the banquet but the king waved him away.

"Hugh, I am tired and weary from travelling. If your petition is so important, I promise. we..." He pointed to the earl at his side. "...will grant you an audience at a more suitable time. Come and see us tomorrow morning."

Hugh knew better than to press the king further. He bowed low and backed away from the top table.

Afterwards, in the kitchens of Lincoln castle, Hugh caught up with the Italian tumblers.

"I thought you were for the dungeons when I saw that man at arms race towards you." Leo grinned at his friend and dug his teeth deep into a bread trencher soaked in meat juices.

"So did I." Hugh smiled with relief as he relived the moment. He put down the lamb bone he had been gnawing and took another mouthful of small beer from a pot jug.

"Well? Did your king remember you? Did you get his attention?"

"Yes. Thanks be to St Jude, he did! He remembered me and took the time to listen to my plea."

"Is this Giles to go free, then?"

"Hold hard, Leo. We didn't discuss that. A feast is not the place to present evidence on a murder. No, I have the promise of an audience with the earl tomorrow morning. That is all I could have hoped for."

"Will your king be there?"

Hugh shrugged his shoulders. There was no way of telling if Edward would bother with such a trivial matter, but he had spoken quickly to him and had hinted he would like to have spoken at greater length. "I don't know," he finally answered between mouthfuls of food.

Chapter Twenty Two

The dawn broke grey and damp over Lincoln. Hugh stretched himself in the straw of the hayloft and massaged his damaged knee to get some life back into it. He left the other Spalding men still sleeping and clambered down to the yard, where the landlord was flushing the remains of last night's meals down the drain.

"Good morning to you, sir." The man sounded almost cheerful.

Hugh pulled his fingers through his hair to tidy himself up a little. "Is the lady about yet?"

The man raised an eyebrow and looked puzzled.

"You remember Lucy Moulton and her son. We brought her here with us."

"Oh arr, I remember her." He grinned as if at some private joke.

"Well?" Hugh was getting tired of this conversation.

"Well, she ain't here no more."

Now it was Hugh's turn to look puzzled.

"She paid for her room and said she was moving into quarters in the castle."

"Well, I am dumbfounded." Hugh could think of nothing else to say to the man.

After a breakfast of cold fat pork and rye bread, washed down with small beer, Hugh washed and tidied himself in preparation for his audience with the earl. He was just finishing his ablutions when the other Spalding men rolled out of their hay beds, bleary eyed and full of sleep.

"You missed a good night here last night, master Hugh. We didn't stop drinking 'til the city watch called midnight."

"I know. I was up here trying to sleep!"

"Why didn't you join us then?"

"Some of us have business to sort out and need a clear head."

The fisherman looked sheepishly at his feet. "Giles, you mean?"

"Aye Giles. I managed to get to see the earl last night at the banquet. I have an audience with him this morning. But what's happened to Lucy and the boy?"

"Oh! She's fallen on her feet. She's lodging at the castle."

"Did she tell you that, herself?"

"She did. I bumped into her as she was paying the landlord for her room. She had money, lots of money. She saw Lady Margaret de Lacy, and she and the boy have been given lodgings."

"Good, then she will be at the castle if I need to call her to confirm what I say. I'm sure she will speak for me." Hugh fetched the grain sack from where he had hidden it in his saddlebag, and tucked it under his jerkin for safekeeping.

The city was busy, considering the early hour. Hugh struggled up to the castle, making hard work of the walk as the slope increased towards the curtain wall. Already traders where shouting their wares. Bakers offered hot pies and newly baked loaves, the aroma of their wares speaking as eloquently as the tradesmen's cries. Fishmongers laid out freshly caught herrings and eels. Hugh threaded his way through the throng of early risers and made his way slowly to the castle gate.

"I have an audience with the Earl." Hugh explained to the man at arms who barred his way. "And with the king." He added that to lend more weight to his story.

The man eyed him up and down then smirked knowingly. "I hardly recognised you out of your clown outfit. You were entertaining at the banquet last night, weren't you?"

Hugh nodded.

"I was the one who tried to stop you."

Hugh grinned disarmingly at the young soldier. "No offence. I'm sorry I had to knock you over."

The guard shook his head, unable to believe this old man had overpowered him. He stepped aside and waved Hugh through.

"You realise you're far too early." He said, pointing at the watery light of the sun, still very low in the sky.

"I know. I have some work to do first." Hugh passed into the outer courtyard and made for the kitchen.

At the kitchen door he looked for Hal, the cook who had served him his food the evening before. The man was about his own age and an old soldier.

"Hugh. Back so soon?" The cook spotted Hugh first and called across to him.

"Hal. I need to talk with the earl's miller. Do you know much about him? What kind of a man is he? Where can I find him at this early hour of the day?"

Hal wrinkled his brow at this barrage of questions. "I'd have said he was tucked in his bed, if he had any sense, but with so many mouths to feed he's no doubt been hard at work for hours, just like me! What kind of man is he? Well, he's like you and me. He's no youngster. I believe he was a pikeman in the King's army at one time."

Hugh was pleased with this information. "Can you direct me to the mill?"

"I can do better than that." Hal smiled, looking over Hugh's shoulder into the yard. "There's John the miller just coming into the yard with a delivery of fresh flour for me."

Hugh turned to see a cart piled high with sacks of flour just entering the main gateway. Two horses strained to pull the wagon across the cobbles. The driver, a large man covered in a fine dusting of flour from the top of his grey hair to the soles of his white speckled shoes, pulled on the reins to halt the cart in front of the kitchen doors.

"Morning, John." Hal shouted to the miller.

"Is it?" John sounded very grumpy. "I've been at it half a day already. It's all very well them throwing lavish banquets and feeding hundreds of the king's followers. A bit more warning wouldn't go amiss."

Hugh stepped away from the doorway so that the kitchen servants could unload the huge sacks of flour from the wagon. John stepped into the kitchen and was handed a large mug of beer, without another word being spoken. Finall,y as he drained the mug, tipping it upside down over his mouth, Hal spoke to the man.

"That's settled the dust."

"Aye." The miller wiped the back of his hand across his damp lips. "That's the first today and I needed it."

"Someone here wants to speak with you, John." The cook introduced Hugh to the miller, who eyed the stranger up and down suspiciously.

Hugh smiled disarmingly and held out his hand to the man. "I'm Hugh Pinchbeck. I'm an old soldier like yourself."

The miller's severe expression softened. He shook Hugh's hand vigorously. "Where did you serve?"

"The crusades at Acre and Nazareth. I was a bowman. Got this..." Hugh slapped his damaged knee..."at Acre. Took a lance through it."

John nodded sympathetically. "None of us is as young as we used to be."

Hugh pressed on with his questions. "When you were in the eastern lands did you ever come across Saint Anthony's Fire?"

"Yes. I came back through Spain." He pulled hard on a thong he had around his neck and showed Hugh a metal badge shaped like a scallop shell. "Saint Iago of Compostella" He explained proudly.

Hugh fingered the worn talisman and nodded that he understood. Every pilgrim who visited the famous shrine of Saint James in the Spanish City of

Compostella, brought back such a token to prove he had made the pilgrimage there. Men did say a pilgrimage to that holy shrine was worth many indulgencies.

"I saw whole Spanish villages wiped out with the Fire."

"You sound as if you are my man." Hugh said.

John raised an eyebrow questioningly.

"I may not need to bother you at all, but I have an audience with the Earl later on this morning and I may need some advice from an expert. Can I call on you?"

"Oh! So you're going to meet our 'enri are you. He's not so bad, I suppose. He's a good soldier, and as one old soldier to another, aye, I'll help you if I can"

"Where will you be?"

"At the mill. All damn morning!" John spat on the cobbled yard and climbed onto his empty cart. He flicked a whip at the horses and the wagon clattered out of the castle yard.

Hugh had several hours to wait before Henri de Lacy was ready to receive him. He sat on a block of stone by the kitchen door and rehearsed what he hoped to say, then made his way to the servants' quarters to try and see Lucy.

"Master Pinchbeck!" Lucy ran to greet him when he was shown into the room where she was working.

Hugh looked at her and smiled his approval. She had been given a new dress and her hair was tied up with a green band. "I hardly recognised you, Lucy. Are you and the boy well?"

"Oh yes! Thanks to you bringing us here. We have met the Lady Margaret and I have a position as a serving girl in her household."

"And your son?"

"He is learning to help with the horses. And you? Have you seen the earl yet?"

"No but I have an appointment this morning. That's what I wanted to see you about. You will remember you promised to corroborate my story, if need be?"

"Of course."

"Good. I may not need your word but it is better you are prepared."

Hugh left her getting on with her chores and limped back to the kitchen to wait.

Chapter Twenty Three

It was mid-morning before Hugh was shown into a small audience chamber off the earl's private rooms. He was left alone a few minutes while the earl was told of his arrival. At last a squire entered the room, flung back the door and ushered in his master.

Hugh inclined his head to show respect and waited to be asked to speak.

Henri filled a goblet with wine then sat in front of the fire. "Right, Master Pinchbeck. You want to see me about a felon, I believe?"

"A suspected felon, my Lord."

Henri grinned at this obvious correction. Licking his lips he looked Hugh straight in the eyes.

Hugh didn't flinch or drop his gaze. He'd fought alongside nobler men than this and he knew his own worth.

"I understand you were a bowman at Acre? Edward tells me it was you who sliced part of his arm away when he was stabbed by an assassin with a poisoned knife? You saved his life, he tells me."

Hugh nodded. "For my sins, I did cut the king. I was helping tend the wounded, because I was one of the walking wounded myself." He tapped his damaged knee.

Henri inclined his head for him to continue.

"The surgeons argued that Prince Edward must be cut to stop the gangrene, but none of them dared do it. What if he didn't recover? Would they be held responsible for killing the heir to the throne? So I volunteered. I'd had experience of removing arrows from the battle wounded. They say it saved his life. If they had hesitated much longer he would have died anyway."

"You were a brave man." The earl nodded slowly to reinforce those words. "Now what do you wish to ask me?"

"My lord, I am here to plea for a young man from my home town of Spalding. He is wrongly accused of murder and has been sent here to your court."

The earl raised an eyebrow and put down his glass. "Murder, you say? That is serious. On whose authority is he sent here?"

"The Lord Prior of Spalding, my Lord."

"And why didn't the prior try him at his own assizes?"

"Giles – his name is Giles Fisher - is accused of murdering one of your lordship's kinsmen."

Henri really did sit up and take notice at this answer. "Who has been murdered?"

"Ivo Longspee, a neighbour of mine at Wykeham."

"Oh! Ivo Longspee, my wife's kinsman!" Henri's tone of voice changed to one of resignation.

Hugh smiled to himself. The Earl knew of the dead Norman, and it was obvious he thought little of him.

"I think, to save us both time, I will send for this prisoner." He summoned the squire who was standing just out of earshot behind the door, and sent him to the castle dungeons to bring the prisoner up to them. Turning back to Hugh he said. "This could take some time. We have full cells down there, awaiting my return. Meet me back here in an hour. I will get a servant to take you to the kitchens for some refreshment."

Thus dismissed, Hugh sat in the kitchen, drank a little wine and ate some bread and cheese while he watched the cooks preparing yet another huge feast. It was plain the king and his many followers were not yet ready to depart from Lincoln.

It was less than an hour when an agitated page rushed into the kitchen to find Hugh.

"Sir. You are requested to attend on the earl at once." The young man started back at a run, until Hugh shouted him to stop.

"Son, I have an old battle wound. If you go at that speed you will lose me. What's the hurry?"

"The king is with the earl, sir. They are both waiting for you."

"The king knows I have a damaged leg. He saw enough of me dragging it around his sick bed on the crusade. He will wait for me, never you fear."

The page slowed his pace but still looked harassed and unconvinced.

"Come in Hugh." Edward greeted him at the door. "I'm intrigued at this murder charge."

Hugh bowed as low as he could, struggling to stay upright on his crippled leg. He looked around the room and was surprised to find only the king and the earl were present. There was no sign of Giles. He frowned, betraying his unease.

"Well Hugh, as you can see, your felon is not here in Lincoln."

"But he was dispatched under guard the day before I left Spalding, my Lord."

"That I don't doubt, but he never arrived here."

"Where is he then?"

"It seems the wagon was swept away trying to cross the Hammond beck."

"Oh. God preserve him!" Hugh put his hands up to his mouth. Of course, there had been mention of a wagon getting into difficulties at that spot. "Is he drowned?"

"No. He was untied for the crossing and he made his escape." The earl hesitated for a second to let the impact of that news sink in, then he repeated pointedly. "He made his escape…Does that sound like an innocent man to you?"

Hugh thought fast. "That doesn't prove he's guilty, my Lord. He probably thought he had no chance to prove his innocence and took his only chance of living."

"That may be so." Henri tapped his fingers on a roll of parchment set on the table by his side. "One of his escorts carried on here to Lincoln to report the escape. He brought the details of the crime for us to read. Your prior seems in no doubt there is a case to answer, but without the accused it hardly seems worth going on."

Hugh bowed his head and said nothing, but he shot a pleading glance at the king.

"I think, as he's come all this way to see you, it would only be fair to hear him out." Edward suggested quietly.

"Very well. I will tell you what the prior has written about this crime and you can correct me if I am wrong." Henri unrolled the deposition and read out the evidence against

The king listened with a furrowed brow. Finally, he spoke to Hugh. "This Giles Fisher has a lot against him. He had opportunity, he had good reason and he had a virulent poison at his disposal. Monkshood is one of the most virulent of poisons. It seems there is little doubt that the dead man died from poisoning. Are you arguing with any of these facts, Hugh?"

"No sir. But I think I can prove that Ivo Longspee died from a poison accidentally added to his food."

Both the king and the earl raised their eyebrows.

"Go ahead then. We are listening."

Hugh pulled the grain sack from under his jerkin and placed it on the floor. "This sack came from Ivo Longspee's home. He had been eating bread made from the contents for several days before his death. His last meal was a large amount of this same bread." Hugh opened the sacks and shook the contents out onto a clean napkin. The two listeners bent over the small heap of rye and eyed it thoughtfully.

"I suppose you can prove this, Hugh?"

"You have Lucy Moulton, Ivo Longspee's woman and his son under your protection, my lord. She cooked the bread. She can verify all I have said."

"It smells fusty!" Edward wrinkled up his nose at the grain and poked his finger into it.

"Exactly, Sir!" Hugh jumped at this corroboration.

"So what exactly does that prove? I have eaten worse on a long campaign."

"Have either of you ever heard of Saint Anthony's Fire?"

They both looked doubtful.

"St Anthony's Fire, caused by ergot poisoning. It's very common on the continent. It causes burning sensations all over the body, images of devils and finally death."

The king dipped his hand into a finger bowl and wiped his fingers vigorously on a napkin. "Yes, I do recall it now. If the ergot gets into the ears of rye as it grows, and it is not detected by the miller, whole villages can be wiped out."

"But didn't you say this scourge was in the warmer countries of the continent?" Henri asked.

"Yes my lord. Spain and Portugal as well as parts of France have had outbreaks of it."

"So?"

"This was Spanish rye, my lord. The sacks bear the imprint of a Spanish seal."

Both noblemen leaned over and checked the sack. The earl scratched his head thoughtfully but said nothing.

Hurriedly, Hugh carried on with his explanation. "It seems this flour was claimed to be salvage from a wrecked Spanish merchant ship in the sea off Lincolnshire. Ivo Longspee claimed he rescued the cargo, but none of the crew reached land alive. If they had been eating such flour that seems very possible."

Henri nodded his head vigorously. "I have just read a report of the non-delivery of a large cargo of Spanish spices which was intended for me, which never reached Boston docks. I knew I had seen that imprint before. That is the seal of one of the Spanish shippers we trade with on the continent."

Hugh coloured slightly at the mention of the missing spices but he carried on with his defence of Giles. "Ivo Longspee had a certain unsavoury reputation along the Lincolnshire coastline, my lord."

"Go on."

"He sailed out of thieves creek, according to the local fishermen."

Edward shot a puzzled glance at the earl, who looked embarrassed.

"I know as much already, my liege. If my wife had not pleaded for him in the past he would probably already be in gaol."

Hugh breathed a sigh of relief at this comment. He had taken a chance hinting that the earl's kinsman was a criminal.

Edward grinned at the earl's admission. "We don't choose our relatives, do we, Henri."

Edward turned to Hugh. "Go on. Prove to me that this flour contains enough ergot to kill a man."

Hugh hesitated. He knew he had only a small amount of the rye and the particles of fungus were small and diffused. He sifted the grains though his fingers and tried to point out the tiny pink and black granules in it.

"No. I am not convinced." Edward said at last, after peering at the napkin for several minutes, by the light from a window.

"I'm afraid I must agree with him." Henri said.

"Maybe if I can ask your miller, my lord. He will know if anyone does."

"Right, send for the miller." Henri's voice sounded bored with the whole thing, but he gave his permission.

The king smiled at Hugh. "I will see you get a proper hearing, Hugh. Now, while we wait for the miller, tell me about your holding at Spalding. Is it enough to keep you comfortable as you grow older?"

Hugh hesitated. He did not wish to sound ungrateful to the king, who had procured the land for him from a reluctant Lord Prior. He hedged his answer. "In these bad times who couldn't do with more land, my lord?"

"I see." The king said no more.

Eventually John the miller hurried into the room, out of breath and flustered. He shot a black look at Hugh then bowed low before the king and his lord.

"Get up man. We don't want to see your back, the king and I want your advice."

John sprang to his feet, belying his advancing years.

"Take a look at this rye sample and tell us what you think."

The miller squinted at the small heap of grains and rubbed a little between his fingers, bringing it to his nose to sniff. "It's contaminated with some kind of fungus, sir. It ain't none of my grain!"

"No John. No one is accusing you of anything. As a miller have you met ergot contamination before this?"

"Yes, my lord. On the continent."

"Good! Then you are just the man we need. Is that fusty smell due to ergot?"

John sifted the rye yet again and sniffed at it tentatively. Finally he straightened up and said. "It could be, my lord."

"Only could be? A murder charge hangs on this, John. Can't you say either yea or nay?"

"There's so little of it, my lord. If there were more..." He spread his hands in a gesture of helplessness.

"Well, master Pinchbeck, we must return to you. Is there no more of this sample?"

"There were two whole sacks of it, one of which Ivo Longspee kept for his own use. He ate it all. That's what killed him."

"What happened to the other sack; you say there were two?"

"It was spoilt with sea water, my lord. It was fed to the swine."

"And they survived?"

"I don't know about the rest of the herd my lord, but the runt of the litter had lost its tail. It looked just like frostbite. That was the Saint Anthony's Piglet."

"Lost its tail? Saint Anthony's Piglet?"

"Animals do lose limbs when they eat ergot. My lord." John broke into the conversation.

"The runt of a litter is called Saint Anthony's Piglet in some areas." Hugh added, trying to be helpful.

King Edward was also growing tired of the affair. He spoke sharply. "All of which gets us nowhere. Have you any other suggestions to prove your point, Hugh?"

Hugh could see he was failing to get his argument across. In desperation he tried to think what to do. Suddenly an idea came to him. "There is one possibility, sir. If I can separate the ergot from the flour, John can take a closer look at it."

Both noblemen looked doubtful. "That will take you all day, sorting it grain by grain."

"No my lord. I will try to sort it like they sort amber from stone on the eastern shoreline."

"What do you need?" Edward's interest revived again at this novel suggestion.

"A bowl of cold water and some salt, my lord."

"Sounds simple enough."

When a page had brought the necessary items. Hugh stirred a handful of salt into the water until it had all dissolved. With a silent prayer to Saint Anthony, who seemed to be taking a special interest in this affair, he stirred in the whole of the remaining rye. At first it looked to be a mess of rye grains and water but slowly the coarse particles of rye sank to the bottom of the bowl, leaving a scum of small black and pink pieces on the surface. Hugh scooped these pieces off the top of the water and placed them to dry on a clean napkin.

"Amazing!" Henri was very impressed. He fingered an amber cloak pin at his shoulder. "You say men separate amber in this way?"

"Yes, my lord. The salt water lets the amber float and allows pebbles of stone to sink."

"And you knew this would also work with ergot?"

Hugh shuffled his feet and looked down. "Not exactly my lord. I prayed it would. I prayed that the pure salt would reject the bad poison and keep the good rye grains. And I was proved right. I must admit, I did take a chance."

"A man with a cool head indeed. It's a pity you are too old and infirm for war. A man with such a brave heart could lead a company of archers with distinction."

Hugh blushed crimson at the compliment.

It was then that John, who had been engrossed in an inspection of the scum, interrupted them. "That's definitely ergot, my lord." He spat out the particles he had placed on the tip of his tongue, to taste. "And there's enough there to kill a few men, if the sack was full of the same rye."

The earl and the king walked to the far side of the room and held a whispered consultation. Hugh strained to hear the conversation but could only catch odd phrases. The king seemed to be convinced of the truth of Hugh's case but the earl seemed doubtful. At last the two men turned towards him.

The king spoke first. " I would…indeed I have, trusted Hugh with my life before now. If he vouches for this Giles I believe him."

Henri de Lacy addressed Hugh. "That's settled then. Ivo Longspee died from ergot poisoning and probably obtained the rye by piracy in the first place. Your Giles has no case to answer."

Hugh bowed his head and asked. "Don't you want to question Lucy Moulton, my lord?"

"I have wasted enough time on this 'murder' charge. I am sure you have told me the truth, Hugh. Who can doubt you, with the king as a character witness? It is a pity your man made his escape before he arrived here. He is a free man but doesn't know it. Let's hope he doesn't fall in with outlaws and commit more serious crimes."

Hugh bowed again and thanked the king and the earl for giving him a fair hearing. The elation he should have felt at proving Giles innocent was tempered by the knowledge of the boy's escape at the Hammond brook. He had more urgent work to do. He must now try and trace Giles and give him the good news.

The drama over, both the earl and the king turned to other documents they had beside them on the table. Hugh and John backed out of the room and walked down the corridor.

"I'm glad that's over." John sighed.

"No more than me. But at least I proved my theory. Thanks for your testament, John. It needed someone wise in these things to convince the king."

"I think a drink is called for. Let's get to the kitchen, that's if you have time before you go chasing across the country for this Giles fellow."

Hugh grunted. He had no real idea where Giles might be after four days on the run.

John, relieved to be out of the king's presence, chattered on . "Who is this Giles, anyway. Your son or a close relative?"

"No, not exactly. He's betrothed to my niece."

"Your niece? You must be very fond of her."

"I am. Elizabeth is my sister's only child and I have no children."

John shook his head sadly. "I have five. You can have any of them if you want them."

In the kitchen, John told the cooks how Hugh had stood up to the earl and the king and had proved the prisoner was innocent. It made a good tale and it grew in the telling. The relating was worth several more mugs of small beer. They were just finishing their last drink when the earl's page rushed into the room and ran up to Hugh.

"Hugh Pinchbeck?" Without waiting for confirmation the boy gave his message. "The king wishes to see you now, sir."

Hugh frowned, and John looked suitably sorry for his new drinking friend.

"Hurry sir. He insisted you must see him before you set out for Spalding."

Hugh limped after the lad, wondering what could have happened since he last spoke to Edward that could be so urgent.

The king was alone in the same small private chamber, when Hugh arrived. He wasted no time on formalities.

"I have letters here from your Lord Prior, Hugh. He is begging permission to fortify parts of the priory. What's going on at Spalding?"

Hugh nodded, he had been expecting as much. He licked his lips and searched for the best way to explain it without mentioning the new taxes the king had imposed to finance his wars. "There is unrest because of poverty and starvation, sir. The prior has increased the taxes and will have to do so again because the drains and bridges have been badly neglected for years. I think he is being prudent and anticipating trouble. The local farmers are finding it impossible to meet the increases. There could be trouble."

Edward nodded sagely. "As I thought. I have drafted a reply to the prior. I want you to deliver it for me. Make sure you do it in person." He held out a roll of parchment sealed with the royal seal.

Hugh took the scroll and pushed it safely under his jerkin. He bowed his head and started to back out of the room.

"Mind you deliver it to the prior in person. And don't waste time searching for that young runaway on your way home. There will be time for that after you have finished my business."

Hugh held the package close to his chest and went back to the kitchen. John had already left to return to his milling. Hal was busy preparing food for hundreds of hungry people. He left the castle and made his way to the Tabard inn where he found the Spalding men who had accompanied him to Lincoln.

"Hugh!" Robert the fisherman was the first to notice him as he entered the stable at the Tabard. "Back already. How did it go? Is Giles a free man?"

"It went well. Giles is free."

The man frowned. "Where is he then?"

"You tell me! Giles never came to Lincoln. He escaped at the Hammond beck. You remember we were told there was a problem with a wagon the day before we crossed the floods there?" Hugh explained how Giles had made his escape in the confusion of the river crossing.

Robert slapped his thigh. "Good for Giles..." Then he realised the full implications of the news. "...but he wont know of this. He thinks he's still a felon?"

"Exactly. We need to get a message to him before he falls in with proper outlaws or before he's robbed and killed by them."

"Where do we look for him?"

"Your guess is as good as mine. I am returning to Spalding with all speed. We'll look and ask for Giles on our way home."

Hugh got together his few things and started to prepare his horse for the return journey. His companions quickly followed suit.

Chapter Twenty Four

Hugh arrived back in Spalding after a gruelling two-day ride. He had forced the pace of their return and as a result his leg was even more swollen. He stopped in the market stead outside the market tavern and gently lowered himself to the cobbles. His horse had been heard inside and Elizabeth rushed out to greet him.

"Uncle Hugh! You are back already. We've been worried about you."

Hugh could see the girl's roving eyes searching the market place for signs of Giles.

"Isn't Giles with you?"

"No. I must come inside and sit down. Then I will explain."

Elizabeth supported the old man and helped him struggle to a chair. "Would you like a drink and food, uncle Hugh?"

"Please, my dear. But first get your mother. I have some news for you."

She ran off to the kitchen to fetch his sister.

Maud was red faced and sweating from preparing hot food. She wiped her hands on her apron and drew up a chair beside her brother. "No Giles with you? Is the boy free?"

"Maud, hear me out then you can ask all the questions you like." He broke off his explanation and took a draught of small beer that had been brought to his table, along with a small loaf, still warm from the oven, and a chunk of fresh cheese. "That's most welcome." He wiped his mouth on the back of his hand and broke off a piece of the cheese to stem his hunger.

"Uncle Hugh! What's happened?" Elizabeth jumped up and down, unable to contain her curiosity.

"I saw the earl, and the king for that matter. As a result, Giles is no longer suspect for the Norman's murder, but..."

Elizabeth flung her arms around his neck and hugged him tightly. Maud, sensing her brother had not said all that needed to be said, pulled her daughter away and wagged a scolding finger at her.

"Give Hugh some space. There's more to this, I'll be bound."

Hugh recovered his composure and continued. "Giles is free, but where is he?"

"Where is he? Didn't you bring him back with you from Lincoln gaol?"

"No. He never got to Lincoln. He escaped his escort at the Hammond beck on the way there and was not recaptured. He's on the run."

Elizabeth shrieked and then covered her mouth. Maud frowned deeply. "The silly boy. I suppose he doesn't know he is now free to come home?"

"No. I managed to persuade the earl that Giles was not guilty of this murder but that was long after he'd fled. How could he know?" Hugh took another sip of the beer and broke off a piece of the bread, which he topped with a morsel of cheese and popped in his mouth. "I don't suppose he's contacted you, has he?" He turned hopefully to his niece.

"No. I have heard nothing from him."

"Then we had better put out the news that he is a free man and hope he hears of it. Perhaps you can go and see his mother and father, Elizabeth. I intended telling the good news to the Fishers but this leg is getting too painful to move." He rubbed his damaged knee gently and grimaced with the pain.

"I will, gladly." Elizabeth was ready to rush off that very minute.

"Finish in the kitchen, daughter. A few minutes delay will not hurt anyone."

"On your way out, you can do another errand for me." Hugh shouted after her. "Go to my house at

Eau Side and tell my housekeeper that I am back in Spalding. Tell her to prepare warm water for a wash and to lay out some clean clothes for me. I have business with the Lord Prior."

Maud raised her eyebrows at this last remark. Hugh patted her arm and explained. "I have a message for the prior, direct from the king." He tapped the documents concealed beneath his coat.

"You are carrying the king's messages? Fancy, my brother being so honoured."

Hugh gave her a withering look and addressed the remains of the bread, cheese and ale.

Later that same day, when Hugh had rested and deadened the pain in his knee with monkshood salve, he washed and changed. He sent John, the yard boy, ahead of him to prepare the Lord Prior for his visit.

"Tell the monks I have letters from the king." Hugh had insisted the boy repeat the message to him. He did not want to have to wait in a cold draughty corridor while the Lord Prior was found. By the time he finally arrived at the priory his visit was eagerly awaited.

Clement of Hatfield, the Lord Prior, arranged to see him in the chapter house, which was on the ground floor and had an entrance directly from the yard. Hugh smiled with satisfaction, obviously John had told them he was not able to walk well and they had taken that into account. A lay brother rushed to help him dismount and tethered his horse. Inside the chapter house there was a deputation awaiting him. The grey haired prior sat on a wide wooden chair, looking every inch the wise and important figure he was. On each side of him were his officials. Among them Hugh recognised Thomas Bohun, the steward, Brother James the librarian, and the cellarer. There were also two other monks from the Mother House in Anjou, who happened to be paying a visitation to Spalding. The Prior spoke first.

"Welcome Hugh Pinchbeck. We understand you have been to Lincoln to plead for Giles Fisher."

"Yes, my Lord." Hugh inclined his head, that being as close as he could manage to a bow. He gritted his teeth but the pain showed on his face.

"Get the man a chair." Clement of Hatfield ordered.

Gratefully, Hugh accepted the offer and sat in the front of the small semi-circle of priory officials.

"Now Master Hugh Pinchbeck what occurred in Lincoln?"

"I saw Henri de Lacy and King Edward to present my evidence. The boy is free to go."

The Prior nodded and looked pleased. "Good. We would not wish to see an innocent man punished. Now, I understand you have letters from the king for us."

Hugh reached under his jerkin and took out the bundle of documents. He handed them to Thomas Bohun who had stepped forward ready to take them from him, saving him the pain of rising from his seat.

The Prior turned the documents over and checked the royal seal, which was still visibly intact. A small smile of satisfaction crossed his face. He broke the wax seal and unfolded the letters. Silence fell on the room as the old man read. He took his time, reading the Latin script most carefully to understand exactly what the king had agreed to do. He passed each page to his steward as he completed it. Finally, he handed the last letter to Thomas Bohun and bade him deal with the matter it concerned.

"Thank you, Hugh. That is what we had hoped for." Clement rose from his seat and swept regally out of the chapter house, followed closely by the monks. Thomas Bohun remained behind with Hugh.

When the clerics were out of earshot, Thomas spoke. "I suppose you know what was in the letters?"

"No, not really. The King did mention that the Lord Prior wanted royal permission to fortify the priory, but I know nothing else."

"That's correct. We now have that permission, but at a very high price."

"More taxes?" Hugh grimaced.

"Yes. The king constantly needs money for his Scottish campaigns. His favours always come with a heavy price on them."

Hugh thoughts were with the local peasants and townspeople who would bear the brunt of any new demands. His concern showed on his face.

Thomas understood his concerns and voiced them aloud. "I know. More taxes on you poor farmers when many of you are practically destitute. That is the way of things with the kingdom constantly on a war footing, but you have cause to celebrate, haven't you?"

"Me? You mean getting Giles free? I suppose so." He had not told Thomas about Giles' escape. That fact alone spoiled his triumph.

"Oh that, yes of course." Thomas tapped the folded parchment in his hand. "No, I was referring to this letter from the king."

Hugh shook his head, bewildered by the comment.

"Oh! I see the king did not make you privy to this news." The Steward grinned. "I'm very pleased for you, Hugh."

Hugh frowned even more.

Thomas laughed aloud. "Don't look so worried my friend. The king has ensured you can live out your old age in comfort. He's ordered the Lord Prior to let you have the tenancy of the old Longspee holding next to your own, in the fen."

Hugh was astounded. No wonder the king had asked him how he was managing on his original grant of land. He smiled in gratitude, then remembering the bad state of that holding, he shook his head sadly.

Thomas understood Hugh's reservations. "Yes, I know it's in a parlous state. My men have inspected it. I've had reports about it; no livestock, the buildings in disrepair, the land sour and unploughed, even the fishing boats ruined. That's not a happy inheritance for anyone in these hard times. But hear me out. I'm sure we can come to some arrangement. You are the obvious tenant for that land as it joins your own and you will look after it properly. The prior has asked me to deal with it personally."

"What had you in mind?" As he spoke, Hugh made some quick estimates of the extra men and materials he would need to farm the holding successfully.

"No rent or tithes 'til next Michaelmas quarter day. How would that suit you?"

Hugh absorbed the implications of the offer. A whole year cost free. It would probably be enough if he took full advantage of it. He knew the Longspee holding was capable of sustaining more crops than his own land once it was back under the plough. There was another salt pan and there were at least two sea going boats, if they proved to be repairable. "What about the boats and materials? Can I have them all?"

"For what they are worth, they are yours. But from the reports I have, they are in a bad state. Anything worthwhile they stole or destroyed before those pirates left the area."

Hugh remembered the fast boat that had attacked the krugge only weeks before. Surely that must be seaworthy? It would be a shame if that boat was damaged beyond repair.

"By the way. My back is healing beautifully. You have my heartfelt thanks and my recommendation to anyone who needs a healer." Thomas smiled again. "Even allowing for my unpalatable diet these days!"

Hugh sat and digested the news. He was now the owner of three times as much farmland as before. He rose from his seat, temporarily forgetting his damaged knee, but his leg gave way under his weight. He immediately sat down again, racked with pain and unable to get up.

With the help of two lay workers, Hugh managed to get back onto his horse and ride the short distance from the priory to his home on Eau Side. There he was carried into the house by two of his own men and put to bed. Margaret fussed over him like a mother hen and insisted he had the soup and bread, which she had prepared especially for him.

"You don't look after yourself, master. You are not as young as you think you are. You need a good woman to look after you." She clucked over him as he lay helpless in bed.

"I am fine. Give me a day or two's rest to get over that ride from Lincoln and I'll be as good as new. Now leave me in peace and send your son up here. I want him to do some errands for me."

Unhappy that her master had dismissed her so quickly, but mollified that he wanted her son to help him, she left him in peace and retreated to her kitchen where she took out her frustration on the pots and pans, clanging them unnecessarily as she worked.

"John, we have much to do. I need you to ride to Wykeham and fetch Joseph the reeve here. Can you do that?"

"Yes, master. Do you want me to go now or first thing in the morning?"

Hugh glanced out of the window and realised it was getting dusk. There was no way the boy could reach Wykeham and return with Joseph before darkness fell.

"Tomorrow. First thing in the morning, mind you. Joseph and I have much business to discuss. Now look in the oak chest at the bottom of my bed and pass me the small green glass bottle from the corner."

Hugh took the pot of monkshood salve from the boy and rubbed some of the strong analgesic into his knee joint, then he lay back and closed his eyes while he waited for the preparation to do its work.

John left his master, who finished his soup then settle down to a fitful sleep, where nightmares about the king, Giles and Ivo Longspee alternated with sharp pains in his knee, which woke him up in agony. It was a long and painful night.

Chapter Twenty Five

Next morning Hugh woke up late. The sun was well over the rim of his window and he could hear voices downstairs. He leaned out of bed and reached for the monkshood salve, which he applied liberally to his swollen leg. The rest overnight had eased the pain a little and the swelling had gone down. He felt slightly better. Recognising the deep tones of Joseph's voice, he shouted loud enough to be heard downstairs.

"Ah! You are awake again." Margaret hurried into the room. She plumped up the blanket roll under his head and straightened his bedding, fussing over him far too much for his taste.

"Send Joseph up, woman." Hugh tried to sound sharp with her, but she just smiled at him.

"I will, when you've eaten, master. You need to look after yourself better."

Hugh scowled at her but she took no notice of him. When she had gone to the kitchen to fetch him some breakfast, he had to admit he quite enjoyed being waited on after the hardships of his trip to Lincoln.

"Oatcakes, fresh from the baking stone and a mug of beer, master." Joseph brought the breakfast up to the bedroom with him.

Hugh ate heartily. His knee was sore but that didn't affect his appetite. Joseph sat patiently by the bed and waited for him to finish eating.

"I gather you were successful in Lincoln, master."

"Giles you mean? Yes, but I suppose you've heard he ran off and doesn't yet know he's a free man?"

"Aye. A funny business all together, master."

"Yes, Joseph. But that's not what I wanted to talk to you about."

The reeve shifted uneasily on his chair. He knew there were rumours of more taxes, He was apprehensive.

"How do you feel about more land?"

"More land, sir?" Incredulity showed in Joseph's voice. The reeve was not prepared to hear those words. He had been expecting to hear they must tighten their belts and some of his men must go.

"Yes, more land. The king has ordered the Lord Prior to offer me the old Longspee holding. What do you think?"

Joseph said nothing while he considered this mixed blessing. Finally, he answered. "It could be much better for us. The land was very good once, before that Norman ruined it. But we haven't the men or the resources to use it and we certainly can't make enough to pay the rent and tithes."

"Exactly my sentiments, Joseph."

The reeve shrugged his shoulders. "So, what can we do, master? I would love to get my hands on the holding and work it for you, but can you afford it?"

"Well, the steward fully understands the problems, he's had the farm surveyed."

"I know. I saw his men there last week."

"He has offered me the land free of all taxes and tithes for the first year. Do you think we can get it ploughed and sown to bring in enough to make it viable? Have we kept enough seed to do that?"

Joseph's face broke into a grin. "I don't see why not, sir. God be praised. I may need to take on an extra man or two for a start, but I know we can work it."

"Good. I'd hoped to hear that." Hugh pushed himself upright in bed and shouted for John to come to them. "John come up here and bring another jug of small beer. We have something to celebrate."

The morning passed quickly with Hugh and his reeve making plans and discussing what must be done urgently to the new land to get it in working condition. Time passed quickly, it was soon mid-day and time for another meal. Hugh remained on his bed all that time. Once he had attempted to get up but the pain in his knee defeated him, so he sat upright on the top of the covers and talked though his plans with Joseph.

"What about that fast boat? Is it too damaged?"

"I haven't inspected it properly and I'm no seafarer myself, but you can see light through the side where it's been smashed. You need a shipwright to have a look at it, master."

"I suppose I do really. If you pull it up above the tide line so that it suffers no more damage, I will have a look at it when I'm about again."

Joseph looked doubtful.

"That won't be long, never you fear. I will get out and about if only to stop Margaret fussing over me like a broody hen with only one chick!"

Joseph laughed heartily at that promise.

Chapter Twenty Six

For three days after his return from Lincoln, Hugh had to remain on his bed. His temper got shorter and shorter at the enforced rest. He tried to take his weight on his damaged leg on several occasions but the pain defeated him. The members of his household grew tired of his constant shouts for attention but no one dare voice their frustrations. Finally, John came up with a solution. He ran up the stairs to Hugh room and stood beside the bed waiting for his master to wake up.

"What do you want? I'm not asleep, just resting my eyes. I'm dying from boredom!"

John reached over and lay a thick branch of a tree on the bed cover.

Hugh looked at him sharply, demanding an explanation.

"I was chopping more wood when I found this unusual shaped branch, master. I wondered if it would serve as a crutch for you?"

Hugh eyes opened wide. The lad had come up with a good idea. He sat upright and inspected the branch closely.

John waited patiently for the verdict.

"Good idea, my boy. Help me measure it up." Hugh placed the bar of the branch under his armpit and lay the limb of the branch along the top of the bed. "It's just slightly too long. Make a mark level with my foot and cut it to the correct length for me."

John indented the wood with his fingernail and ran downstairs to the yard to cut the crutch to size. By the time he returned, Hugh was sitting on the edge of his bed, impatient to try the new aid.

"Hold onto my other side." Hugh ordered the boy. He stood up on his good leg and pushed the crutch under his arm. Leaning forward, carefully he took his weight on the branch and his good leg then swung himself forward across the bedroom. "It works! Wonderful!" Hugh stopped to regain his breath. The effort was proving as much as he could manage, but he was smiling. "Get my clothes, John. I'm going downstairs."

The boy looked doubtful at this suggestion. A few steps across a level floor was one thing, tackling a flight of stairs was entirely another. He said nothing, but he put his master's clothes beside him on the bed and ran downstairs to the yard.

Hugh dressed slowly because of his painful knee. By the time he was ready to try his crutch again, John had returned with one of the yard men.

"What do you want?" Hugh barked at them.

"If you are going to walk downstairs master, I will go in front in case you fall."

Hugh scowled at the man, but he could see the sense in the suggestion. He waved his hand towards the doorway, to show he was going to attempt to go through it, then lurched onto his feet. Slowly he made it to the top of the stairs then, step by step, he eased himself down to the ground floor. John and the man hovered in front of him, ready to break his fall if he slipped.

Margaret, who had heard the commotion, came running in from the kitchen and stood at the bottom of the stairs with her hands covering her face and her lips mouthing a silent prayer.

Once safely at the bottom step, Hugh hesitated and sat down to regain his breath. "Move my...chair over in front...of the fire " he panted.

John rushed to obey.

Hugh swung himself across the room and sat heavily on his carver chair, letting his crutch clatter to the floor. With a sigh of relief, he grinned at his helpers and looked around the familiar room. It was good to be back at the centre of his world again, sitting in his hall, on his chair in front of a blazing fire. Thinking back, he realised he had not spent so many days in his bed since his leg was wounded in the first place. This would have to be a lesson to be kinder to himself. At fifty five he was an old man and getting worn out.

"Would you like some beer, master?" Margaret deposited a jug and a mug beside his chair, anticipating his next request. He smiled and nodded. That was better. Now he was at the hub of things. Now he felt back in control. He may not be able to move far but he had plans to perfect and things to oversee. All his life he had been independent. In his days as a bowman he had stood in the ranks of his fellow archers but he still felt he was an individual, not like the massed pikemen. He knew his arrows could make all the difference to the outcome of a battle. This streak of independence was what made him, and those like him, a fighting force to be feared. But old bowmen do make terrible patients, he reminded himself.

Three more days passed before Hugh could think of leaving the confines of the house. During that time he slept in his chair in front of the fire, with John always by his side in case he wanted for anything in the night. He had had plenty of visitors to keep him occupied. Elizabeth came frequently, but her news was not good. No one had heard from Giles and the enquiries his father had made in the

Hammond beck area produced nothing new. Giles seemed to have vanished completely.

Will the fletcher called to deliver a dozen new arrows and to regale him with the gossip from the tavern and the market. Little had changed in Spalding. The townspeople were anticipating a heavy tax burden because the prior, as warden of the waterways, was insisting they shouldered their responsibility to reinforce the fallen banks and to dredge out the debris in the clogged-up streams and drains.

"It's no more than many of them deserve." Hugh had little sympathy with his fellow townsmen. "Maybe they'll keep on top of their duties in future."

Will nodded agreement. He was drinking free ale and happy to agree with anything his host suggested.

"If the drains aren't cleared, we shall have flooding again and a great loss of goods and maybe even life." Hugh had been born a few miles from Spalding, in the village of Pinchbeck. He was a true fen man and understood the continued prosperity of the area depended completely on the fens being well drained.

"I've made that small bow for you, and a dozen short arrows."

"Ah! I'd forgotten about that. Good man." Hugh had promised to teach John to shoot in the bow when he had time. Now he felt that he owed the boy even more, after the way he had rallied to help him in his illness. "Bring them over. I will start training the boy when I'm able."

Joseph took time off from the busy autumn period at the farm to ride into Spalding to give Hugh a report on how things were progressing.

"Any nearer starting on the new holding?" Hugh enquired.

"I've been over the creek several times to take a look, master. We had better put a man in the house soon, I'm thinking."

"Why, Joseph? Problems with the rats?"

"Possibly, master, but there are signs that someone has been sleeping there."

Hugh raised his eyebrows. "Landless tramps or maybe one of those pirates has come back again?"

"I can't say. Could be either. I just noticed signs of a recent fire in the corner of the main hut, and I felt I was being watched as I moved about the holding. I don't want to lose any more of our sheep."

"Well, don't go over unarmed and don't go alone. I wouldn't want anything to happen to you."

"I have several things to show you, master. When do you think you will be fit enough to travel to Wykeham?"

Hugh sighed. He was impatient to be walking the new land and making plans for it. "Give me two more days. If I can't ride in the saddle, I'll use a wagon, but I'll get there, never you fear."

Joseph seemed relieved at this reassurance. He was a good reeve but he missed Hugh's guiding hand when it came to the big decisions. He drained his mug and left, a much happier man than when he had arrived.

That afternoon, Hugh felt much better and decided to try a few steps out of the house. He still relied on the make-do crutch but he took some of his weight on his damaged leg and managed to progress slowly down the yard to the riverside. There he sat on a wooden stump and surveyed the river.

The river Welland was as busy as ever. Grain boats came up from the sea, fishing boats brought in their catch of herring, barges were loading pelts from Richard the skinners warehouse on the far side of the river. Further inland there were several barges laden with sandstone blocks for the masons at the priory.

"Still the building prior!" Hugh said to himself. "I suppose we shall have even higher walls and battlements now he's got the king's permission to fortify." He knew there would be much unrest in the town over these new taxes. Who could blame the prior for protecting his priory or for that matter, the locals for objecting to the crippling taxes? His thoughts were distracted by one of the Fisher's boats gliding back to the quayside. As it passed him by,

Robert, the fisherman who had accompanied him to Lincoln, waved to him from the prow. Hugh put up his hand to greet the man.

Hugh was just about to leave his riverside seat and limp back up the yard to his fireside chair when Robert came jogging along the towpath towards him.

"Are you feeling any better, master?" Robert stopped in front of Hugh to regain his breath.

"Much better, thanks. Any news of Giles?"

Robert hesitated, just long enough for Hugh to be suspicious. Then he answered. "No. I've not seen him. Have you heard anything? Has he contacted Elizabeth?"

Hugh looked at the man and quizzically cocked his head on one side. "I thought you were going to tell me something new just then. What's worrying you, Robert?"

The fisherman grinned. "There's not much you miss, is there, master." He sat down on the riverbank. "I was not thinking of Giles especially. Two nights ago someone untied several of the smaller boats and let them loose on the tide. Most of them have been found, in various parts of the river, but one of ours is still missing. It's a special one"

"Ah! Do tell."

"We had a small boat stolen...well, I think it was stolen. That's all."

"Go on. There must be more to it than that. How do you know those boats didn't just drifted upriver on the tide?"

"I can't be sure, but I myself tied our boats to the quay and I don't usually make that sort of mistake...besides, it's Giles own boat. It's one he had as a young lad."

"Ah! Now I see. You are adding two and two and making five."

Robert frowned, not understanding the reference.

"You are jumping to conclusions." Hugh explained.

"I suppose I might be...but I have an uneasy feeling about that boat. If Giles came back this way what better way to leave than in his own boat?"

"Precisely!" Hugh smiled at the man. "I have just come to the same conclusion. It's suspicious enough to interest me greatly."

When he was alone, sitting once more by the fire, Hugh thought over the information he had gleaned. Several small boats had been set adrift but only one was still missing. Was that just a coincidence? There was no way of knowing when the boat was stolen and thus the state of the tide and whether it had gone upstream or downstream. His common sense told him it had probably been taken upstream towards Stamford and inland, because there was only the estuary and the sea in the other direction. The open sea was no place for a small open boat. If Giles had taken the boat, he could be far inland by now. If he had come back to Spalding it was a shame he hadn't contacted any of his friends who could have told him he was no longer a wanted man.

Chapter Twenty Seven

That night, for the first time since his return from Lincoln, the acute pain eased in his leg and Hugh slept well. When he woke up at dawn he felt refreshed and much better, so much so that when he'd eaten breakfast he decided he was feeling well enough to drive a wagon over to Wykeham.

"Margaret. I am going to Wykeham today. I will take the small wagon and be there until this evening. I will not be here for a mid-day meal but I will eat tonight."

Margaret shrugged her shoulders at this. She did not think he was well enough to go, but she knew better than to argue with him when he was in so positive a frame of mind.

"Will you take anyone with you, sir?"

"No. Why should I? I'm fine now." To prove his point Hugh threw away his crutch and limped down the yard to the stables. Soon after dawn he was on his way, but he took the precaution of placing his crutch on the back of the wagon.

Joseph was pleased to see his master. There were so many questions he needed to discuss. "Good to see you, sir. Come in, you're just in time for some oatcakes and beer."

Hugh had a second breakfast. It warmed him up and gave him a chance to recover from the bumpy ride.

"Are you feeling well enough to walk the farm?"

"I'll walk to the high ground and you can point out all I need to know from there."

The two men made slow progress to the top of the sea bank, then turned to view the holding from that vantage.

"Everything looks fine, Joseph. The sheep are close in to the yard, the cattle we need to overwinter are in their winter quarters. Tell me, have you slaughtered and salted all the beef we will need to last us the winter?"

"Aye, master. All done."

"Good man" Hugh turned to face across the creek. "Now, tell me about that trespasser we think we have on the far holding. Any more signs of him?"

"I'm not sure. There was a small boat washed up on the beach recently. No signs of anyone with it, mind you."

Hugh stroked his chin thoughtfully. "Could be a boat that broke its moorings in Spalding several nights ago. They lost several, but only one is still unaccounted for."

Joseph nodded. Many strange things floated down the river and out to sea on the high tides, especially after a storm or heavy rain inland.

Hugh used his crutch and limped down the sea bank out of sight of the Longspee holding. At the bottom he stopped for breath and took hold of the Reeve's arm to stop him walking further over the holding. "I need to see the state of that sea going boat that the pirates used to use."

"It's on the other side of the creek!" Joseph sounded extremely surprised at the request. "Are you sure you are walking well enough, master?"

Hugh shook his head and grimaced. "You sound just like my housekeeper. Let me be the judge of that."

Hugh limped down to the water's edge where Joseph kept a small boat moored. With a struggle, he managed to clamber aboard and was paddled across. He directed the man to pull alongside the hull of the beached boat, so that he could inspect the damage.

Joseph leaned over the side of their boat, grabbed the top plank of the fishing boat and pulled them closer. He leaned over the side and inspected the damage. "There's a hole in the other side. Looks as if it's been deliberately scuttled to me."

Hugh balanced on his good leg and checked the damage for himself. Sure enough, there was a gaping hole in two of the side planks, but the boat had not been left long enough for the sea to damage it beyond repair. If it was rescued soon, it would prove a valuable item to exchange or sell, and he needed all the valuable assets he could wring from this run-down holding. He sat back heavily in the rowing boat. "Now I want to see that hut and the embers of that fire you found."

Joseph shook his head in disbelief. "Are you sure...?" Hugh silenced him with one withering look.

Getting to the bank of the Longspee holding was no problem but disembarking on the muddy bank was another matter. Hugh struggled and slipped in his efforts to get out of the boat and up the bank. Eventually, with the reeve pulling him and the other man pushing him from behind, he made it to the top of the bank, where he stood regaining his breath, looking out over the deserted land.

"Looks bleak."

"It does, Master. It doesn't take long for the weeds to take over and the land return to nature once it's left empty."

"Let's look in the main hut." Hugh tucked his crutch under his arm and limped towards the largest structure on the farm, followed closely by his two workers. He stopped near the pigsty and glanced in, where the runt had been found. Now fresh grass shoots were growing over the mud ruts where the pigs' snouts had rooted.

Behind the pigsty, close to the main hut, he stopped and poked the ground with his crutch.

"What's that?" Joseph bent down to look.

"Fresh remains of some fish, if I'm not mistaken." Hugh pushed the bones about with the tip of his stick.

"Rats? Maybe seagulls dropped them here."

"Hm!" Hugh grunted in disbelief at this suggestion. "They're not from a raw fish. That's been cooked. It's more likely some two-legged rat whose been fishing!"

The two farm workers looked about them nervously. There had been traces of someone at the holding, and those fish remains were certainly recent.

Hugh hesitated just inside the hut door and glanced around. At the far side of the room, the curtain, which had hidden the Norman's body, was still hanging from the rafters. The old ashes of Lucy's fire were still in the middle of the earthen floor but there was a smell of fresh smoke in the air. He walked over to another fresh heap of ashes in the far corner, and held the palm of his hand above them. "Still warm!"

Joseph pulled out his dagger and glanced nervously around the inside of the hut, although there was really nowhere where anyone could hide.

"He's not here now. I think he heard us coming, which means he can't have gone far. Where did you say that small boat was beached?" Hugh asked.

"On the foreshore. Why?"

"Because I think our visitor arrived in it and is using it to fish. I think we'd better get to it before he does." Hugh hobbled out of the hut and made for the shore. His two companions walked along beside him, unsure of what he wanted them to do.

"Don't wait for me! Get down there as fast as you can" He waved his companions on to run to the boat.

By the time Hugh arrived at the beach the two workers were standing on the edge of the water looking out to sea. A few hundred yards out a solitary figure was paddling rapidly away from them, helped by the fast receding tide, which was running offshore and carrying everything out with it.

"There he is."

"The devil! We missed him." Hugh cursed.

"Well I for one am not sorry. I'd rather see his back than tangle with him. I'm sure he'll not come back now we've chased him off."

"But I want to catch him. Don't you understand. Hugh stamped his good foot on the wet sand. "That is probably Giles!" He cupped his hands and yelled at the top of his voice to attract the fleeing man's attention, but it was useless, the sound of the waves breaking on the beach and the sound of the wind drowned his cries.

Joseph looked bewildered by it all.

Hugh shielded his eyes and looked out to sea after the tiny boat, which was then hardly visible, it had floated so far out from the shore. He saw the wind was getting up and the waves were rolling in with white plumed tops. It was a heavy sea to sail in a small open boat. He cursed silently. He should have anticipated this. If only he had been more mobile he may have managed to get a message to the man fleeing in the boat. He struggled back to his own holding in despair.

Chapter Twenty Eight

Hugh hurried back to Spalding without waiting to take a meal with the reeve's family. The fact that he had probably just missed saving Giles, weighed heavily on his conscience. He had gone to the holding half expecting to find Giles there but he had still failed to speak to the lad. Now things looked bleak. Whoever had been sheltering on the empty Wykeham holding was now far out to sea in a small, open boat. The wind was freshening and he knew that the Wash could be a treacherous place. Hugh recalled the waves he had encountered on Erik van Driell's krugge on his way back from Amsterdam. The thought of tackling those high seas in a small open boat, was frightening. He whipped the horse to make it hurry along and drove the wagon at break neck speed.

"There's no meal ready for you." Margaret stood with her hands on her hips and glared at Hugh. "You told me you would not be home until this evening."

"Hold your tongue, woman!" Hugh scolded her sharply. "I'm not interested in food when a man's life could be at stake" She coloured up in her confusion and rushed back to her kitchen to hide from him.

"John! John! Unharness this horse and saddle me another one." Hugh stood in the yard and bellowed his orders. Soon he was in the saddle and trotting up to the market tavern, where Elizabeth and her mother came out to meet him.

"Any news, Uncle Hugh?" Elizabeth was the first to reach him.

"No. I have not seen or spoken to Giles yet." He saw no sense in raising her hopes about the fugitive at Wykeham. The man he disturbed at Wykeham, may or may not have been Giles It was all academic now. He'd missed his one chance to communicate with the fellow, whoever he might prove to be.

"Have you had a meal?" Maud was much more practical.

"No, not yet, but I must speak with Giles' father first. I'll be back here shortly, then I'll eat here."

The two women watched him as he left the market stead and set off for the Fishers' home.

At Giles home there was a family conference in progress. With no news of their son, his parents had called all their men together to discuss what they might do next. Hugh's arrival caused some excitement.

"It's Hugh Pinchbeck." A young lad shouted the news to those inside the house.

Gilbert Fisher, Giles' father, rushed out to greet him, closely followed by his wife and several of their fishing crew.

"What news? Any sighting of him?" Such questions were asked before Hugh had had time to slip from his horse to the ground. He limped across to the doorway and sat down heavily on a bench seat by the door.

"Any news?" Mistress Fisher asked softly.

"Yes and no. I may have caught sight of him. I'm not sure."

There was a general hubbub of voices at this news.

"Where, man?"

"Possibly at Wykeham."

This caused even more consternation as that meant he would have come through Spalding first. The babble of voices rose and drowned out any further conversation.

"Shut up, all of you! Give the man quiet." Giles father took control of the situation and the noise quietened down. He turned to Hugh and asked "Now then, what has happened?"

"Robert there..."Hugh pointed to the fisherman..."told me Hugh's rowing boat was missing. I had heard a whisper that a tramp or someone was hiding at the old Longspee holding. I went over today to take a look." The hum of conjecture broke out yet again. Hugh held up his hand until they fell silent, then continued. "We went over to the holding and found recent traces of fish remains and of a fire. While we were there someone must have spotted us before we saw him. He made a run for it."

"Did you see him?"

"No. By the time we got to the foreshore he'd launched his small boat and was way out to sea."

"Was it my Giles?" Giles mother asked, hope filling her voice.

"I honestly don't know. But whoever it was, he could handle a small boat well."

Once again the hum of voices drowned out anything further Hugh wanted to say. Robert, the older fisherman who had accompanied Hugh Lincoln, sat down beside him to talk to him privately.

"How's the leg now?"

"It's mending. But I am worried about Giles. If that was Giles we saw, he's in great danger. That boat was fast drifting out to sea on the outgoing tidal currents. There are strong rip tides along that coast, as you well know, the wind is getting up and the sea is rough. I don't give a lot for anyone's chances in a small, open, boat in that weather."

Roberts nodded grimly. "I agree. The weather is blowing up for a storm. That's why we are not out fishing. I'd better have a word with the old man and see what's to be done."

Hugh nodded his head vigorously. This is exactly what he had hoped would happen. He was no sailor and things were now beyond his help.

By the time Hugh had eaten and returned to Eau Side, the Fisher's fishing boat was heading out of the dock and along the river towards the sea. Hugh trotted his horse along the towpath and stopped to pass the time of day with one of the local fishermen who was working at mending his nets.

"Was that the Fishers boat I just saw heading out?"

"Aye. Rather them than me! It's not going to be fishing weather out there on the open sea. Not the way the sky's looking."

Hugh watched the boat vanish around the bend in the river towards Wykeham. He said a silent prayer for their safety and for Giles safe home coming. What the chance were of them spotting a small boat in the rough, open sea, was anybody's guess, but he understood why Giles father had felt he must try. Now it was out of his hands completely. He sighed at the way things had turned out, gave his horse its head and let it make its own way home. He was aware that his leg was beginning to throb again. He knew he had overdone it.

Chapter Twenty Nine

The Fisher's boat, with the fish painted on its prow, did not return to Spalding quays that night. It was late the following afternoon before it came upriver on the incoming tide.

Hugh who had spent the day quietly resting and talking with his old friend Will, had asked John to keep an eye out for the boat's return.

"It's the fishing boat, master!" John ran into the hall with the news. "It's just rounded the bend down river. It will be here in a few minutes."

Hugh threw the last few dregs of his beer onto the smouldering turf fire, took up a walking stick, which he'd had cut, and followed the boy out into the yard. By the time he had limped down to the quay the boat was coming alongside.

Everyone on the docks stopped their work and waited for what news the boat would bring. Everyone in town had heard about Giles and his predicament and all sympathised with the lad and wished him well. Hugh eyes searched the boat deck for signs of Giles or for some signal that all was well but he was to be disappointed. From the serious look on Gilbert Fisher's face and the closed expressions of his men, it was obvious their search had not been successful.

Hugh hobbled down the steps to the dockside and waited for their news.

"No luck?" He asked the inevitable question but he knew the answer before he asked.

Robert shook his head sadly. "We have quartered the Wash for miles out to sea but we've seen hide nor hair of him or his boat"

Giles father shook his head emphatically but looked too upset to speak.

Hugh said nothing. He had feared as much, but he had hoped against hope and prayed for a miracle.

Just then, Elizabeth arrived at the quay, out of breath and anxious. News of the return of the boat had reached the inn almost as soon as it was sighted.

"Any news, Uncle Hugh?" Her face was tear stained and her eyes red rimmed from crying.

"No not yet." Hugh put his arm around her shoulder and hugged her to him.

"What do you think will happen? Is Giles lost to us?"

Robert, who had jumped onto the quay to make the boat fast, came over to them and answered her question. "Don't give up yet. Giles knows those waters. It is possible he is already ashore somewhere towards the Norfolk coast." This assessment cheered the girl up visibly. Only Hugh noticed the desperation in the man's eyes.

"I must go back to help mother. Let me know if you hear anything new." She turned and walked wearily back to the market stead.

Hugh and Robert stood and watched her until she was out of sight.

"Well? What do you really think?" Hugh asked.

"I don't give him much hope. It's rough out there. Waves like small mountains. We had a job keeping the prow into the swell. The only ray of hope is the fact that we did not spot the wreck of his boat."

Hugh shrugged his shoulders in despair and said lamely. "Of course, I may have been mistaken at Wykeham. It may yet prove to be some landless beggar that we saw on the shore."

Robert shook his head. "It sounded like Giles boat and it was taken from here. I think you understood the situation all too well."

When the crew had disembarked from the fishing boat and he had passed the time of day with Giles father, Hugh made his way slowly back to his home. With his difficulty in walking and his worries for Elizabeth and Giles, he felt a very old man. The spring had gone from his step and the joy gone out of his life. Even the prospect of a more secure future with the new land the king had secured for him, gave him little cause to celebrate.

Chapter Thirty

Next morning on the incoming tide, Erik van Driell's krugge edged its way once more into the docks at Spalding. It was heavily laden with barrels of wine and bolts of finished cloth, all roped securely down against the autumn gales they had encountered in the North Sea.

Hugh was in the yard teaching John to string his new bow.

"I don't want to leave your service, master." The boy blurted out.

Hugh frowned. "Why should you be leaving my service, John? I am very pleased with your work. There's no question of it, lad."

John shrugged his shoulders helplessly. "My mother is talking of marrying again. If she gets married she will go and look after her new husband. I will probably have to go with her."

Hugh stayed silent for some minutes while he digested this unwelcome news. He could replace Margaret easily enough but she was a good worker and he was comfortable with her. First, he reassured the boy. "I see no reason at all why you can't remain here, John, whatever your mother decides to do." He stroked his chin thoughtfully. "Do you know who your mother wished to marry?"

"Yes master. It's your friend Will the fletcher."

Hugh frowned. Will had certainly made complimentary comments about his housekeeper but he hadn't realised things had gone so far. He looked at John and smiled. "If your mother and Will wish to get married I wish them both well, but that will not affect your place in my household, unless you want it to, of course."

John looked very relieved. He took the bow in his hands, eager to get on with the lesson.

Hugh carried on instructing him. "Stand with your legs well apart for balance, lodge that tip of the bow under your instep. Pull the centre of the bow towards you with your right hand, while you push the tip away from you with the left one." John didn't seem able to follow these instructions so Hugh took the small bow from him and demonstrated. "Pull the bow up at the centre and slide the top loop of the string up over the nock." Hugh strung the light bow easily in spite of the strain on his bad leg. He unstrung it and handed it to the boy to try again. John was about to try again when his sharp ears heard the sound of a man shouting from the bottom of the yard. He relayed the message to his master.

"Master Hugh, sir. That Amsterdam krugge you sailed on. It's back in the docks."

Hugh smiled at this news. Erik should have brought him the proceeds from the sale of the cloves he had shipped to Amsterdam. He left John struggling to string the bow, took his stick and walked slowly down to the quayside.

"Erik! Good to see you." Hugh shouted across the river to the master of the boat.

"And you, my friend." Erik kept one hand on the tiller and waved the other in greeting.

Hugh sat on a bollard on the quay and watched Erik manoeuvre his boat alongside. Once it was tied securely, Erik jumped ashore and joined Hugh on the quay.

"You look in pain, my friend. What's happened?"

"It's a long story, Erik. My old battle wound has come back to haunt me."

"This will cheer you up." Erik undid his jerkin to reveal his money belt. He counted several gold coins into Hugh's hand.

"That much? Have you taken your share?"

"Of course. You know me. Those cloves made a very good price. They were top quality."

"Good, my friend. Will you come with me to celebrate at the market tavern?"

Erik shook his head. His face took on a very serious look.

"What's the problem?" Hugh asked, surprised at his friend refusing a celebratory drink.

"Come with me on board the boat for a moment. I want to talk to you in private."

Hugh was surprised at this request. Erik was aware of his injured leg and the difficulty he would have climbing down onto the deck of the krugge. He hesitated momentarily and was about to apologise for his lack of agility, when the Flemish sailor lifted him bodily in the air, carried him gently to the edge of the quay and lowered him onto the deck.

Hugh was not pleased at being manhandled like that. He turned on his friend. "What the devil do you think you're doing?"

Erik met his eyes and held a silencing finger up to his lips. "Come over here to the prow." He walked to the front of the boat. When Hugh had caught up with him, he gently lifted the edge of a pile of sheepskins to reveal what was underneath. Hugh bent over and cautiously peered under the covers, not knowing what to expect.

"My Lord!" Hugh straightened up. "Is he dead?" He was shocked to see the body of a man lying on the deck beneath the sheepskin covers.

"No, but he's close to it. I took you into my confidence because he said he knew you."

Hugh pulled back the top corner of the cover again and took a closer look.

"It's Giles!" He let the sheepskin drop from his fingers and turned to Erik. "Where did you pick him up?"

"Out at sea. He was adrift in an open boat, well out of sight of land."

Hugh nodded. "Was he conscious when you found him."

"Hardly. We had to lift him bodily into the krugge. I gather he was telling me the truth out there. You do know him. That's very obvious from your reaction."

"Yes. He is betrothed to my niece, Elizabeth."

"Ah! Now I understand. He has been mumbling that name and he mentioned Spalding, among other things..."Erik glanced furtively around the dockside to check that no one was watching them. "He is a fugitive, he told me. He is wanted for murder."

Hugh nodded. "He was on his way to Lincoln to be tried for murder when he escaped."

"If you like, I can give him safe passage back with us to Amsterdam. That's if we can keep him alive and undiscovered until we make the return trip."

Hugh shook his head emphatically. "No need, Erik. Much as I appreciate the offer, Giles if a free man. He is not wanted anymore for that crime." Hugh pulled the covers off the unconscious figure and bent down to examine him closely.

Erik was puzzled. "In his more lucid moments he was insistent that he would be hanged for a crime he had not committed. I don't understand how he is now free?"

"I went to Lincoln and pleaded for him. The victim of the so-called murder was poisoned by accident. Now stop asking so many questions and help me get him ashore and into bed."

Erik picked Giles up easily and jumped ashore with him. "Tell me where you want him taken and I'll bring him."

Hugh made a quick decision. "Take him to my home. I can look after him better there."

By this time several bystanders at the docks had noticed the sick man and a few had recognised him. They crowded around the Flemish sailor and his burden.

Hugh dispersed the crowd. "Give him room. Giles is very sick and needs immediate attention." He led Erik along the towpath to his home, where they put Giles onto Hugh's own bed.

Margaret followed them up the stairs, anxious to see what she could do to help.

"Bring water and get me extra woollen blankets for him. He's been exposed to wet and cold weather at sea. He could die from the cold." Hugh shouted his instructions to his housekeeper as he stripped the damp clothes from the still figure. He rubbed Giles arms and hands to get some warmth back into them then covered him over with warm blankets.

"This is going to be touch and go, Margaret. When you've brought more bed covers you'd better get some strong beer heated up. Then you can send John to tell Giles' parents and my niece that we have him here."

Hugh sat on the bed and examined his patient. He did not like the colour of the boy's skin, which had a blue tinge. He listened to his shallow breathing, which rasped at each exhalation. It was obvious that Giles was very ill. Only youth was in his favour. If Giles had been an older man, Hugh would have given him little chance of surviving.

Within the hour, Gilbert Fisher and his wife arrived to see their son. They were shocked when they saw how ill he looked.

"Will he live?" Gilbert asked in a whisper.

"Maybe." Hugh was honest with them. "Meanwhile, he's in the best place here, where I can keep an eye on him."

Giles' mother buried her face against her husband's shoulder and broke into sobs.

"Don't let him want for anything." Gilbert said fiercely, making a supreme effort to hold back his own tears. "Anything he needs, you must give him. I will pay."

Hugh nodded and smiled. "The best thing for him is good care, and he will get that here. He can have my bed. I will have my chair brought up here so I can keep a watch over him."

"I thought we'd lost him to the hangman, but thanks to you he is a free man. Now we could lose him to illness. We are indebted to you once again. When this is over you must let me repay you, Hugh."

Hugh shook his head emphatically. "If he recovers and makes my niece happy, that will be reward enough for me."

The mention of Elizabeth was very timely. From downstairs they heard a loud knock on the front door followed by a muted conversation with Margaret. Hugh recognised the voice of the visitor. He shouted down the stairs

"Come up Elizabeth. We are in my bedchamber."

She came up the stairs quickly, taking the steps two at a time. "Where is he?"

"In bed." Hugh put his arm around her shoulder to comfort her. "He's not conscious yet, but when he's warmed up we may see an improvement."

Elizabeth stood and looked at her young man. She had thought she would never see him again, but to see him looking so ill took her completely by surprise. "Is he dead, Uncle Hugh? He's so pale and I can't see him breathing."

"He's breathing. It's shallow but it's regular. I think you should tell him you are here, then we had all better go downstairs and let him rest."

Elizabeth frowned at this suggestion. "Will he be able to hear me?"

"Most probably. It's amazing what the senses can pick up. If he hears your voice it's sure to help and he will know he is in safe hands."

Giles remained unconscious for two whole days after his return to Spalding. His parents kept calling at Hugh's home and Elizabeth visited whenever she could be spared from her chores at the tavern. Hugh kept a constant vigil by his bedside, mopping his brow when he developed a high temperature and moistening his lips with water or beer whenever he seemed to be thirsty. Hugh had his own meals served in the bedroom so that he need not leave his patient. At night he dozed fitfully in his oak chair beside the bed, keeping his vigil by the light of a candle.

In the early hours of the morning, on the second day, Giles temperature broke. Hugh was pleased with this turn of events, but disappointed when he showed no signs of regaining consciousness. The constant sitting and immobility took its toll on Hugh's damaged leg. He had to get up from his chair occasionally and pad quietly up and down the room, to keep his joints mobile. It was while he was on one of those walks, he thought he heard a murmur from the bed. He took up the candle and hurried over to check his patient.

"Giles! Giles! Can you hear me?"

The patient murmured again. This time it was a definite attempt to speak.

"Thanks be to God!" Hugh sat on the bed and leaned over the boy "You were close to death, Giles. But now you are back with us, you stand a fighting chance of recovering."

"Where... am I?" Giles managed the question in a barely audible whisper.

"You're safe. You're in Spalding at my home."

Giles opened his eyes, took one look at Hugh, then shut them again tightly. He turned and sobbed into his pillow.

"Come on Giles. No need to fret. You are safe and you are a free man now."

"Free?" The boy turned his face towards Hugh.

"Free. I'll explain when you are fitter, but you are not wanted for the murder of Ivo Longspee. He died of accidental poisoning."

Giles smiled for the first time in days, shut his eyes and drifted into a deep sleep.

Hugh limped downstairs and shouted for Margaret to bring him some wine. He poured himself a glass, his first for two days. Raising the glass, he looked through the red liquid at the spluttering candle flame and mouthed a silent prayer of thanks to Saint Anthony.

"Will that be all, master?" Margaret stood and waited for any further orders.

"Yes thanks...No... I think congratulations are in order Margaret. I should have spoken to you before this but things have been very hectic with this business with Giles."

"Congratulations, master?"

"Your marriage to Will."

"Oh that." She looked sheepishly down at her feet.

Hugh smiled secretly to himself. He had his suspicions about the marriage, especially as Will had made no mention of it. Maybe it was just Margaret's way of trying to make him jealous? Perhaps she was hoping to shock him into asking for her hand? From her demeanour he guessed he was right. He played her at her own game. "I'm thrilled for you both,

Margaret. I'll tell Will so when I next see him. And you needn't worry about John, his position here is secure even when I replace you."

Margaret coloured up and shook her head "I'm not getting married, master. There's no need to replace me."

Hugh smiled. "Oh good! Will can't afford to keep a wife and I would have a job finding anyone as efficient as you are, Margaret."

She stalked back to the kitchen, her head bowed and her eyes downcast. Hugh took another mouthful of the wine, pleased that the confrontation had gone so well.

Chapter Thirty One

Over the ensuing days, Giles gained in strength and health. One week after he regained consciousness, he was well enough to be transported to his own home, a move that pleased Hugh immensely, for sleeping in a wooden chair had played havoc with his joints. After a further week the patient was walking about and pestering his father to be allowed to return to fishing. Elizabeth, who visited him daily, was not happy with this suggestion.

"No! Don't take any notice of him. He needs to build up his strength more." She remonstrated.

Giles mother tended to agree with her. "Maybe another week or two at home, Giles. You have been very ill you know."

"I am well again." Giles protested. "I need to get back to work or we will never get married."

Elizabeth found herself torn between her worry for his health and the logic of what he had said.

Giles turned on them both. "I am going out for a walk today. I need to discuss something with your Uncle Hugh."

Just you wrap up well and don't tire yourself." His mother told him.

Hugh was busy at Eau Side. He had erected a straw target half way down the yard and was teaching John how to shoot a bow properly. The lad had shot a bow before but had never been taught the correct technique.

"Stand like this, with your feet well apart and your left shoulder facing your mark." Hugh took up the traditional stance of a bowman to demonstrate.

"Take an arrow and nock it on the string with the cock feather facing outwards." Hugh placed the arrow across his bow and pushed the nock onto the waxed linen string with the dark coloured cock feather outermost.

John copied his teacher but took his eye off the target to see the arrow onto the string.

"No lad! Learn to nock by feel alone. In the field when you are hunting, you never take your eyes from the mark. In battle there isn't time for such niceties. If you learn properly now, it will save you developing bad habits that you will have to correct later."

John tried again and after one or two false starts managed to get his arrow firmly onto the bowstring without looking at it.

"Good." Hugh smiled at the lad. "Now place the fingers of your draw hand on the string, with the first finger above the arrow and the second and third fingers below it." Hugh demonstrated. "Now twist the bow string as you curl your fingers, that way the shaft is held firmly against the belly of the bow by the tension in the string."

This skill took John a little longer to learn. Several times his arrow fell away from the bow until he had mastered the trick.

Hugh drew back his arrow, anchoring the fletchings against his cheek just below his right ear. He held the bow at full draw while he sighted along the shaft.

John watched closely.

Hugh sighted on the straw target and loosed the arrow cleanly into the centre of the target.

"Now you." Hugh ordered.

The lesson went on for an hour. After a slow start the boy learned quickly. He was full of enthusiasm and forever pestering Hugh for details of the crusades and the battles he had fought.

"Did you kill many of the infidel, master?"

"Enough."

"Tell me again about..." John didn't finish that question because Giles entered the yard from the towpath and interrupted the lesson. Hugh was thankful for the interruption.

"Giles! Good to see you up and about again."

"It's good to be out again, master."

"Come into the house and have a mug of beer with me." Hugh dismissed John and led his visitor into the hall. "How are you? Fully recovered?"

"More or less. I'm better than my mother or Elizabeth will admit and perhaps a bit worse than I pretend to be."

Hugh grinned and slapped him on his back. "Women folk do mither, lad."

Giles sipped his beer and waited for an opportunity to share his thoughts with Hugh. "I wanted to come and thank you personally for all your help. You freed me from that murder charge and you saved my life. I can never repay you."

Hugh shook his head and smiled. "I don't want paying. You and Elizabeth seem very happy together, that is reward enough. She is my only niece and I think the world of her, as you know. Let's say I did it all for her."

Giles nodded that he understood, then changed the subject. "When I was at the Longspee holding I noticed there was a fishing boat they had damaged and left in the creek."

Hugh raised his eyebrows in surprise. He hadn't realised that Giles had seen the boat. He himself had made tentative plans for that boat. It was a shame to let it lie there and rot. He was sure the damage was not beyond repair and it was now his, along with all the other equipment at the farm, so it was up to him to make the best use of it.

"What had you in mind, Giles?"

"If the Lord Prior would sell it to me, I know that I could get it seaworthy. You know I am looking for a boat of my own to provide a living for Elizabeth and me, so that we can marry."

Hugh grinned. "Could you afford to buy it?"

Giles shrugged his shoulders.

Hugh guessed the lad did not have the money and was only day dreaming about buying the boat, but he conceded that everyone needed dreams, especially the young. He decided to tell the lad what was happening to the old Longspee holding. "The Lord Prior doesn't own that boat. It goes with the holding."

Giles looked crestfallen. He shrugged his shoulders. "It was just an idea."

"It's a good idea, Giles. Maybe the new owner is a farmer and doesn't want to catch fish. Maybe he would come to some mutually agreeable arrangement if you asked him."

Giles frowned. "Do you think so? Who shall I ask?"

"Try me, Giles. I have the tenancy of the holding and all the fittings that go with it."

"You?" Giles looked dumbstruck.

"Yes me. And I was thinking along similar lines myself for that boat. What if I had it repaired and went into partnership with an experienced fisherman? It just so happens I have the money." Hugh tapped his money belt. "I will supply the boat and this partner would work it. We could come to some agreement on how we divided the catches and the profits."

Giles sat down at the table and shook his head in amazement. "You mean me? You'd go into partnership with me?"

Hugh nodded.

"You are the most wonderful man I know, Uncle Hugh...I hope you don't mind me calling you Uncle Hugh?"

Hugh laughed aloud. "Don't get sentimental, Giles. When I said we would come to a mutual arrangement that is exactly what I meant. You must work out what size catch we could expect from that boat and how much that will pay us. Then we can discuss terms."

"I will. I will. Thanks for the chance. I can't wait to talk this over with Elizabeth."

Chapter Thirty Two.

"Raise your hands and drink with me to the happy couple." Hugh raised his wine and drank to his niece and her new husband. All the wedding guests at the market tavern joined in with the toast. Hugh held up his hand again and proposed yet another toast. He pointed to the remains of a cooked pig, set on a dish in the centre of the wedding feast. "Here's to the Tantony Piglet. Without its inspiration there would have been no wedding." Most of the guests were puzzled by this remark. The few who understood the reference, joined in with vigorous applause.

With the sound of clapping still ringing in his ears, Giles leapt onto a table and held up his hands for quiet.

"My wife and I..." He got no further with his speech. His voice was drowned by laughter and screams of delight. Temporarily unable to continue he beckoned his bride to join him and stand beside him on the table.

Elizabeth jumped up beside her new husband and blew kisses to the crowd of friends.

Hugh slapped his thigh and shouted his approval.

When the noise had died down, Giles continued. "Elizabeth and I want to thank you all for a day we will never forget. We are so lucky to have so many good friends. Now, as a special surprise, I would like you all to accompany us down to the quay."

Hugh looked at his sister and shrugged his shoulders. She shook her head, for she had also been taken by surprised at this request.

"Why, Giles?" Hugh shouted.

"You'll have to come and see." Giles and Elizabeth chorused together as they jumped off the table and ran hand in hand out of the door and down the market stead towards the river.

With much singing and hilarity, the guests tumbled out of the tavern and followed the young couple to the water's edge where they crowded onto the dock overlooking the moorings.

Giles held up his hand for silence.

"My friends, you all know Elizabeth and I have wed thanks to the generosity of her Uncle Hugh. He has supplied a fishing boat for me to use. The craft has been at the boatyard the past few months. They have been making it seaworthy. Today, the day of our wedding, I want you to join Elizabeth and me in launching the boat and in giving it a name."

Hugh, who was sitting near the water's edge, glanced down at the prow of the newly repaired craft, but he was unable to read the name painted there because it was hidden behind a cloth.

Giles continued his speech. "Please Uncle Hugh, will you come and unveil the new name?"

Hugh walked to where Giles was standing and grabbed the rope he was offered.

"I name this boat..." He pulled the rope and uncovered the name... "The Elizabeth... A very fitting name for a beautiful craft."

Other Historical Novels by this Author

Deeping Fen ISBN 9781902474243

A novel set in the early 1600's when an attempt was made to drain the 30,000 acres of Deeping Fen in South Lincolnshire.

It was a time of great upheaval with resistance and riots from the local people, who made their living and fed their families by fishing and wildfowling on the fen.

The Alchemist's Tale ISBN 9781902474342

- Set in Spalding, in the Lincolnshire fens in the reign of Edward 1st. A mysterious Augustinian monk arrives in the town offering to demonstrate Alchemy; the art of turning base metal into Gold. The locals are intrigued and hope to gain from this. When the monk proves to be a trickster and is found murdered, a local man is accused of the crime. Hugh Pinchbeck, a healer and a survivor of the Crusades, uses his skill to try to prove the man's innocence.
- The story unfolds against the hectic Christmas celebrations when Henry de Lacy, the Earl of Lincoln, and his retinue spend Christmas at Spalding priory.